BREATHLESS

Treet kissed her until they were both breathless. He pulled away an inch, staring into her alarmed eyes. "Why do you insist on fighting such a good thing?" His voice became a sex-roughened rumble. "If I make you half as crazy as you make me . . ."

"I explained it to you before, Treet," she whispered, moistening her lips. "I don't think it's a good idea for us to complicate an already complicated situation."

"How about if we just kiss?"

"I've heard that line before."

"It's not a line, it's a promise. I'll leave it entirely up to you to go further than kissing."

"That's not fair."

Treet lifted a brow. "So you admit it wouldn't be easy?"

"No, I don't admit anything!" She gave a half-hearted chuckle. "Treet, you're impossible."

"I'll take that as a yes," he whispered, lowering his hungry mouth to hers again.

SHERIDON SMYTHE

Those Baby Blues

LOVE SPELL NEW YORK CITY

LOVE SPELL®

July 2002

Published by

Dorchester Publishing Co., Inc.
276 Fifth Avenue
New York, NY 10001

ISBN 0-505-52483-X

Printed in the United States of America.

Visit us on the web at www.dorchesterpub.com.

In loving memory of my own perfect hero,
Herb Davidson, grandfather and friend.
1913-2002

—Sherrie Eddington

Those Baby Blues

Prologue

"Don't think about the pain, Hadleigh, concentrate on the contractions. She's crowning nicely. A little more help from you and we'll be done here."

Don't *think* about the pain? Hadleigh Charmaine, in the grip of the most agonizing contraction yet, had but three choice words for her infuriatingly cheerful obstetrician, Dr. Cole.

Gasping as she surged forward, she ground out, "Go . . . to . . . hell!" Her face felt as if it would explode. She strained and heaved, vowing to kill her coward of a husband—if she ever saw him again—and all three of her lying friends.

"Nothing to it," Doreen had assured her.

"Just wait until the contractions are close together before you go to the hospital," Barbi had advised. "I've heard that first babies take forever, and you'll go stir-crazy sitting in the hospital."

And the mother of them all, Karen's smug assurance that once they administered the epidural, she would feel little or no pain.

"Again, Hadleigh. Push again—and hold that breath until you have to let it go. One more should do it."

Hadleigh grabbed the handles as another contraction snagged her tortured body. Between her bent knees and over the mountain of her belly, she saw Dr. Cole shake his head and exchange an exasperated look with one of the hovering nurses.

"Looks like we missed again. You didn't push long enough."

"I *hate* you!" she gasped out as she released her breath in a whoosh. And she hated her friends. In their infinite, smug wisdom, they'd failed to mention that the epidural could not be administered after a certain point.

She was beyond that point when she'd checked into the hospital an hour ago because Barbi had advised her to wait as long as she could.

Someone, it seemed, had failed to inform this baby that she was supposed to take her own sweet time.

"Come on, Hadleigh," Dr. Cole said. "My butt's growing numb sitting on this stool."

If her hands hadn't had a death grip on the handles attached to the bed, Hadleigh would have checked her ears to see if they were clogged with something. *He* was uncomfortable? While she was being relentlessly ripped apart, the *doctor* was complaining about his—

his *butt* growing numb? Red spots danced before her eyes. Oh, she'd show him discomfort! She'd rip his heart out and—

"That's my girl! Get mad! Come after me. I'm insured."

The chuckle that followed his outrageous taunt was the last straw for Hadleigh. The insensitive, not-so-funny Dr. Cole had to die.

With a hiss of rage, she followed the contraction forward, lunging for him and unwittingly propelling the baby into his waiting hands.

In smug triumph, he held the newborn high.

And in shock, Hadleigh stared at her daughter. She was covered in blood and a white, cheesy substance that did not inspire in Hadleigh instant motherly love. *This* was her baby? Once again, it seemed, her three best friends had omitted a few important facts. . . .

Slowly, the bright fluorescent lights began to recede.

"I think she's going to faint."

"It wouldn't be the first time," Dr. Cole said, sounding amused. "Check her blood pressure and give her a shot of happiness. She's earned it."

Damned right I have, Hadleigh thought, fighting to stay conscious. She felt cool hands on her shoulders, easing her against the mattress. After all she'd been through, the sharp prick of a needle against her skin hardly registered.

Almost immediately, her eyelids grew heavy. Her body began to feel as if it were floating, her previous aches and pains fading away. Happiness . . . oh, yes, this was definitely a happy feeling.

The nurses worked around her, chattering and gossiping as they went about their routine cleanup. Floating leisurely through the clouds, Hadleigh fought to stay awake and enjoy the feeling.

"Have you seen him yet?"

"You mean, Treet Miller? I heard the rumor, but I didn't believe it. What's the scoop?"

"His girlfriend's having a baby in 315."

"*His* baby?"

"Maybe, maybe not. Depends on which rag you believe."

"The *Galaxy* said he's denying the baby."

"Yes, but the *Hard Truth* says he's overjoyed at impending fatherhood," another nurse interjected. With a wistful sigh, she added, "*I'd* have his baby any day. He's cuter than Richard Gere, and believe me, I'm *crazy* about Richard."

Hadleigh smiled, picturing Treet Miller in her mind. Yes, he was definitely hot. And it wasn't just that he was gorgeous, she thought. It was the way his baby-blue eyes smiled along with his incredibly sexy mouth, as if he knew secrets—delicious secrets—no one else knew. Hadleigh licked her dry lips. Imagine, Treet Miller, right here in the same hospital. Incredible.

And probably a hallucination.

"Well, I heard the truth straight from the horse's mouth." Frowning, Hadleigh tried to fit a face to this new, hard-edged voice. She struggled to open her eyes, but her eyelids felt as if they were weighted with something thick and heavy. Like cold cream, maybe. Or cucumbers. The image made her giggle.

"Tell us, Nurse Priscilla!"

"Cheyenne Windsor just delivered a seven-pound girl, and *she* claims that Treet Miller is threatening to take her baby. We've got security on watch."

There was a round of gasps, and Hadleigh would have joined them . . . except she felt more like giggling. She couldn't imagine the self-assured movie star pacing the waiting room of a county hospital, issuing threats. The only role she pictured him in was the devil-may-care one she'd seen him play in his movies.

"He can't do that, can he?"

The grim new voice continued. Nurse Priscilla, Hadleigh thought, tickled that she could remember.

"Not at this hospital, he can't. He'll have to settle this in court." She snorted. "I don't care how rich and famous he is, Miller won't upset *my* patient again without answering to *me.*"

Of this, Hadleigh had no doubt.

"Why would he want the baby? I read—"

"Forget what you read, Josie. You should know better than to believe those ridiculous rags. Miss Windsor said he tricked her into having this baby, promising to marry her. She's a model, you know, and now it will be months before she can work again. All Mr. Miller cares about is getting the baby."

Murmurs of disappointment swirled around Hadleigh. She sympathized with them. The great Treet Miller had fallen from his pedestal in *her* foggy eyes as well. Or was that her foggy brain? Right now, she mused with another drug-induced giggle, it was her foggy everything.

5

"Cheyenne swears he won't get her baby. I just hope she has a good lawyer."

Me too. Hadleigh continued to resist the pull of sleep. She was exhausted, but too intrigued by the conversation to give in to the sandman. At least *she* wouldn't have to worry about Jim fighting for custody of Samantha Leigh. Since she'd told him she was pregnant, it was as if he'd disappeared from the face of the earth. The coward.

And Treet Miller was an arrogant ass, if Cheyenne Windsor could be believed. Humph! It would be a cold day in hell before Hadleigh watched another one of *his* films. . . .

Men. Even when they did stick around, it seemed they were a pain in the butt.

"Let's put her in the room with Miss Windsor. Maybe that will help keep the woman calm and you-know-who out of there."

"Good idea."

Hadleigh wasn't so certain she agreed, because after hearing their conversation, she wasn't too keen on being in the room with anyone remotely connected with the baby-stealing, promise-breaking Treet Miller.

But she was too tired to argue.

Chapter One

"I'm afraid the DNA testing shows that Jim is not Samantha's father."

Hadleigh's first, instinctive response to Dr. Manubay's grave announcement was to laugh. She was joking, of course. She had to be. But someone definitely needed to tell her this was not the time or place for humor—although Hadleigh would be the first to agree that Jim's return from abroad after nearly a five-year absence and subsequent demand for a paternity test *was* a joke—a cheap attempt to humiliate her.

Of course Samantha was Jim's child! She had never even considered being unfaithful during their brief marriage. There was, however, considerable suspicion regarding Jim's fidelity.

"Are you certain, doctor?"

Jim's terse question jarred Hadleigh with the ridiculous realization that they were *both* serious. She glared at Jim, who had changed little in the time he'd been absent from their lives.

Thank God Samantha was nothing like him.

"Of course Samantha's your child," Hadleigh snapped out. It would be convenient for her *and* Jim if Samantha wasn't, because then Jim could do another disappearing act with a clear conscience. But after the doctor's silly statement, Hadleigh felt a perverse need to convince Jim *and* Dr. Manubay.

The doctor shook her head. "There's no mistake, Mrs. Charmaine, and I'm afraid there's more bad news."

"Miss Charmaine," Hadleigh corrected automatically, feeling as if she'd stepped into the twilight zone without a script. Inwardly, she braced herself for another blow. "What—what do you mean, there's more? Is—is something wrong with Samantha?" Panic sank its teeth into her. Had they found something in Samantha's blood?

"No, there's nothing wrong with Samantha." Dr. Manubay paused, obviously reluctant to continue. "But according to the extensive DNA tests your ex-husband demanded, Samantha couldn't possibly be *your* child, either."

The room tilted wildly. Hadleigh squeezed her eyes shut. "Not . . . my . . . child?" she repeated over the buzzing in her ears. "What a ridiculous thing to say!"

"What in God's name do you mean?" Jim demanded, for once in harmony with Hadleigh.

8

Dr. Manubay looked from one bewildered face to the other, her expression one of sincere sympathy. "The only plausible explanation I can think of is that you brought the wrong baby home from the hospital. It's rare, but unfortunately, it does happen, despite every precaution."

"Impossible!" Hadleigh nearly shouted. The panic dug its claws in deeper. "I've raised Samantha for *four* years. I think I would know my own child!"

"Does she favor you—or your husband?"

"Well, no, but—"

"Have you recognized any obvious traits in Samantha?"

Cold fear clutched Hadleigh's heart like a vise. It was true that Samantha's volatile nature and high energy had baffled her from the beginning, and she had just assumed that somewhere in a past generation she or Jim had had an ancestor with red hair, which would account for Sam's auburn tint. Samantha's crystal-blue eyes had been even more perplexing, as Jim's eyes were brown, and Hadleigh's were green.

But these disturbing facts didn't mean—couldn't mean—"Samantha's my child," she heard herself state with a tinge of desperation. "Do the tests again, and you'll find that you've made a mistake."

"We've performed the test three times, Miss Charmaine. I had my own doubts about the results. We could do it again—at your expense, of course—but these tests are rarely wrong."

Three times.

"No, that won't be necessary." Hadleigh halted her trembling bottom lip with her teeth and glanced at Jim. The tight compression of his mouth signaled disapproval, and when they were married, had prompted in her instant feelings of ineptitude and bewildering guilt.

She was relieved to note that his reaction meant nothing to her now.

Numb with shock, she turned back to Dr. Manubay. "What do we do now?"

"We sue the damned hospital, that's what!" Jim said.

Dr. Manubay sighed. "Can't say that I blame you. But in the meantime, it's the hospital's responsibility to find out where your real baby is. They'll have records of who delivered around the time Samantha was born." She sat back in her chair and placed a finger on her rounded chin. "Don't worry, they'll find your child."

Hadleigh took a deep breath, struggling against an overwhelming urge to throw up. Something vital had just occurred to her. Something horrendous, and ugly. Something unthinkable.

"No!" she burst out, jumping to her feet and startling the doctor and Jim. "I won't give Samantha up—she's *my* daughter! I can't just hand her over to strangers!"

"Hadleigh, she's not ours. We know nothing about her parentage," Jim said in that pompous, patronizing tone Hadleigh didn't miss one bit. "In fact, we have no idea how our real daughter has been raised—" He was stopped by a quelling look from Dr. Manubay.

"Miss Charmaine, I'm afraid we have no choice. Somewhere out there someone else has your child. That means *you* have their child. Ethically and lawfully, we have to let them know."

"How . . . how much time do I have?"

"Until we find the other child. I'm sorry, Miss Charmaine."

Without responding, Hadleigh rose and stalked from the room. If she didn't have much time with Samantha, then she didn't want to waste another moment.

As for Jim and his not-so-gallant attempts to reconnect with his daughter, she had a very strong feeling that after today, she would never have to worry about Jim or his scheming, childless wife again.

"Daddy, is this a boat?"

Sitting in the director's chair with Caroline on his lap, Treet Miller glanced at the book in her hands. "That's definitely a boat. See the paddle wheels?"

"Peddle wheels? What's that?"

Smiling, Treet explained, knowing he was paving the road for a whole new set of questions. It didn't matter; he never seemed to tire of answering.

"Treet! Break's over. We need to shoot this scene before midnight." Sands Echo, the youngest director in history, waved at him from across the set.

Caroline curled her little fingers around his arm and whispered, "No, Daddy. Not yet!"

Treet's heart melted at the sight of her upturned, earnest face. With a wink, he called out to Sands, "Give us another five, will ya?"

Sands let out a dramatic sigh as he walked in Treet's direction. "Okay, but I'm sending makeup over. Oh, and you have a phone call."

Frowning at the intrusion, Treet took the cell phone and jammed it between ear and shoulder so that his hands would be free to continue turning the pages. Caroline didn't seem to notice his preoccupation, pointing at pictures and asking questions with a relentlessness that continued to astound Treet.

"What's this, Daddy?"

"A shark." He pressed the phone closer to his ear. "Hello? Treet Miller here."

"Does it bite?" Caroline persisted, forcing his face downward again with her chubby little hands.

"Hold on one sec," he instructed his mystery caller. Laughing, Treet kissed Caroline's nose. "Only if you bite first," he whispered. The official-sounding voice in his ear snagged his attention.

"Mr. Miller? This is Wade Collins. I'm the administrator for County Central Hospital. I need to meet with you about a serious matter concerning your daughter."

Treet's eyes narrowed. He stiffened in the chair. "What about her?" he demanded, silently signaling his bodyguard, Brutal, with a snap of his fingers. If this was a threat, it wouldn't be the first Treet had received, but when it involved Caroline he didn't take chances.

When the big, burly black man reached his side, Treet shifted Caroline into his massive arms. Caroline opened her mouth to protest, but immediately clamped it shut as Treet put a finger to his lips. She regarded him with dark eyes as if she sensed his sudden urgency, one arm linked trustingly around Brutal's thick neck.

"I'd prefer to talk to you in person," Mr. Collins stated.

"And I'd prefer that you didn't bullcrap me." Anger hardened Treet's voice. "So whatever you have to share with me will have to be over the phone—*if* you have anything to share, that is."

Silence. Treet counted his heartbeats as he waited, and forced himself to smile at Caroline.

Her gaze remained pensive and unwavering. She was nobody's fool, Treet thought with a surge of pride.

"Very well."

Mr. Collins cleared his throat, and the agitated sound sent a shiver of premonition along Treet's spine. He stifled the urge to hang up.

"I don't guess there's an easy way to say this."

"Just get to the da—" Treet's angry gaze collided with the bodyguard's. Brutal had been after him to clean up his language. He gritted his teeth and amended his words in deference to his listening daughter. "Just get to the point."

"You currently have custody of Caroline Nicole Windsor, correct?"

"Incorrect. It's Caroline Nicole *Miller*. Miss Windsor granted me full custody."

"She's not your daughter."

For a full thirty seconds Treet couldn't speak, and in those tension-fraught thirty seconds he thought of every nasty name he could remember from childhood and beyond, then directed them at his agent, Todd Hall.

Unfortunately, the unlucky agent was in Australia at the moment. But he'd have to come back to Hollywood eventually, and when he did Treet planned to tear him a new—

"I know this is going to sound like something straight from the headlines, Mr. Miller, but there was a mix-up at the hospital the day your daughter was born." Mr. Collins, apparently oblivious to Treet's boiling fury, continued. "Your daughter went home with someone else."

Treet nearly dropped the phone. "Excuse me?"

"Your daughter—your *real* daughter—went home with someone else." When the silence stretched again, the administrator prompted, "Mr. Miller? Are you there?"

"Yes." Treet closed his eyes, reeling from the news. Caroline wasn't Caroline? Caroline wasn't Cheyenne's daughter?

When he opened his eyes and focused on Caroline, she blew him a kiss and grinned as if to reassure him. A wrenching pain grabbed his heart as another, more staggering thought occurred to him.

"What—" He cleared the hoarseness from his voice. "What does all this mean?" He couldn't give her up. Not a chance. She had changed his life, brought out the good that had been hiding in his soul.

She was his light.

When his friends called his house, they heard Caroline's sweet, piping little voice on the announcement.

His video library overflowed with cartoons and Disney movies. He had watched *The Lion King* fifty-five times, and could recite the dialogue by heart.

Caroline's little pink princess robe hung on a hook in the bathroom next to his own. There was a doll in every room of the house, and jelly stains on the kitchen counters that his housekeeper declared would never come out.

"Well, we'll have to get this straightened out. We have an excellent counselor here at the hospital that can help the two of you figure out the best way to work through this."

"The two of us?"

"Yes, you and Miss Charmaine. She's the woman who has your real daughter. She's already been informed. I—I didn't tell her who you were, because I didn't want to overwhelm her further. If you've got a pen handy, I'll give you her number. You should get in touch with her within the week and set up an appointment to see our counselor. We'd like to make this as painless as possible for the children."

Treet fumbled in his shirt pocket and extracted a crayon. He stared at it. Green, Caroline's favorite color. Another pain squeezed his heart. His mind went into overdrive as he scrambled for an alternative.

Miss Charmaine. *Miss.* A single mother. Maybe he could work out a deal with her, get her to forget the whole crazy revelation.

Or persuade her to give him *both* daughters.

"Mr. Miller? Are you ready for the number?"

"Yes, I'm ready." Treet flipped to the back of Caroline's picture book and began to scribble.

His hands shook.

Chapter Two

At one o'clock in the afternoon, the hospital cafeteria at County Central resembled a morgue.

Hadleigh sat staring at the glass of iced tea on the table in front of her, wondering how she would survive the next thirty minutes—and the meeting thereafter.

It was so quiet she fancied she could hear the ice melting.

"You look like you're going to shatter," Karen observed, breaking the silence. "Everything will work out, you'll see."

Hadleigh rubbed her burning eyes, unaccountably irritated by her friend's remark. "How could this mess possibly have a happy ending, Karen? Either I'll get to keep Samantha and always wonder about the . . . other

16

child, or I'll have to make the trade and start all over again with a child I don't even know."

Just saying the words sent a cold chill down her spine. She'd tried not to think about it, reminding herself that Samantha was all that mattered. She didn't know the other child, and the other child's parents didn't know Samantha. The logical thing to do would be to keep it that way. Yes, this is what she had decided. If they wouldn't give her both children, then she would fight to keep Samantha.

"It's got to be confusing," Karen murmured sympathetically.

"That's an understatement." Hadleigh let out a harsh breath. "I can't believe this is happening to me!" For two weeks she'd lain awake long into the night, remembering the two o'clock feedings, the many hours walking the floor with Samantha through a bout of colic.

Samantha's first step, her first words, her first birthday party. Were the other parents thinking the same things? Did their daughter—*her* biological daughter—feel like their own flesh and blood? And how could she not, after four years?

Across the table, Karen fidgeted. "Did you see the television movie where the babies got switched—"

"Yes," Hadleigh fairly snapped. She grabbed her warmed tea and took a gulp, her hands shaking. "I saw it, and this isn't a movie. This is real life."

"I believe the movie was based on a true story," Karen argued. "And in the end they shared the kids."

"I don't want to share Samantha. For all I know, these people are descendants of the Manson family."

And they were raising her daughter. Hadleigh took another big swallow of her watery tea, but the dryness remained.

Karen echoed her thought. "Doesn't that bother you? Knowing your *real* child might be in the hands of unfit parents?"

Before Hadleigh could answer that, yes, it bothered her immensely, Karen gasped, her gaze riveted to a point beyond Hadleigh's shoulder.

Her voice so faint Hadleigh had to strain to hear, Karen whispered, "You won't believe who just walked into the cafeteria. You won't believe it. In fact, *I* don't believe it!"

At the moment, Hadleigh didn't care, but to pacify Karen, she cast a casual glance over her shoulder.

And froze.

Two men paused at the entrance to the cafeteria, surveying their surroundings. One she didn't recognize, a huge monster of a man with shoulders the width of a Mack truck. He was completely bald, his skin the color of fresh-ground coffee, and his arms the size of telephone poles. No doubt about it, the suit he wore had to be custom made. The man with him was understandably smaller in comparison.

Nevertheless, Treet Miller turned heads and stopped hearts.

Hers included, but not entirely because of his considerable appeal. His appearance had triggered a disturbing memory.

Treet Miller was here, at County Central Hospital. Hanging around in a deserted cafeteria.

"Wonder what he's doing here. Oh, God, who cares? I've got to get his autograph—"

Without taking her eyes from Treet, Hadleigh grabbed Karen's arm and pushed her back into the chair with more violence than she intended. "Don't move a muscle," she ordered in a hoarse whisper.

Treet Miller. At County Central.

"But, Hadleigh! It's *Treet Miller!* Barbi and Doreen will *kill* me if I don't get an autograph. In fact, I'll kill *myself!*"

"Karen—"

"God, he's even sexier in real life!" Karen snatched up her soggy napkin and fanned herself. "I think I'm going to have a heart attack!"

"Karen . . ." Treet Miller, here, at County Central on the day she was supposed to meet with Samantha's parents, and on the day Samantha was born, she had roomed with Cheyenne Windsor—Treet Miller's girlfriend and the mother of *his* baby.

The coincidence was too great. Too horribly, horrifically, great. *Oh, dear God!*

"And look, Hadleigh! I won the bet with Doreen. She bet me that he wore tinted contacts, but I'm here to tell you those baby blues are one hundred percent authentic! I've *got* to get his autograph—"

"Karen!"

Karen stopped ranting abruptly and looked at her, her eyes huge in her heart-shaped face. "What?"

19

Hadleigh tore her gaze from Treet and leaned close. Her heart was pounding so hard it hurt. "What color are Samantha's eyes?"

Frowning, Karen said, "Baby blue, just like—" She drew in a noisy gasp, her gaze sliding to where Treet wound his way through the deserted cafeteria. "No!"

"After I delivered Samantha, I roomed with his girl-friend, Cheyenne Windsor." Hadleigh whispered the reminder through her constricted throat. Her friends knew the story of how Treet Miller had threatened to steal Cheyenne's baby. And Cheyenne . . . Cheyenne had vowed he'd never get her.

"The supermodel." Karen shook her head. "This is unbelievable."

"Believe it." It was all circumstantial, of course, but Hadleigh was certain she'd hit the nail on the head. Cheyenne must have switched babies with her to keep Treet from having what he wanted, even if he didn't know he had the wrong baby. The supermodel must have pulled the switch while Hadleigh was still under sedation.

No matter what Treet's transgressions against Chey-enne, it was a rotten, devious, vengeful, horrendous stunt to pull. Because of Cheyenne, two innocent little girls' lives were about to be turned topsy-turvy, and she and Treet would be responsible for setting things right again. A monumental task, to say the least.

Hadleigh, normally slow to anger, felt a blast of fury so potent that if she hadn't been sitting, she was con-vinced it would have knocked her to her knees. If Cheyenne were before her now, she would take great pleasure in pulling her masses of beautiful red hair out by the roots.

She felt Karen's hand on her arm, shaking her.

"Hadleigh, you look murderous. It's not Treet's fault, is it? I mean, if you're thinking what I'm thinking, Cheyenne made the switch to get back at Treet. God, this sounds like a soap opera."

She was right—both times—but Hadleigh couldn't forget that if Treet hadn't tricked Cheyenne, then Cheyenne wouldn't have felt compelled to get revenge. It didn't excuse Cheyenne, of course, but it gave Treet his rightful portion of the blame.

And it gave Hadleigh a target for her immediate fury.

"Boss, do you know that woman? The fox with the dark hair?"

Treet glanced at the two women sitting at a table across the room. He hesitated a second. The one Brutal described did look vaguely familiar, and she was definitely a looker in a Meg Ryan sort of way, but he couldn't honestly say he knew her. "No, I don't. Why? Do you?"

"No, but she looks mad about something. That's twice I've caught her glaring at you." Brutal muttered a curse beneath his breath. "Damn, I told you we should have brought Trick and Antsy with us."

Slowly, Treet's brow rose in a mocking challenge. "If those women decide to pounce, I'm confident you can take care of it." He drummed his fingers on the table, restless and tense. "I need a cigarette."

"You quit four years ago."

"And your point is? I still need a cigarette."

"Caroline hates cigarettes."

Caroline . . . A vise clamped onto his heart. Somehow, some way, he had to convince Miss Charmaine to let him keep Caroline. Maybe she needed money.

The thought of *buying* his daughter put a nasty taste in his mouth.

"What time is it?"

"You've got a watch on."

"Oh. Right." Treet glanced at the Micky Mouse watch Caroline had proudly presented to him on his thirty-fourth birthday and saw that it was fifteen minutes past one.

"Don't worry, boss. I'll cry if I have to, get down on my knees and beg the woman to let us keep Caroline. When she sees a big man like me sobbing like a baby, she's sure to—"

"Be quiet, they're coming over."

"Who?" Brutal straightened in a hurry. He pasted a mean look on his broad face and flexed his massive arms—as if his sheer size weren't enough. "You want me to scare 'em off, boss?"

"They probably just want an autograph."

Brutal wasn't convinced. "Or a piece of your shirt, or a wad of your hair torn out by the roots. You can't be too careful, boss. Women go crazy when they see you. You have to remember that."

Sometimes Treet wished he could forget. "Just be cool, okay? I don't want to make a scene. It's almost time for the meeting."

The two women reached their table. Treet launched his for-fans-only smile, his gaze lingering with mild curiosity on the dark-haired woman hovering behind the blond. His heart gave a funny leap at her chilly look. Apparently she wasn't a fan of his.

"God, it *is* you, isn't it?" the blond gushed. "Treet Miller!"

The dark-haired woman rolled her eyes, folded her arms, and turned her back to them. Then, to Treet's astonishment, she began to tap her foot. "Come on, Karen. Get your autograph and let's go."

"Yes, can I have it? Your autograph, I mean?"

Treet took the pen she offered and quickly signed his name across a napkin. He handed it to Karen, glancing up just as the other woman turned around again. Her frosty green eyes resembled one of those packaged lime Popsicle sticks Caroline loved.

On impulse, Treet reached for another napkin. He poised the pen over the paper and stared straight at the mystery woman. "And your name is?" he inquired softly.

Green eyes glimmered with something that looked surprisingly like contempt as they swept over him. "None of your business." Grabbing Karen's arm, she urged her forward toward the exit door.

Brutal nudged him in the side. "I don't think you're her type, boss, if you know what I mean."

He started to agree, watching her slim hips rock from side to side with an appreciation he hadn't felt in months. Finally, he shook his head. "I think you're wrong about that."

23

"I don't think so, boss. I ain't never seen a woman turn away from you, not unless she likes her own kind better." Brutal stood and stretched. "We'd better get going."

Reluctantly, Treet rose from the chair and pushed Frosty from his mind. He'd sobbed his heart out before millions of viewers in the movie *Too Late*, and he'd walked buck naked into the ocean during a poignant suicide scene in the blockbuster flick *Trouble in Paradise*, yet he knew these challenges would pale in comparison to what he was about to face.

His knees were literally trembling—and it wasn't an act.

Chapter Three

Caroline's mother.

She was seated in front of the counselor's desk, profile slightly turned in his direction, a short, uneven swath of dark hair hooked over her ear.

And it was her exposed *ear* that Treet noticed first. Not usually the first thing he noticed about a woman, but this time he did. He stared, transfixed, by that ear.

It was shaped exactly like Caroline's ear: small, dainty, like a fragile seashell one might stumble across on the beach. He'd traced that shape many times, trying to remember Cheyenne's ears . . . and failing.

Now the puzzle was solved.

He stopped so quickly in the doorway that Brutal ran into him with a grunt. If Treet harbored any lingering doubt about the authenticity of the bizarre story, it was quickly fading.

And then the "fox" from the cafeteria turned to look at him.

The breath Treet had been holding whooshed out of his lungs in a burning hiss. Yes, he'd looked at her in the cafeteria when Brutal drew his attention, but that was before he knew who she was—Caroline's biological mother. Then he'd been looking at her as a man looks at an attractive woman. Now other details came under his scrutiny, details that might otherwise go unnoticed at the first appreciative glance.

Like the shape of her green eyes.

Caroline's eyes were brown—a rich chocolate brown that danced with merry lights or grew somber and fathomless, depending on her mood—but they were almond shaped like this woman's. In fact, when Caroline smiled, they tipped up at the corners in an adorable gamine way that never failed to make Treet smile.

Treet took another wobbly step, shaking off Brutal's sympathetic touch on his shoulder. He made it to the chair opposite Miss Charmaine's, hopefully without giving himself away. When he was seated, the counselor's rather chiding voice reminded him that he and Miss Charmaine were not alone in the room.

Amazingly, he'd nearly forgotten.

"Mr. Miller, I don't think there's any need for a bodyguard," Mrs. Shoreshire said dryly. "I hardly think you're in danger from either myself or Miss Charmaine."

Treet wasn't at all certain about the latter, if the jut of Miss Charmaine's chin and the frost in her eyes were any indication of her present mood. He glanced at her hands, noting the way she dug her nails into the leather arms as if to hold back a scream. She had an artist's fingers, long, slim, and beautiful.

Spotting Treet's barely perceptible nod, Brutal grumbled and backed from the room, leaving Treet alone to wonder why in the hell Miss Charmaine was mad at *him*. And if he knew his bodyguard and friend, Brutal would have his ear pressed to the door wondering the same damned thing.

Mrs. Shoreshire, a petite, middle-aged woman with short, iron-gray hair, clasped her hands in front of her and began her speech. "First, I want to apologize on behalf of County Central for this tragedy."

"My daughter isn't a *tragedy*," Treet growled at the same instant Miss Charmaine did the same, using nearly the exact same words.

"Sam isn't a tragedy!"

Unruffled, Mrs. Shoreshire gave her head an impatient shake, glancing from Treet's angry face to Miss Charmaine's equally furious one. "What I *meant* was, the tragedy that brings us here today."

"Are you implying that it would have been better if we hadn't found out?" Treet asked truculently. He was beginning to think this meeting was a bad idea, because the counselor seemed to be saying all the wrong things. Things that ticked him off.

"No, Mr. Miller, I wasn't implying—"

"Sounded like it to me," Miss Charmaine cut in with a challenging jut of her chin. She stared squarely at Mrs. Shoreshire in a gutsy way that ignited instant admiration in Treet. This woman was a fighter . . . like his Caroline.

"I think we've gotten off on the wrong foot," the counselor said. "Let's start over. We're all here today with Caroline's and Samantha's best interests at heart. Am I correct?"

Treet nodded. Miss Charmaine, he saw, reluctantly followed suit.

"We are all aware the hospital made a grave mistake, although how it could happen with the security we use these days is beyond me."

From the corner of his eye, Treet saw Miss Charmaine's mouth open, then close, as if she changed her mind about what she wanted to say. The odd action aroused his curiosity, but he kept silent as Mrs. Shoreshire continued.

"Regardless of how or why, it happened, and now we have to decide the best course of action. You may or may not be aware that you are both within your legal right to immediately reclaim your biological child."

"I don't think so," Treet said softly, yet distinctly.

"Over my dead body."

At her low-voiced, yet violent statement, Treet angled a brow and looked at her. She glared right back as if *he* were the enemy. Maybe she was confused. Maybe she thought *he* had something to do with the switch four years ago. Her obvious paranoia and unjust

28

hostility reminded him of Cheyenne, and that wasn't a pleasant thought.

"Miss Charmaine, I know how you must feel, and you too, Mr. Miller."

"Do you?" Miss Charmaine challenged, her voice brittle, her eyes glittery with tears. "How could you possibly know? Has this ever happened to you?"

"No, but—"

"Then you don't know. Samantha's my daughter. I don't care who her biological parents are. I'm not going to just hand her over—especially to *him!*"

Treet straightened in his chair, bristling at her implied insult. "Just what the hell do you mean by that? I don't even know you."

"But I know *you,* and *my* daughter—"

"You mean *my* daughter?" Treet cut in angrily, goaded into recklessness.

"No, she's mine! I'll fight you every inch of the way, and I'll win. No court will give a man like you custody of a small child."

Animosity crackled between them, heating the air.

Eyes narrowed, Treet said softly, "I have custody of my daughter, so apparently you're wrong." He waited a heartbeat, then added, "And I don't intend to give up Caroline, either."

Miss Charmaine's eyes widened. Her jaw dropped, then snapped shut. "You don't?" she squeaked, the anger fading from her eyes.

"Please, at least hear—"

They both ignored Mrs. Shoreshire.

"No, I don't."

"Then . . . then I can keep Samantha?"

"If I can keep Caroline."

Silence fell in the small office. Mrs. Shoreshire blew out an exasperated breath and drummed her fingers on the desk to get their attention. "Please, at least listen to me before you make such a hasty decision! If you both decide to keep the daughters you have, then you will have to legally adopt them."

"Fine."

"Okay." Treet tore his gaze away from Miss Charmaine's. Her beautiful eyes were almost hypnotizing in their intensity. That she loved her daughter—*his* daughter—he had no doubt. The realization made him feel oddly warm all over. But then, it was an emotion he understood, because he loved Caroline every bit as much.

"I see that you both think you have your mind set on this decision." Mrs. Shoreshire sounded resigned. "But I'm going to give you my counsel anyway.

"Right now you probably feel as if you could leave this office and forget the entire episode ever happened. But you won't, and you can't." She had their attention now. "When you leave here, Miss Charmaine, you'll start asking yourself little things. What color is Caroline's hair? Does she look like me? Is she happy? Well fed? Cared for? In a safe environment? Will she find out later that I didn't want her, and hate me for it? Will the knowledge ruin her life?"

Miss Charmaine inhaled sharply at the counselor's blunt words. Tears shimmered in her eyes. Watching her, Treet felt an unexplained anger toward the counselor. Before he realized it, he found himself saying, "She's playing on your guilt, hoping you'll change your mind."

"Am I?" Mrs. Shoreshire asked, pinning him with a glacial stare. "And what about you, Mr. Miller? Aren't you curious at all about Samantha, your own flesh and blood? Can you truly walk out of this room and never wonder about Samantha again?"

Treet sighed inwardly. He hated to admit it, but the old battle-ax had a point; it would drive him insane, more than either woman could ever imagine.

He settled his ankle onto his knee and said, "I guess you have a brilliant plan?"

"Maybe not brilliant, but something to consider. It won't cost you anything to listen." She focused on Miss Charmaine, who still looked as if she would burst into tears any moment. "Miss Charmaine? Are you willing to hear my suggestion?"

"If you're willing to accept the possibility that I may not agree," Miss Charmaine answered in a decidedly wobbly voice.

Treet resisted the urge to reach out and touch her—anywhere. He hadn't felt the need to connect with another person besides Caroline in so long, the urge surprised him. After Cheyenne, he found it hard not to be suspicious of women. It wasn't an episode in his life he cared to repeat. In fact, he preferred not to think about it at all.

"Fair enough. My advice is this: get together, the two of you, with Samantha and Caroline. Go some place private"—she slanted a reproving look Treet's way as if he were solely responsible for the paparazzi frenzy surrounding the mere mention of his name—"away from the media. Spend quality time together as if you were a family. In fact, the friendlier you appear to each other in front of the children, the more relaxed and safe they'll feel."

"You mean . . . tell them?" Miss Charmaine asked faintly. Her knuckles had turned white where she gripped the chair.

"Not right away, and maybe not ever. That would depend on your final decision. All I'm asking is that you at least get to know your biological daughters, see them, appease your curiosity about where they live and how they live, and assure yourselves that you can live with your decision." She paused a moment to let the information sink in, then added, "I'll be honest with you. This hospital doesn't need the publicity should this get out, and with Mr. Miller's background, it would be especially damaging."

Treet flashed her a humorless smile most of his fans would not have recognized. "You lost me. Tell me again why I should be concerned about the hospital's reputation? In fact," he continued softly, "what makes you think my lawyers aren't waiting outside that door right now, preparing to sue the pants off the hospital?"

"Because our security watched you enter the building, and we know you and your bodyguard came alone," Mrs. Shoreshire admitted candidly.

To Treet's surprise, Miss Charmaine came to her defense.

"She's right, if the media gets wind of this, we won't have a choice about telling our daughters the truth. I don't want to put Samantha through that."

It was on the tip of Treet's tongue to ask why she hadn't included Caroline, but then he realized how hypocritical he'd sound. Like him, she had probably been trying to ignore her instincts concerning her real daughter in favor of the one she'd loved and raised for four years. He of all people understood her angst, the torn emotion, the unavoidable guilt, and yes, the growing curiosity. These same emotions had bombarded him since the phone call two weeks ago.

Mrs. Shoreshire was giving them a chance to satisfy that curiosity, but at what cost? Would either of them be capable of walking away once they'd gotten to know their real daughters?

One truth kept emerging in Treet's mind: he knew his life would be horribly empty without Caroline. It was one of the reasons he'd hired a full-time nanny, so that he could take her with him on location and keep her with him as much as possible.

He also knew that Mrs. Shoreshire was right—he would never be able to pretend he didn't know the truth.

"Are we willing to give it a shot, then?" Without waiting for their response, Mrs. Shoreshire stood, signaling the conclusion of the meeting. She indicated a document on the desk. "If you'll just sign this statement saying that I explained the legal ramifications and gave you counsel to the best of my ability, then we're through here."

Slowly, Treet rose. Beside him, Miss Charmaine stood as well. He couldn't help noticing how pale she looked, just as he couldn't help noticing that one of the buttons of her blouse had come undone. The third one from the top. It gaped just enough to give him a glimpse of mystery and shadow.

Mustering his willpower, he looked away; he'd been successfully sued for less, as Brutal constantly reminded him.

After skimming the brief document, he signed his name and stood aside, watching as Miss Charmaine took her time reading before she picked up the pen. So that's where Caroline came by her caution, he mused, his gaze drifting to the curvy bottom revealed by the stretch of her skirt as she bent over the desk.

Heat flared in his groin, instant and surprising. No doubt about it, Miss Charmaine not only intrigued him, she appealed to his dormant libido. An interesting twist to an otherwise nerve-racking day.

She turned abruptly, nearly catching him in the act of ogling her. Treet backed up and almost stumbled over his chair, an uncharacteristically clumsy move for him.

Their eyes met, locked.

A tingle of awareness raced down his spine. Treet found himself saying, "Would you like to have dinner? We should talk about how to approach this—this—"

"Straight-from-the-headlines adventure?"

And then she smiled. Her almond eyes tipped up, just like Caroline's. Of course it was what one might call a "ghost" of a smile, rather sad and frightened.

But it was enough of a smile to make Treet go weak in the knees again, and this time this had nothing to do with nerves or fear of losing Caroline.

"Yes, I guess we'll have to talk."

Well, she could have sounded a tiny bit more pleased and a little less resigned, Treet grumbled to himself as he led the way to the office door.

It came open all too easily beneath his hand.

Brutal grabbed the doorjamb on the way down, catching himself before he fell across the threshold. He didn't look a bit embarrassed to be caught eavesdropping. "You read that document first, didn't you, boss?" he demanded.

"Believe it or not, Brutal, I *can* read," Treet drawled. He thought he heard the ghost of a chuckle behind him to go with that ghost of a smile, but he couldn't be sure.

Perhaps it was just wishful thinking.

The limo seemed to have every luxury with the exception of a bathroom. At least, there wasn't a bathroom that Hadleigh could see.

A long time ago in high school, her prom date had picked her up in a rented limo. She'd been uncomfortable then, and she was uncomfortable now.

A roomy station wagon was more her style. Okay, so maybe she'd take a Park Avenue if someone gave it to her, and she certainly enjoyed the stylish Intrepid she owned, but anything bigger seemed like a waste of space and money.

"Do you need to call someone and let them know you'll be late?"

Hadleigh gave a start, glancing at the compact cell phone in his hand before she shook her head. She deliberately avoided eye contact. Looking into his baby blues was paramount to looking into the sun, beautiful and blinding.

Dangerous and unsettling.

"No, thanks. Karen volunteered to pick Sam up from preschool."

"Karen . . . the girl that was with you in the cafeteria?"

Detecting a trace of amusement in his voice, she bristled on her friend's behalf. "Believe it or not, she's the most levelheaded person I know. I've never seen her so . . . flustered."

"You sound shocked."

"And *you* sound far too certain of your own appeal." She watched the Beverly Hills traffic through the heavily tinted window, trying to ignore the ominous rustling sounds coming from his direction. She didn't know what he was doing, but it sounded as if he were undressing.

"You weren't impressed."

"Good observation."

"At the risk of sounding conceited, may I ask why?"

Hadleigh choked on a derisive snort and finally forced herself to look at him so that he wouldn't suspect what a liar she was. She did a double take. He had disguised himself by stuffing his dark hair beneath a baseball cap, and gluing a thick mustache onto his upper lip. He still wore faded, butt-hugging jeans, but instead of the navy blue sweater, he now wore a checkered flannel shirt, rolled at the sleeves with the shirt tails out.

But his most vivid, memorable feature was still exposed.

Hadleigh stared into those baby blues and swallowed dry. "For starters, I'm a grown woman with a child, not a hormonally charged teenager. I don't have the time or the inclination to get gooey-eyed over a movie star, or any other man for that matter." Her pompous, self-righteous announcement might have worked—if her husky voice hadn't betrayed her.

"So you *are* single."

He had long black lashes to go with his killer eyes, Hadleigh couldn't help noticing. She also noticed the satisfaction in his voice. Why he would be satisfied to learn about her single status was beyond her, and she most certainly wasn't flattered. Flirting was probably as natural as breathing for a man like Treet Miller. A habit. Perhaps even an addiction.

Deciding the best—and safest—course of action would be to ignore his curious statement altogether, she changed the subject by asking, "Does your disguise usually work?"

Before he could answer, the glass door dividing them from the driver slid aside. The man he'd called "Brutal" spoke. "Boss, you want me to go in ahead and get you a private room?"

Treet Miller shook his head as he produced a pair of dark sunglasses from a side pocket in the limo door. "No, I'll take my chances." He flashed her a quick, boyish glance that made her heart play leapfrog with her lungs before adding, "Sometimes I get lucky."

"Boss, you're in a *limo*, for heaven's sake!"

"Just let us out at the next block and we'll double back to the restaurant."

Brutal's jaw went slack with disbelief. He snapped it shut and glared at Treet. "If you think I'm going to leave you, you're crazy. Don't you remember what happened last time you tried this?"

"It was an accident."

"Yeah, right."

"The girl didn't mean any harm."

"Still hurt, didn't it, boss?" Brutal taunted. "And what if this time it's your face instead of your arm?"

"Don't be such a pessimist."

As Hadleigh listened to their byplay, her curiosity got the best of her. "What happened?"

"It wasn't a big deal . . . until Brutal *made* it a big deal," Treet groused.

But Brutal appeared to take great satisfaction in relating the tale. "The last time he pulled this stunt, the waitress recognized him. She got all flustered and dumped hot linguini on his arm. Burned the hair clean off."

"It grew back, and it didn't scar," Treet added with a long-suffering sigh. "Drop it, Brutal, before I tell her what I caught *you* doing last Christmas."

Brutal's coffee-colored eyes narrowed threateningly. "You start spreading that story and I'll snatch you bald-headed myself, boss, and that's a fact."

"Then shut up. You're scaring Miss Charmaine."

Hadleigh bit back a smile at their bickering. The brotherly love between them was obvious. "I don't scare that easily, Mr. Miller."

"Call me Treet."

"I don't think—" She sucked in a sharp breath as Treet Miller, superstar, voted one of the top ten sexiest men in the world, thrust his face close and pinned her with his famous baby blues.

The breath remained in her lungs as his fingers curled around her chin and angled her face upward. Closer to those blindingly blue eyes. She watched in helpless fascination as his mouth curved in a bone-melting smile that had sent millions of women of all ages into a swoon.

And just as she remembered, his eyes smiled right along with it, as if he possessed delicious secrets.

"Say it," he commanded softly.

It was a command no sane woman could resist.

And as any sane woman would in the face of such sensual beauty, Hadleigh breathed, "Treet . . ."

With a superhuman effort, she jerked free and scrambled from the car before Brutal could open the door. She slammed it behind her and leaned against the limo, expelling the breath she'd been holding.

No doubt about it, her knees were definitely shaking. She passed an equally shaky hand over her face and muttered an uncharacteristic curse, followed by a rueful chuckle. So much for maturity, she thought, blown away by her surprising reaction. The girls would have a field day if they knew that she—the same woman who had chided Karen over her silly, juvenile reaction on meeting the star—had melted like a hot candle at the touch of his fingertips.

Not that Hadleigh would be foolish enough to tell them. Oh, no. *Some* sanity remained!

Chapter Four

"So . . ." Hadleigh cast a deadpan look at Treet over her menu, opting for humor to ease the incredible tension in her belly. Since Treet had announced he wasn't going to give up *his* daughter, either, most of her earlier animosity had faded, leaving in its wake a dangerously giddy relief. "Do I dare order linguini?"

There was a slight flaring of his eyes before one eyebrow shot upward beneath the shadow of his cap. He'd laid his sunglasses aside to look at the menu. "The mystery lady has a sense of humor."

"I'm no mystery lady," Hadleigh quipped, focusing on her menu and *not* on the brilliance of his eyes. "Just a plain, hardworking mother of a rambunctious four-year-old."

The moment the reminder was out, a charged silence fell between them. Now the exchange of information would begin and there would be no turning back, Hadleigh thought. Until this moment, Caroline was the name of Treet Miller's daughter, someone she'd read about, but had never met and didn't know.

If it were possible, her stomach knotted even more tightly.

The arrival of the waitress was a lifesaver, in Hadleigh's opinion. She needed a moment to adjust to the fact that she was having dinner with Treet Miller in a public restaurant—before they began exchanging facts about their mutual daughters.

How totally bizarre.

With a faint shake of her head, Hadleigh resisted the urge to pinch herself. This was truly happening, and she might as well make the best of it. Something to relate one day to her grandchildren . . . who would in reality be Treet's grandchildren.

She ground her teeth and chided herself. No, nothing had changed; she was still determined to keep Samantha, and that would make Samantha *her* daughter. Still, if she could find a way to have both, all the better.

In a perfect world, Treet would put his menu aside and confess that he didn't have time to continue raising his daughter, that his lifestyle wasn't a good environment for a small, impressionable child.

In a perfect world . . .

Treet broke the new tension in a way that quickly dispelled Hadleigh's dangerous fantasies and made her smile. He kept his eyes on the menu as he gave the waitress his order. "I'll have the *cold* linguini shrimp salad and a glass of iced tea."

It was nice that he could joke about his fame, Hadleigh mused. Holding the menu high to hide her impish smile, Hadleigh said, "Good choice, *Ronald.* I think I'll have the *steaming* linguini with the clam sauce."

When the waitress had gone, Treet leaned forward. "Ronald? Is that a former boyfriend?"

"No." Hadleigh laughed at his absurdly disgruntled expression. "I just plucked the name from my head."

"Thanks."

"You're welcome."

"You act as if you've done this before."

"Well, I haven't. I guess I was just born with the talent," she added breezily. Hadleigh avoided his gaze and reached for her water.

"Sassy woman."

She darted a quick look at him—it was the most she could handle—and tried to sound casual. Inside, her heart was racing. "You don't even know me."

"I'd like to."

Habitual flattery. Hadleigh heaved an inward sigh. Too bad he was who he was, and they were here for the reason they were here. Otherwise . . . otherwise she might have relaxed and enjoyed the flirty, chance-of-a-lifetime interlude. Like most women, she had had her share of fantasies about movie stars. And like most of her immediate friends, they had often included Treet Miller.

At least they had before she found out his feet were made of clay. A sobering reminder.

"I guess your curiosity's understandable, given the circumstances." But Hadleigh didn't want to talk about herself, not that she didn't lead an interesting life. But compared to his own—well, her existence would probably sound pretty dull. He might do something humiliating, like fall asleep on her. He was, after all, *Treet Miller.*

To distract him, she whispered, "Don't look now, but I think someone's recognized you!"

Treet froze, then carefully followed the direction of her eyes. Hadleigh watched his shoulders relax when he spotted Brutal sitting at a table a few yards away. She quickly dropped her laughing gaze when he turned to look at her.

"Sassy, humorous, *and* a trickster," he observed in that deep, sexy drawl of his. "What other secrets are you hiding, I wonder?"

"Sorry. Guess I'm just nervous."

"You could have fooled me."

His fingers did a rapid tatoo on the table, filling the sudden silence. "Is she . . . really rambunctious?"

Hadleigh took a deep breath. This was it. She couldn't put it off any longer. And now that the drawbridge was down, it all came spilling out. "Yes, she is. And very bright. She's been reading since she was three and a half." She took another gulp of her water to ease the sudden dryness in her throat. "How about . . . Caroline? What's she like?"

As she waited for him to speak, a fist slowly closed around her heart until her chest hurt. It was at that moment that Hadleigh realized just how perceptive

Mrs. Shoreshire was. Never in a million years would she be able to forget about Caroline now that she knew. The shock of finding out was wearing off and reality was sinking in.

"She has her moments of extreme energy, but for the most part Caroline's the quiet type. A little bashful until she gets to know you. Then she'll talk your ears off. She's very bright, too, and loves books."

Hadleigh listened to the loving pride in his voice. The fist around her heart slowly began to ease. A new mixture of feelings moved in, pushing her anxiety aside. Tenderness. Wistfulness. Regret. Jealousy.

Terror.

"She keeps after me to teach her to read, but I don't think it ever occurred to me that she *could* learn this early."

"Samantha wouldn't take no for an answer. In fact, sometimes I wonder if she hears the word *no* at all." Hadleigh smiled faintly in remembrance. "I have to practice reverse psychology to get her to do anything."

"That sounds familiar."

Surprised, Hadleigh looked at him.

And wished she hadn't. His blue, blue eyes were shimmering with something that looked suspiciously like tears. She pretended not to notice—for his ego's sake. As for the sudden lurching of her heart, she decided not to notice that either. "You were like that as a child?"

He grunted and glanced away as if embarrassed. "Was and still am, according to Brutal, my agent, and just about every director I've worked with."

"That explains it, then." Hadleigh forced a chuckle. "I couldn't figure it out. Jim's a quiet, orderly person, and I'm not usually so—so—"

"Animated? Funny?" Treet supplied gallantly. "Does this mean I bring out the best in you?"

He sounded ridiculously hopeful . . . considering they'd only just met. A very good reminder. "I was just trying to ease the tension."

"So you noticed it too."

"Not *that* kind of tension," she blurted out, then flushed. She hadn't meant to admit that she knew what he'd meant. And what if he *hadn't* meant it?

"If you say so."

Exasperated and embarrassed, Hadleigh said, "Look, we've got a serious situation on our hands, so could you please lose the charm? I'm not . . . I mean, you don't have to . . ." Hadleigh floundered, then tried again as he folded his arms and looked amused. "I'm flattered, but I don't think we need to complicate things."

He shrugged . . . and continued to look at her in a way that made her shiver inside. As if he liked what he saw, and liked it a lot. How many women had seen that look? Hundreds? Thousands? Probably millions.

"Okay, I promise not to say anything that I don't mean. Fair enough?"

For a moment, Hadleigh simply stared at him. Finally she gave her head a rueful shake. "It's scary to think that my clever little monkey is going to grow up to be a clever *big* gorilla like her father."

Those Baby Blues

He flashed her a million-dollar smile that she'd recently seen on the cover of *People* magazine. "I can't wait to meet her." His smile faded all too quickly. "Caroline looks like you. When I saw you in the cafeteria, I thought you looked familiar. Her eyes are brown, but shaped like yours. Her hair is a similar shade of mahogany, and her ears are *exact* replicas of yours."

Hadleigh gave her ear a self-conscious tug. "Oh, no. Bless her heart. I've always hated my little ears."

"You're kidding. I think they're delicate and beautiful. Very feminine."

Another flattering remark Hadleigh wisely ignored. "Samantha has your eyes—those famous baby blues. Of course, not in a million years would I have made *that* connection."

The waitress arrived with their food, her platter of steaming linguini transferred to the table without mishap. They ate in silence for a few moments before Hadleigh ventured hesitantly, "How—how is Caroline coping without a mother?"

Treet stabbed a shrimp and popped it in his mouth. When he pulled the fork away, his mustache came with it. With a quick, boyish smile he tucked it out of sight beside his plate. "She's a daddy's girl, and she loves Miss Trudy, her nanny."

Instantly, Hadleigh envisioned a tall, sleek blond with a soft voice and big breasts. She winced at the image and shoved it away; it was none of her business if he employed a dozen blond bimbos.

"How about Samantha? All you have to do is read the papers to know what's happening in *my* life, but I

47

don't have that luxury. Does your ex-husband share the responsibilities with you?"

Hadleigh's throat closed at the mention of her ex-husband. She laid her fork aside. "It was Jim that demanded the DNA testing. He left before Samantha was born, but recently remarried and decided he wanted to play Daddy. Samantha doesn't even know him." She tried to keep the bitterness from her voice as she added, "After finding out about the switch, I don't think I'll have to worry about Jim coming around again."

"So that's the way it is." Treet sounded as disgusted by Jim's actions as Hadleigh felt. He removed his hat, swept his thick dark hair from his forehead, and then replaced it.

It proved to be a big mistake.

"Hey, aren't you—oh my God, it's Treet Miller!"

A bloodcurdling scream followed the young girl's shrill announcement. Chairs scraped the floor, and voices rose from a comfortable murmur to an excited roar within astounding seconds.

Like the genie of fairy tales, Brutal appeared as if by magic at Treet's side and yanked him out of his chair. Before Hadleigh could fully comprehend what was happening, Treet reached out and grabbed *her* arm before Brutal could drag him away.

"Let's get out of here, boss, before they tear you limb from limb," Brutal shouted. He pulled them through the swinging doors into the restaurant's kitchen, startling the cooking crew into silence.

The silence didn't last long.

A plump, middle-aged woman wearing a stained apron and a hair net over her iron-gray curls turned from her task to stare at them. Her eyes widened in instant recognition. "Look! It's Treet Miller, by God! Right here in our kitchen!" The spoon she'd been holding clattered to the floor as she started in their direction at a lumbering run. Along the way her hip bounced off the handle of a big pot on the stove, sending it crashing. Steamed lobsters washed across the floor beneath the force of the boiling water.

The urgency of their situation finally sank in. Hadleigh, pressed against Treet's back, glanced frantically around, looking for the back door as Brutal tried to block the woman's path.

She spotted a small storeroom off to the left. Grabbing a fistful of Treet's flannel shirt tail, she shouted, "Come on! This way."

They made it inside just as the growing crowd burst through the swinging doors of the kitchen. For the moment, Hadleigh didn't think they had spotted them.

Brutal appeared in the doorway of the storeroom, blocking the crowd's view. "Lock the door," he instructed. "And don't move. I'm going for backup."

Before Brutal could get the heavy door shut, Treet thrust out his booted foot and grinned at Brutal. "Aren't you going to say I told you so?"

The big bodyguard appeared speechless. Finally, he sputtered furiously, "Boss, one of these days I'm gonna—"

"There he is!" someone screamed behind Brutal, effectively ending his tirade.

"Treet! Treet Miller!"

Hastily, Treet removed his foot and shut the door, bolting it from the inside.

Stunned, shaken, still reeling from the bizarre events of the last few moments, Hadleigh found herself alone in a very small space with a man who could arouse millions of otherwise sane, mature women to a frothing, crazy frenzy.

America's number-one heartthrob.

A superstar.

A sexy, drop-dead gorgeous hunk with blazing blue eyes and a killer smile. A man who obviously possessed an irresistible charm, not to mention the fact that he filled out his jeans like nobody's business—front *and* back.

Samantha's *father*.

She put a hand to her throat, not surprised to find her pulse pounding in a crazy, erratic rhythm. It was a brutal reminder that she, too, was a woman. Did she really think she was immune where others were not? Even now, the crowd outside continued to chant Treet's name as if their lives would change dramatically if they could only touch him.

When he turned from securing the door and leaned his back against it, Hadleigh blurted out the first silly thing that came to her mind, which just happened to be a corny cliche. "Do—do you come here often?"

Her eyes were huge in her pale face, a heart-shaped face framed by thick hair the color of dark chocolate.

She was frightened, that much Treet could see. And shocked, as could be expected. But he thought he saw something else in the luminous depths of her eyes . . . something not unlike fear, but not exactly fear.

Wariness. Reserve. Determination.

Interesting, Treet mused, admitting to himself how refreshing it was to see something other than blind adoration on a woman's face. The fact that she was wary interested him most of all, because if she was wary, that meant she was worried about something.

And since he was an optimistic kind of guy, he chose to believe that her worry stemmed from the attraction she'd have to be blind, deaf, and dumb not to notice. He didn't think she was any of those things.

With a barely perceptible move, Treet shifted his back against the light switch digging into his spine.

The room went dark. She let out a tiny shriek of surprise, then fell silent.

"You see?" Treet heaved an exaggerated sigh. "That's why I stopped coming here. They not only let strangers tromp all around their kitchen, they never pay their light bill."

"You're not funny. What—what do you think happened to the lights?"

"I don't know. Maybe they're hoping one of us is claustrophobic. Sort of like a smoke-out."

Behind him, the fans continued to chant his name, their voices rising and falling. He felt a rumbling against his spine as someone beat on the door and demanded he open it. As *if*.

"If *you* were, they'd know it," she pointed out matter-of-factly.

"What about you?"

"Not claustrophobic, no."

Striving to keep the hope out of his voice, he asked, "Afraid of the dark?"

"Not—not really."

He shamelessly pounced on that tiny hesitation. Gauging the distance between them, he reached her and gently snagged her waist with his arm. Very, very slowly, he pulled her in his direction, relying on instinct and smell alone to guide her to him. She wore expensive perfume—something light and tantalizing.

Her breath exploded against his neck as she whispered, "What—what are you doing?"

Treet closed his eyes and inhaled the soft fragrance of her hair before he answered. His voice was noticeably husky when he did. "Following Mrs. Shortshirt's advice."

She awarded him with a nervous chuckle. "You mean Mrs. Shoreshire, don't you?"

"Do I?" Treet countered teasingly, bringing her just a little closer. They were nearly touching now, and he could feel his body straining toward hers. He hoped Brutal had a hell of a time finding someone to help him control the crowd outside. With Hadleigh in his arms, he could stay here all night. "Didn't she suggest we appear friendly?"

"Yes, but—"

"She said we should look convincing, too."

"Hmm, but—"

"You said yourself that my daughter is extremely bright." He felt her stiffen and he knew he'd said something wrong. It didn't take him long to figure out what it was, either. "I meant *your* daughter, not *my* daughter." Although her daughter *was* his daughter. Or could be.

"It's okay. I just—I'm just not used to sharing her with anyone."

"Me either. It's just been me and Caroline for a long time now." Her silence was telling, and prompted him to ask, "You don't believe me?"

"Your personal life is not my business, Treet."

He liked the way she said his name, drawing it out as if she liked saying it. Wishful thinking, he supposed. Still, a man could wish. "Rule number one if we're going to be friends: don't believe anything you hear, see, or read about me." The darkness masked her expression, but Treet sensed her skepticism.

She didn't bother hiding it from her voice. "Photographs don't lie."

"The hell they don't. Five years ago they featured me on the front page of *Sizzling Star* with Lady Diana. I'd never met her in my life."

"Did you sue?"

"No." She shifted restlessly in the loose hold of his arms, but to his delight, she didn't move away.

"Like I said before, it's not really my business what you do. I may know you, but I don't *know* you."

"Which brings me back to the point at hand. I think we should start right now getting to know each other."

53

Her soft, helpless laughter sent a thrill right down to his toes.

"Just like Samantha—too impatient to start at the beginning."

Treet shrugged, grinning to himself. He inched his hand along her spine until he reached her shoulder. Her delicate bones shifted beneath his fingers. "We had dinner, didn't we?"

"Do you always go straight from dinner into bed?"

"Do you always read people's minds?" he countered softly. Cupping her chin, he brought her face close to his; he could feel her warm breath against his mouth, excited little puffs that gave him hope. Prudently, he checked his urgent impulse to plunge ahead and kiss her. "I don't think we're going to have a problem convincing our girls that we like each other."

"Liking is as far as it's going to go, Treet. I'm not a sleep-around kind of woman." Her voice dropped to a squeaky whisper as Treet nuzzled his mouth against hers.

"Thank God. But a little hugging and kissing won't hurt, will it? Just to show them what great friends we are."

"I'm beginning to think you have a devious mind."

She inserted her hand between them and pushed gently at his chest, but her breathing wasn't anything close to normal, Treet noted with supreme satisfaction.

"Look, I don't think it would be a good idea to become involved like this."

"Why not?"

"Because you're *Treet Miller*, and I'm just—just Hadleigh Charmaine." She sounded exasperated and flustered in the same breath. "We might as well live on different planets."

"Can you be a little more specific?" Meanwhile, Treet had managed to pull her another inch closer. Soon he'd have her fully against him—something he discovered he wanted more than he'd wanted anything in a long time.

Reluctantly, she admitted, "I don't know if I'm reacting to *you,* or to *Treet Miller.*"

Well, she didn't mince words, Treet thought, wincing inwardly, but at least she was admitting to a reaction. After a slight hesitation, he decided a little humor was in order. Humor seemed to be the magic key between them. "The answer to that should be pretty obvious."

"You lost me."

"You're still in your clothes."

Treet braced himself for a slap. Fact was, he wouldn't have blamed her if she had slapped him, because now that the words were out, he realized how crass he sounded. Crass and conceited.

But she didn't slap him.

Instead she gave him his most fervent wish by falling against him and burying her face in his shoulder—laughing.

"You are incorrigible!" she muttered between chuckles. "And I'm not supposed to like you."

Treet was so immersed in savoring the feel of her supple body against his hardening one that he nearly missed her last statement. "You're not?" She shook her head, sending her silky hair cascading across his cheek.

"Never mind."

"Oh, no, you don't. You can't just blurt out something like that and expect me to forget it."

"Let me go and I'll tell you."

"Kiss me and I'll let you go."

"Why do you want to kiss me? There must be thousands—no, hundreds of thousands of women who would give their eyeteeth to be kissed by you."

"And you're not one of them." Treet deliberately injected a note of hurt in his voice. Actually, it wasn't as contrived as he had meant it to be. "Just my luck."

"You only want to kiss me because I'm not falling at your feet. It's that primitive, male conquering thing."

"What are you, a psychologist?"

"No, I'm an illustrator of children's books."

"You're *that* Hadleigh Charmaine?" Treet let out a low whistle. "See, we're of the same species after all, so it's okay for us to kiss."

"You're making fun of me."

But she was chuckling again, which Treet took as a very good sign. He loved this woman's sense of humor. "Seriously, I'm not joking. I've seen your name in several of Caroline's books. That puts you on the Hollywood map, honey, so come here and give me a kiss."

"Stop!" She was laughing against his neck again, obviously unaware of what that did to him.

Treet decided he'd been patient long enough. He cupped her chin in his hand and guided her mouth to his, turning her laughter into a moan of surprise. He kissed her softly, exploring her tender, shapely lips before slipping his tongue between her teeth.

It was a joyous, exciting moment when she gave him access and allowed him to press her tightly against his arousal.

And hell on earth when the door behind him opened abruptly, polluting his small slice of heaven with screaming fans and shouting policemen.

Chapter Five

Hadleigh unlocked her apartment door and stepped inside, dropping her purse on the hall table. She paused a moment, frowning at the unnatural quiet. Apparently Karen and Samantha were gone, probably to get something to eat, she mused.

When she turned around, she encountered two astounded pairs of eyes watching her from the sofa. Barbi Copeland and Doreen Bates, two of her best friends.

As one, they came to their feet and rushed to her side. Doreen had apparently came straight from work; she still wore her paramedic's uniform.

"What happened to you? Oh my God, Hadleigh, you look awful!" Barbi, who owned and operated an exclusive beauty salon, plucked at Hadleigh's wild hair, attempting to smooth it down.

Doreen echoed Barbi's exclamation, indicating Hadleigh's torn sweater. She bent closer to examine a nearly invisible scratch on her arm. "Are you okay? What the hell happened?"

"He wouldn't let go of me."

"Why, that son of a bitch!"

"I *knew* this would happen!" Barbi said. "We've got to call the cops! I don't care if he's the pope, he won't get away with this!"

Dazed, bruised, and still reeling from the day's events—and Treet's kiss—Hadleigh watched in silence as Barbi marched to the phone and snatched it up. Her long red nail tapped an angry, impatient rhythm against the phone.

Finally, Hadleigh found her voice, suppressing the hysterical urge to laugh. This day had been the most bizarre of her life, and it wasn't over yet. She felt like weeping and laughing at the same time. "Treet didn't do this, Barbi, so put the phone down."

Her friend froze with phone in hand, obviously not convinced. "Then what happened? Why are you—you *mauled* like this? Karen said you left with Treet Miller—"

"I did, and yes, I've been with him. But he didn't do this. His fans did." All because he wouldn't let her go. When she had tried to remain behind as Brutal pushed and shoved his way through the frenzied crowd, he'd kept hold of her hand, stubbornly insisting she stay with him. Silly to be flattered, but she was.

"His . . . fans?" Doreen echoed faintly.

Sighing, Hadleigh stumbled to her favorite chair and collapsed. Quickly, she related the evening's events to her eager, curious friends, leaving out the most memorable event of all—the kiss. And what a kiss. Her toes were still tingling in reaction. It would be years before she could forget it, although the sane, logical side of her brain insisted she try.

What a fickle person she was! When she'd first realized Treet was Samantha's father, she was determined to believe every horrible, shocking thing she'd read about him.

Then she'd met him, and he was nothing like what she'd expected.

After she finished with her outrageous tale, Barbi and Doreen remained silent for a moment. Hadleigh suspected they were as stunned as she felt.

"So . . . let me get this straight," Barbi said slowly. "You were locked in a storeroom with Treet Miller for half an hour?"

Hadleigh nodded.

"And you've told us everything?" Doreen asked in a disbelieving voice.

A flush crept up Hadleigh's neck as she nodded again. It wasn't like her to keep things from her close friends, but she wasn't ready to talk about what else had happened in that storeroom—at least not until she'd had time to think about it first.

"So what's he like?" Doreen demanded, apparently satisfied that Treet hadn't manhandled Hadleigh, but not totally convinced he hadn't put the move on her.

If only she knew, Hadleigh mused, imagining their reaction. "He's funny."

Barbi's eyes widened. "You spent thirty minutes in a closet—"

"Storeroom."

"*Storeroom* with Treet Miller and all you can say is that he's *funny?*"

"He reminds me a lot of Samantha," Hadleigh added.

"Oh."

"I see."

Barbi and Doreen exchanged a mysterious look. Hadleigh narrowed her eyes as she glanced from one to the other. "Something you're not telling me?"

"We were just wondering," Barbi began reluctantly, "if you remembered the rumor that was floating around about the time that Cheyenne gave him custody of Caroline."

Hadleigh's stomach bottomed out. She didn't have the slightest idea what Barbi was talking about, but she suspected she was about to find out. "Go on."

"The one about Caroline being another man's baby."

As their meaning finally sank in, Hadleigh closed her eyes against the impact this new realization had on her already overloaded nervous system. "So you guys are thinking . . . that *if* this rumor were true, then he might try to take Samantha from me, even after he assured me that he didn't want to give Caroline up anymore than I wanted to give Samantha up?"

"We're saying that you need to be careful. You can't forget that he planned to take Cheyenne's baby from the beginning."

Hadleigh couldn't resist pointing out the obvious. "Let's say the rumor is true. Do you honestly think Treet would have fought so hard to get custody of Caroline if he knew she wasn't his?"

"He's a public figure," Doreen said. "After making such a fuss about it, what else could he do without damaging his image?"

It just didn't make sense, Hadleigh thought. "You weren't there. He talks about Caroline like I talk about Samantha. He loves his daughter."

"He's an actor," Barbi reminded her bluntly. "Rumor has it they paid him twenty-five million for his brief role in *Doubting Daniel*. And there's something else: while we were waiting for you to get back, someone called asking questions about you. He wouldn't give us a name."

Hadleigh groaned. "Not a reporter!"

"I don't think so. He sounded like an investigator, and when I told him you weren't here, he started asking *me* very personal questions about you. Not that I told him anything."

"Barbi hung up on him after telling him to mind his own damned business."

"You did the right thing," Hadleigh said with a frown. She glanced around the apartment, searching for telltale signs that Samantha had been there. Karen had been instructed to bring her straight home from preschool, but Sam's bright purple backpack was nowhere in sight.

Alarmed, she sat up straight. "Where's Sam?"

Those Baby Blues

"With Karen," Barbi quickly assured her. "After that man called . . . and considering the possibilities, we all thought it would be best if Karen took Samantha home with her until you got back."

"You think he'd try to *kidnap* her?" The very thought was ludicrous. Treet Miller wasn't above the law, and he wasn't stupid. Yet . . . yet Mrs. Shoreshire *had* stated they were both within their rights to immediately claim their biological daughters. What if Treet decided to take Sam, then disappear into oblivion? Hadleigh knew he had the means and the money.

Perhaps she *was* being naive in trusting him.

She jumped as the phone rang. Barbi snatched it up before Hadleigh could remind her this was *her* apartment. Her friends were taking their duties a little too seriously.

"Charmaine residence." Eyes wide, Barbi listened for a few seconds, then covered the mouthpiece with her hand and whispered loudly, "Speaking of the devil. It's *him!*"

No need to ask who *he* was, Hadleigh mused. She took the phone from Barbi, praying her astute friend hadn't noticed her trembling hand. "Hello?"

"Hadleigh?"

Weakness flooded her knees at the sound of his low, sexy voice, despite her best efforts to remain unmoved. "Yes?"

"I wanted to make sure you're all right. I'll replace your sweater—"

"That's all right," Hadleigh interrupted, highly aware of Barbi and Doreen listening. "It was old anyway." A tiny silence fell between them. Then Hadleigh heard a muffled curse.

"Look, I don't blame you for being freaked. It was my fault for thinking I could get away with it."

"I'm fine." And she was. Confused, wary, and emotionally drained, but otherwise fine.

"We didn't get to talk about how we're going to approach this . . . situation."

Because we were doing other things besides talking. Hadleigh wasn't certain she would have been brave enough to voice the thought aloud even if Barbi and Doreen hadn't been listening, but she was sure thinking it.

"So I'm calling to arrange another meeting, this time some place more private."

As if a locked, dark storeroom weren't private. Frustrated by her audience, Hadleigh said, "Okay."

"Okay? Just like that?" He paused a beat, then asked softly, "Are you alone?"

"No."

"Oh. Karen?"

"Um, no, but close."

"Should I call you later on tonight?"

"That would be fine." Hadleigh fancied she could feel Barbi's breath on her neck. And if Doreen leaned any closer, she would definitely tip over and fall into Hadleigh.

"How about if I just come over? I'll bring my pajamas and we'll have a slumber party."

"Very funny." With extreme effort, Hadleigh suppressed a smile. "Later."

The moment she hung up the phone, they pounced.

"You're hiding something," Barbi accused.

"Yeah," Doreen added, narrowing her eyes on Hadleigh's flushed face. "I thought we were your friends."

Hadleigh faced them, arms folded across her middle, legs braced as if taking a stand. Which she suddenly felt she was. Gently, she said, "We're not teenagers, girls. I'm perfectly capable of handling my own business and making my own decisions."

Barbi's jaw dropped.

Doreen snorted.

Before either could argue, Hadleigh held up a restraining hand. "I'm not ignoring your warnings, or your advice. But I *am* going to trust my instincts on this one."

"Like you trusted your instincts about Jim?" Doreen taunted.

"I'd like to think I'm smarter now."

"Let's hope so." Barbi let out a lusty sigh and threw her hands in the air. "Like you said, we're grown women now. I just hope you know what you're doing. He's *Treet Miller*, for heaven's sake, Hadleigh! He probably eats little girls like you for brunch!"

"If you ask me, you're starstruck," Doreen inserted, arms folded in a militant stance.

"I recall a time when both of you thought he was God's gift to women," Hadleigh pointed out. "And I'm *not* starstruck."

Doreen flushed at the reminder, but stood her ground. "That was before our best friend got involved with him. Before he became a threat."

"He isn't a threat." When they both remained stubbornly silent, Hadleigh let out an exasperated breath. "This isn't about me, girls. Treet is Samantha's father. If I don't give her this opportunity to get to know him, she might very well hate me for it later." Her voice thickened with emotion. "And I have to see Caroline. Is that so wrong?"

Doreen stared at her long and hard. *"If* that's what this is all about, and *if* that's Treet's motive as well."

"You shouldn't believe every rumor you hear," Hadleigh chided.

"And *you* shouldn't believe every single word that comes from that million-dollar mouth," Doreen retorted, grabbing Barbi's arm and marching to the door. She looked indignant, a little hurt, and a lot worried. "Come on, Barbi. We can take a hint. Maybe Karen will have better luck talking some sense into her starstruck head than we did."

Hadleigh watched her friends leave, torn between guilt and relief. Lord, she thought with a groan, if things ended badly, they would never, ever let her live this down. She'd have to move to another country to escape the incessant I-told-ya-so's.

"Caught in the witch's evil spell, Princess Aurora reached out and pressed her finger against the point of the spindle." Treet paused in his reading to glance at Caroline. She was fast asleep, her dark lashes resting on her rosy cheeks. With a tender smile, Treet kissed her forehead, tucked the Scooby Doo comforter more securely around her, and turned out the bedside lamp.

He bumped into Trudy in the hall. The diminutive Korean widow flashed him a quick smile.

"She sleeping?"

"Yes." Treet chuckled as he added, "And as usual she fell asleep before the ending. I'm wondering if she's ever going to know what happens to Sleeping Beauty." He'd tried to read the book in stages, but Caroline insisted he start at the beginning every night. The situation didn't seem to bother Caroline, but it was driving *him* crazy.

"She sweet child," Trudy said, in her broken English.

Treet knew that Brutal spent an hour a day working with Trudy on her English. In return, Trudy did her best to satisfy Brutal's sweet tooth by baking cookies and pastries on a daily basis.

"You go now. I watch her."

"Thanks." He turned in the opposite direction, toward the front door.

"And, boss?"

Treet paused.

"Do not worry. Whatever happens, *you* her, um, *fadder*."

It wasn't difficult to translate *fadder* into *father*. Which meant that Brutal had told Trudy about the switch. He shook his head, reminding himself that he trusted Trudy with his daughter. Surely he could trust her to keep the news to herself.

Outside, Brutal waited by Treet's latest indulgence— a sleek black Jaguar. The bodyguard was obviously enjoying the clear, beautiful California night, his broad face tipped upward and his full lips curved in a dreamy smile. The air was a little cool, but above them a blanket of diamond-bright stars was spread across the universe, and smack in the middle hung a full moon the color of sun-bleached brick.

"I'll drive," Treet informed Brutal, who in turn let out a loud groan of dismay. The bodyguard reluctantly folded his big frame into the passenger seat, then very deliberately drew the seat belt across his massive chest and locked it.

Treet grinned as he started the car and pulled out of the circle driveway. "Don't worry, I'm not in a reckless mood tonight."

"Well, thank the Lord for small favors," Brutal muttered sarcastically. "Boss, are you sure about this? I mean, if it's a woman you want, I can get you—"

"Relax. She's Caroline's mother. I just want to get to know her . . . and Samantha." The power of the Jaguar surged through his body as Treet increased his speed on the freeway. Thanks to his resourceful bodyguard, he knew exactly where Hadleigh lived. He settled back with a sigh to enjoy the drive. What a day. And it wasn't over yet.

"It's not you I'm worried about, boss. It's her. You know how unlucky you've been with women."

"This one's different, and Cheyenne was a long time ago. I'd like to think I'm smarter now." Treet took his eyes from the road long enough to cast Brutal a reassuring glance. "Stop worrying."

"You pay me to worry," Brutal argued. "We don't know nothing about this woman. What if she's one of those crazies?"

"Are you forgetting she's Caroline's mother?" The dangerous edge in Treet's voice didn't frighten Brutal.

"That don't mean she ain't crazy, boss. She gets her hooks in you, she's likely to take you for a ride you won't never forget."

The bodyguard's warning prompted a heated image of Hadleigh, naked, straddling him, luscious breasts dangling a hairbreadth from his mouth. Although Treet was fairly certain Brutal wasn't talking about *that* kind of ride, he smiled anyway. "Well, if she does, I'll go down happy."

"Boss!"

Brutal squeaked his outrage, and the tiny sound coming from such a big man made Treet laugh outright.

"See, you're talking crazy already!"

"Calm down, Brutal. Let nature take its course."

"It ain't nature I'm worried about," Brutal muttered. "It's *Treet* I'm worried about, and that gold-digging, devious woman you're about to go see."

Treet sputtered over that one. "You don't know the first thing about Hadleigh Charmaine to be making those accusations, my friend."

"And *you* do?"

"No, I don't. But I'm going to find out, and I'll bet you this Jaguar that you're wrong."

Brutal perked up at the offer. "Really?"

"Really."

"Hot damn!"

Flicking his blinker on, Treet took the Forty-ninth-Street exit at an easy fifty miles an hour before he said, "Be realistic, Brutal. You don't really think that Miss

Charmaine is the mastermind behind some elaborate plot that began over four years ago, do you? That would be more Cheyenne's style."

"Maybe they're in this together."

Brutal was stubborn to a fault, yet loyal as they came, and Treet could see that he wasn't going to change his bodyguard's suspicious mind.

They were a few blocks away before Brutal broke the silence again. "Boss, you gonna see that little girl tonight?"

Treet downshifted and kept his smug grin to himself. Brutal's attempt to sound casual had failed; he hadn't fooled Treet. "You mean Samantha? No. She's staying with Hadleigh's friend, Karen. We haven't decided how we're going to do this yet. That's why we're meeting tonight without the girls."

"Yeah, sure, boss. And I'm Chris Rock."

Ignoring Brutal's insinuation, Treet said, "Fess up, Brutal. You're as curious as I am about Samantha."

"Me?" Brutal squeaked in mock surprise. "She takes one look at me, she'll probably run screaming for her mama." With a grumble, he added, "Not that her mama will notice, because she'll be too busy working at your belt buckle—or your wallet. I just hate to see you get hurt again. I know that it don't matter now, but you were pretty upset when—"

"Give it a rest, will ya?"

"You're the boss."

"Damned right I am."

"You sign the paycheck."

"Damned right I do."

"Don't know why I don't just quit. You don't take my advice anyway," Brutal grumbled.

Brutal's one-track mind was beginning to wear on Treet's nerves. Not bothering to mask his relief, he found a parking spot across from Hadleigh's apartment building and carefully maneuvered the Jaguar between an old pickup truck and a hunter-green Dodge Intrepid that looked about four years old.

He stared at the license plates on the tail end of the Intrepid as the Jaguar's motor rumbled to a stop.

The license plate read SAM.

This was Hadleigh's car, he realized, with her daughter's name on the license plate. When he'd purchased the Jaguar three months ago, he'd thought about putting Caroline's name on the license plate. But in the end he'd voted for prudence. His life was not his own; it belonged to the media and his fans. So far he'd done a pretty decent job of sheltering Caroline from the oftentimes vicious reporters, and his overzealous fans.

"You check the apartment for cameras, boss. At least do that much, okay?"

"Right," Treet lied through his gritted teeth as he unlocked his car door.

"And make sure she isn't taping the conversation."

"Sure thing. I'll frisk her good and proper." He quickly stepped out of the car, but as luck would have it, Brutal rolled the driver's window down and leaned in his direction—no small feat for a man his size.

"Don't sign no papers, either."

Treet checked his sarcastic tone just in the nick of time. "I wouldn't dream of it."

"And if anybody recognizes you, just trigger that alarm."

Frowning, Treet leaned into the window, certain he'd heard Brutal wrong. "What did you say?"

"I said trigger that alarm if you need me. I'll hear it and be there in a flash."

It had finally happened, Treet thought. Brutal had lost his flippin' mind. *"What* alarm?"

"The one in your jacket pocket, boss. The one I put there."

"Damn. I don't believe this."

"Caroline hears you say that—"

"Son of a bitch."

"Boss, you shouldn't—"

"Damn it to hell," Treet added for good measure. He walked away from his crazy friend and bodyguard, stopped after three or four steps, and shouted back, "You need to see a shrink, my friend!"

Brutal nearly spilled out of the car window as he leaned out to yell, "You the one that needs to see a shrink, walkin' around like you ain't nobody! One of these days you gonna get yourself killed, and then maybe you'll believe me!"

Very slowly—so Brutal wouldn't miss the gesture—Treet held up his middle finger. Brutal let out a string of threatening curses and opened the car door.

Treet took off running, laughing as he skipped up the stairs to the apartment building.

For the first time in a long time, he felt on top of the world.

And he didn't have the slightest idea why.

Chapter Six

The coffee was made.

The lights were on in every room of the apartment.

She'd made it a point not to spray herself with her economy-size perfume as she often did out of habit throughout the day. In fact, she had also resisted the urge to brush her teeth.

It wasn't bedtime.

It was definitely not bedtime.

This was Hadleigh's way of keeping the meeting formal—just in case Treet had a seduction planned. The exasperating fact that the very idea of seduction caused her heart to pound made no difference to her determination.

Damn. She was an absolute nervous wreck.

She checked her watch and surveyed her apartment one last time, then glanced at herself in the hall mirror. In striving to appear casual, she found herself wondering if she had gone too far. She had chosen a stark-white, oversize man's shirt and faded jeans. Now she imagined that she looked frumpy. Rumpled. Too casual.

Quickly, she fastened another button at the neck. Another one and she'd be choking.

The doorbell pealed.

Hadleigh put a startled hand to her throat.

He was here. *Treet* was here.

Wiping her sweaty palms on her jeans, she grabbed the knob and opened the door.

She drew in a slow, deep breath. The pressure gathered in her lungs until it began to pound a rhythm in her ears.

Treet Miller had dressed casually too, in black jeans that hugged his butt and thighs, and a black sweatshirt that emphasized his broad shoulders and muscular chest.

Not even the colorful print of a grinning Micky Mouse on the front of his sweatshirt detracted from the sheer sexiness of this man.

Samantha's father.

Determined to keep things in prospective this time, Hadleigh waved him in with a casual hand and turned away from his intense, searching gaze. She headed for her small kitchenette. "I've made a pot of coffee." *Keep it impersonal, businesslike—*

"You've gone all serious on me."

His perceptive observation halted Hadleigh in her tracks. She slowly faced him, bracing herself for the full force of his unsettling gaze. "This *is* a serious situation, Treet."

He nodded, his eyes leaving her face to skim her figure briefly before returning.

A reflex, Hadleigh told herself, but nevertheless she felt as if someone had sucker punched her. Never before had a man's look affected her as this man's look did.

"Yes, it is serious, but I feel confident we can work it out. You love Samantha, and I love Caroline. We won't allow them to be hurt."

"No, we won't." She couldn't doubt his sincerity; it was too obvious. Shoving her trembling hands into her jeans pockets, she nodded in the direction of the kitchen. "Coffee?"

"Got anything stronger?"

"You . . . you're a drinker?" The question was out before she could stop it. Hadleigh flushed at his amused smile. "I mean, it's really none of my business—"

"It's okay. I'm not an alcoholic, so relax."

She felt like a fool for asking. "I don't know why I asked—if you were an alcoholic, I'd—"

"Know," Treet finished with only a trace of bitterness. With a sexy swagger Hadleigh recognized from his various movies, he advanced in her direction.

Hadleigh couldn't help it; she retreated into the kitchen, obviously on the run. He was behind her; she could smell his aftershave, and hear him breathing.

The room felt charged . . . as if an electrical storm were brewing right in her apartment. Could he feel it? she wondered. Did he share it? All questions she shouldn't even be thinking, much less asking herself.

Samantha. Caroline. She took a deep breath and reached for the mugs above the sink. *Keep things in perspective.* If it were any other man, she wouldn't be in this state. It was only because he was Treet Miller.

Incredibly strong arms circled her waist. She let out a shriek and hastily plopped both mugs onto the counter. "What—what are you doing?" she demanded breathlessly.

Without haste, he turned her around so that she faced him. He looked into her startled eyes, then slowly pulled her against him.

"Let's just get this over with, shall we?" he whispered.

Before Hadleigh could protest, his mouth was on hers, warm and gloriously insistent. His hands moved up to frame her face, holding her captive—not that she considered struggling, oh, no—beneath the onslaught of the most pulse-pounding, earth-shattering kiss she had ever had the fortune—or in this case possibly *mis*fortune—to experience.

There was heat. A lot of it.

Sensations. More than she could count. Red-hot desire being the most overwhelming sensation of all. It curled her toes and heated her blood.

Yet even while she was experiencing these feelings and struggling against them, all Hadleigh could think about was how much this kiss would cost her. Anything that felt this wonderful had to have a price.

She suspected the price would be pain.

How many women pined for this man after a kiss like this? How many years did it take them to forget it? Did she truly want to be on that long, long list? The answer was a very definite no.

With a wrenching moan, Hadleigh broke free. She was panting, and so was he. Panting like a teenager in heat. Like someone incredibly aroused, which she couldn't deny that she was. It would be ridiculous for her to try.

Hands shaking, she brought her fingers to her mouth. "This . . . this isn't going to work if you keep doing that." The smoldering look he gave her made her belly somersault as if she'd just turned a double flip on a trampoline.

"We're attracted to each other," he stated huskily, as if daring her to deny it.

Hadleigh wasn't about to embarrass herself by trying. Instead, she opted to go all out in the hope that she would convince *one* of them they were making a mistake. "I'm sure a lot of women are attracted to you."

His brief chuckle curled her toes. "Maybe. But *I'm* not attracted to a lot of women." One gentle, mind-blowing finger traced her lips as he added softly, "Trust your instincts, Hadleigh. You don't strike me as the type to be influenced by fame."

"Is that the attraction for you?" she challenged just as softly. "The fact that I'm not falling at your feet?" When he hesitated, Hadleigh felt a sharp stab of disappointment. Well, she'd wanted honesty, hadn't she?

"I can't deny that it's refreshing to be with a woman who isn't gushing . . . or *falling* at my feet." His handsome lips curved briefly as he quoted her words. "But I don't think that's the main attraction. I think *you're* the main attraction. You're beautiful, funny, intelligent . . . and sexy. Why do you find it so hard to believe I'm interested?"

"Because you can have any woman you want." Hadleigh inched her way to the side until she was free of his hold. Putting distance between them was the only way she could think rationally. "We should get our priorities straight, and think about Samantha and Caroline, and what we're going to do."

His sigh went straight to her heart, flooding it with a dangerous warmth.

"You're right, we should get things settled." He smiled ruefully. "I seemed to get distracted when I'm around you."

"Well, get *un*distracted." She forced a briskness to her voice she was far from feeling. "I'll get the coffee, you bring the milk and sugar."

"No doughnuts?"

She shook her head, the tension inside her easing just a little. "No doughnuts. I've got Fruity Pebbles if you want something sweet."

He laughed. "Caroline's favorite is frosted wheat."

Good, Hadleigh thought, her knees nearly buckling with relief. They were back on track and out of the danger zone. If she had any sense, she would keep it that way.

Because one very important fact was fast becoming clear to her: levelheaded, responsible mother though she might be, Treet Miller was a dangerous threat to her most vital organ—her heart.

Treet had always admired guts in a person, but Hadleigh's show of determination made him gnash his teeth with sheer frustration. Why did she keep pushing him away? Didn't she feel the magic between them? As he remembered her arousing response, he knew the answer to question one, at least.

Hadleigh Charmaine *was* attracted to him.

Maybe he was just moving too fast. Maybe she was right, and he didn't have his priorities straight. He *did* realize the situation was serious, and he *did* want to meet Samantha, but since he'd first laid eyes on Hadleigh, he'd been hooked by her cool green gaze and the burning need to get to know *all* of her.

He set the cream and sugar on the table and pulled out a chair, seating himself across from Hadleigh, who looked adorably flustered and was trying not to show it.

"Patience isn't my strong point," Treet confessed, linking his fingers in front of him to keep from drumming them on the table. She flashed him a glance from beneath her lashes, and Treet thought he saw that ghost of a smile again. It was pure, shy temptation; he clenched his thighs in response.

The woman didn't know her own power . . . or did she?

"I noticed." She added a touch of cream to her coffee, avoiding his gaze as she stirred the caramel-colored liquid. Finally she put the spoon down and stared at him. "I'm not being coy, Treet. Just cautious. Whether you realize it or not, we *are* from different planets. And besides, we have no business making things messy."

"What if they don't get messy?"

"What if they do?" she countered swiftly. "I don't want Samantha hurt, and if we get involved and it ends badly, then she'll get hurt. Caroline will, too. We owe it to them to do this right . . . if we do it at all."

Treet stiffened, although outwardly he appeared relaxed. "Having second thoughts about Mrs. Shoreshire's advice?" Her hesitation hurt more than he cared to admit.

"I'm just worried about us. You're very . . . persuasive."

A flush darkened her delicate cheekbones, and once again Treet lost her gaze as she focused it on the untouched coffee in front of her, obviously embarrassed.

"You think I'm a womanizer," he stated.

Her brow rose. She looked up quickly, then down again. "That's just it. I don't know *what* you are. All I know is what I've read about."

"Then get to know me. Wouldn't that be the fair thing to do?"

"I don't know if I can forget *who* you are long enough to get to know *what* you are," she confessed in a low voice. "So I think it would be better—"

"You mean safer, don't you?" Treet taunted softly.

She ignored him. "It would be better if we started over, I think, as friends. I also think we should keep it that way."

It helped that she sounded disappointed. A little. "Okay. I'll give it my best shot." He nearly laughed at her surprised expression as he offered his hand across the table. It was obvious that she hadn't expected such an easy capitulation. "Here's to friendship in the name of Caroline and Samantha." Gingerly, she slipped her hand in his.

Treet promptly pulled it to his mouth and slowly began kissing the tips of her fingers. She yanked her hand away.

"Treet!"

This time he did laugh, and it came from the heart. "Didn't I tell you? I'm a real friendly kind of guy."

"You—you said—"

"I did, and I will stick to our bargain to the best of my ability." He grinned at her suspicious look. "Hey, all I can do is try. Now, let's get down to business. I was thinking about what Mrs. Shoreshire said . . . about getting away from the media. I have a friend who has a ranch in Montana—"

"Montana?" she squeaked.

He nodded. "Beautiful state. Ever been there?"

"No! I can't just leave my work—"

"Can't you take it with you? Or take a leave of absence?" When she didn't immediately answer, he pressed his point. "This is important, Hadleigh, and I don't think it's something we should rush. The girls need time." Just the thought of spending a lot of time with her—and meeting Samantha—made him feel weak all over. He wanted to scoop them up and take them away *now*.

For an insane moment, he considered doing just that. He could have his private jet ready in less than an hour. As for their clothes, he could buy them everything they needed after they arrived.

Hadleigh dispelled his fantasy with irrefutable logic.

"Samantha hasn't even met you, and Caroline has never met me. We can't just go rushing off and expect them to understand."

"A week, then." Now that Treet had broached the idea, he could barely restrain his impatience. "We'll take a week to let them adjust, go out to dinner, see a movie. Take them to the museum." *Get them to bed early.* Treet knew he should be ashamed of the thought, but he honestly couldn't help himself. He loved Caroline more than anything or anyone, and he was both excited and fearful of meeting Samantha, but he couldn't block out or turn off his burgeoning interest in Hadleigh Charmaine.

And he didn't want to.

"There's something else you should know about Samantha before you meet her."

She sounded so serious Treet felt a chill crawl down his spine. Carefully, he set his cup down before asking, "What is it?"

"She's excessively jealous of anyone . . . that is, of men in general."

"You mean men you've dated." Treet knew exactly how Samantha felt, because he felt it too. Just the thought of Hadleigh with another man made his stomach clench.

"There haven't been many."

"Because of Samantha?"

Hadleigh shrugged. "Partly. She's a very verbal child."

Treet watched with growing interest as Hadleigh's face blossomed with color. "Go on."

"Once, she . . . she opened the door just as my date was attempting to kiss me good night. Before I realized what she was going to do, she punched him in the groin."

He choked on a laugh, earning a chiding look from Hadleigh.

"It's not funny."

Oh, but it was. If only because Treet would have done the same. "Did you punish her?"

"No TV for a week."

Treet winced. "You're tough."

"Don't you punish Caroline when she does something bad?"

It was several moments of hard memory-searching before Treet finally shook his head. "I can't remember the last time." Before she could scold him, he added, "But you have to know Caroline. She's like a small adult." He laughed as he recognized the envy in her eyes. "I'm not saying she's perfect. She's just not . . . not—"

"Rambunctious?" Hadleigh supplied.

"Well, she can be, but not usually, no. She's sneakier about getting her way. When she's mad at me, she ignores me. She can go for hours without talking to me."

This time Hadleigh winced. "I hate that."

"Me too." They shared a moment of mutual understanding before Treet said, "They sound like night and day. How do you think they'll react to each other?"

Hadleigh nibbled her bottom lip, and the unconsciously provocative action made Treet suck in a sharp breath.

"I couldn't begin to guess. Despite her volatile nature, Samantha makes friends easily. How about Caroline?"

"So-so." He flashed her a mischievous grin. "She has your cautious nature, which until tonight I considered an asset."

"Don't start," she warned, but her eyes were smiling. "Since Samantha's like you, Caroline probably won't have a choice."

"Fire and ice," Treet said out of the blue. He didn't have any notion where the words came from, but since he was on the subject . . . "Just like you and me."

Instead of being offended, Hadleigh laughed. "Sounds like Caroline and I will get along fine. But you and Samantha, on the other hand, will be like two bulls in the same pasture."

"Thanks a lot," Treet said with a mock growl. He stretched his long legs beneath the table, bumping his feet against hers. When she quickly jerked them away, he lifted a chiding brow. "If you act this afraid of your dates, then it's not any wonder Samantha reacts the way she does."

Her chin came up and out. "I'm not afraid of you, Treet."

He leaned forward, pinning her with his challenging gaze. "Prove it," he said softly.

"I have nothing to prove."

"Oh, yeah?"

"Yeah."

Treet leaned back with a sigh. "Seriously, from what you tell me about Samantha, your reaction to me will most likely influence her reaction to me."

"You forget. My date was kissing me when she punched him."

"Don't remind me," Treet said beneath his breath. "Sounds like I'm damned if I do, and damned if I don't."

She sounded amused as she said, "Something like that."

"It's not fair."

"She's *your* daughter."

Until this moment, Treet hadn't let himself dwell too much on this significant fact. But now that he knew he would get the opportunity to meet her, get to know her, yet not lose Caroline in the process, the momentous realization flooded his heart with warmth and anticipation. He closed his eyes and let the information soak in. It was a very, very pleasant feeling.

"Treet? Are you okay?"

He managed a nod, but couldn't speak around the lump in his throat.

"It's bizarre, isn't it?" she whispered.

Again he nodded. Finally, he pried his eyes open and looked at her. There were tears shimmering in the emerald depths. His voice was husky as he said, "Pretty fantastic, if you ask me."

He was fairly certain that after meeting Samantha, his life would never be the same. Yet it had already changed for the better, and the reason was sitting across from him, looking frightened and anxious and incredibly beautiful.

Suddenly, the tears spilled onto her cheeks. Treet watched as a single teardrop clung to her sexy upper lip. She attempted to turn her face away, but it was too late. Alarmed, Treet stood and reached her in two giant strides, pulling her to her feet.

"What is it?" he prompted softly.

"What—what if she—Caroline doesn't like me?"

"She will, she will. I know she will."

For the first time since he'd met her, Treet pulled her into his arms with the sole intention of giving her comfort. After a moment, he said, "As a matter of fact, from what you've told me about Sam, *I'm* the one who should be worried."

She sniffled against his shoulder. "Just ignore her. That's the quickest way to get her attention. Most of my dates go overboard trying to win her over."

"And that makes her suspicious."

"I think so."

"Hmm." He lowered his nose to her hair and inhaled. "I'll have to keep your advice in mind. It won't be easy, though."

"I know how you feel. How—what's the best approach with Caroline?" she asked, lifting her head to look at him.

Treet gazed into her eyes, framed by wet, spiky lashes. So distracted did he become, he nearly forgot her question. "Just be yourself. Caroline will probably be a little standoffish at first, but she'll eventually warm up."

"I'm scared."

"Me too." The confession startled Treet. He couldn't remember ever telling another soul that he was afraid.

Yes, this woman was good for him. He felt it.

Now if he could only convince her that *he* was good for her.

Chapter Seven

"Where're we going again, Mommy?"

"To eat dinner at a friend's house," Hadleigh mumbled around the hair band in her mouth. She was braiding Samantha's auburn hair—no small feat with Samantha twisting back and forth. "Be still."

"Who is it? Does she have a dog?"

"It's not a she." Hadleigh was very careful to keep her voice casual. She banded the end of the braid and started on the next one, wishing her stomach would stop rolling like the deck of a ship in high winds. "It's a he, and he has a little girl the same age as you. I don't know if they have a dog. Sam, where's the other hair band? The green one that matches this one?"

"In my backpack. It came off and Drake popped me with it."

"Why did he pop you with it?"

"Because I popped him first," Samantha said. "He wouldn't give me the red crayon."

Hadleigh groaned as she dropped the braid and went in search of the purple backpack. Over her shoulder, she said, "You can't go around hitting people just because they don't do what you want them to do."

"I didn't hit him, I popped him with the band."

"Same difference. Hitting is hitting."

"No, it isn't."

"Yes, it is. Don't argue with your mother unless you want another week without TV."

Like a dream, the threat worked. So far it was the only thing Hadleigh had found that was effective. She used it ruthlessly; Samantha was hopelessly addicted to the Animal Planet channel. Unfortunately, watching it increased Samantha's yearning for a pet. Make that *pets*.

Dog, gerbil, cat, monkey, and even a baby alligator were among the few of her most recent requests.

All of which Hadleigh had to say no to. Her lease didn't allow pets, and they'd had no luck keeping fish alive.

Spotting the bulging backpack tucked into a corner of the sofa, Hadleigh grabbed the strap, pulled it to her, and began to search for the matching hair band.

She removed a wad of clothing and threw it aside, then did a double take on the garment. "Sam! What's my dress doing in your backpack?"

"It was for dress-up day."

"Oh." Later she would have to have another talk with her daughter about respecting other people's belongings. Luckily, it wasn't a dress she wore often, or had to dry-clean.

Hadleigh dug further into the seemingly bottomless pit of Sam's backpack. She unearthed a tube of her favorite lipstick, a wand of mascara, facial cream, a pair of panty hose, and of all things, a sanitary napkin.

The latter was enough to make her face heat with embarrassment at the image of Samantha pulling out such a personal item and showing it to the class, but the disposable razor dangling from the sticky tab of the napkin made her literally growl with frustration.

Grim-faced, Hadleigh decided this particular lecture couldn't wait. She marched to her innocent-faced daughter and held the razor beneath her nose. "Samantha Leigh Charmaine, what on earth were you thinking when you put this into your backpack?"

Solemnly, Samantha stared at the razor, then at her furious mother. Just as solemnly, she said, "Nikki's mommy wouldn't let her bring panty hose."

Hadleigh counted slowly to ten, managing to keep her voice level. "What does that have to do with the razor?"

Samantha tried a smile. When Hadleigh remained stern-faced, she gave up. Her bottom lip began to quiver. "I told you, Mommy. Nikki didn't have panty hose."

"So you were going to shave her legs," Hadleigh concluded, blowing out an exasperated breath. "Sam, do you remember what happened when you tried to shave *your* legs?"

Tears shimmered in Sam's big blue eyes. "I cut myself, and you had to put a Band-Aid on it."

"And do you remember how much you cried?" Hadleigh persisted.

"Uh-huh. You had to kiss it before it got better."

"And do you also remember your punishment?"

Samantha remained stubbornly silent.

"Sam?"

Finally, Sam nodded. "Uh-huh. No critter shows for a week."

"Did Miss Jewel see the razor?" Hadleigh asked, referring to one of the preschool teachers assigned to Sam's group.

Sam shook her head. "Nikki said I'd get in trouble."

"Nikki was right. In fact, you could get kicked out of school, and then Mommy would lose her job because I'd have to stay home and take care of you."

"Oh." Samantha frowned. This bit of information was obviously beyond her realm of understanding. "Mommy, do they have a dog?"

Hadleigh gave her head a rueful shake and pulled her daughter in for a hug. "Sam, from now on, ask me before you take anything to school, okay?"

"Okay. Do they have a dog?"

Like father, like daughter, Hadleigh thought. They both possessed a one-track mind. "I don't know, darling."

"Maybe they have a cat."

"Maybe. Be still now and let me finish your hair. We'll just have to use the blue band."

"Blue's my favorite color. What's her name?"

It took a moment for Hadleigh to catch up with Sam. Her fingers grew still. The butterflies in her belly multiplied. "Caroline. Her name is Caroline, sweetheart."

"Caroline Sweetheart," Sam repeated. She let out a peal of delighted laughter that would have made a mortician smile. "That's a funny name, Mommy!"

"What if they don't like our spaghetti?"

In the midst of tossing a huge salad, Treet glanced at Caroline, who was carefully folding cloth napkins. Despite her concentrated efforts, they looked nothing like the creased, elegant model Treet had set before her. Poker-faced, he said, "Then we'll take them to the dungeon and lock them up. Eventually they'll get hungry enough to eat it."

Caroline giggled as she admonished, "Daddy!" Suddenly, she frowned. "What's a dun-dungeon?"

"It's—" Treet paused, remembering all the horror stories he'd read about dungeons. Nope, he wasn't ready to go there. "Never mind, precious. How are those napkins coming?"

"Almost done. You didn't put yunions in the salad, did you? She might not like yunions. I don't, you know."

Hiding a grin at her mispronunciation of *onions,* Treet asked innocently, "Who?"

"Daddy! You know who. That little girl who's coming to eat with us."

"You mean Samantha?"

"Yeah! Santha."

"I'll bet she wouldn't mind if we called her Sam."

Caroline let out a relieved breath and wiped imaginary sweat from her brow. "Good, 'cause I have trouble saying that other name."

Treet watched as she shoved the napkins alongside the plates, her face flushed and excited over the prospect of company. She bounded from the room, returning a moment later dragging two identical miniature high chairs behind her. Huffing and puffing, she situated them at the table on either side where she had already declared she and Sam would sit. She disappeared again, only to reappear carrying two dolls dressed in identical pink dresses.

"I'm gonna to let Sam feed Gertrude," she announced importantly, stuffing the dolls into their respective high chairs. "Amber don't like strangers, so I'd better feed her. You think Sam would like that, Daddy?"

"I'm sure she would. Who could resist Gertrude? Especially when she cries." Many times he'd been tempted to drown the noisy thing himself. Whoever had invented the clever little microchip dolls obviously didn't have a daughter who took her mothering duties seriously.

But of course he wouldn't dream of telling Caroline. She'd be horrified to know he'd contemplated violence toward any of her "children."

Caroline had over a dozen dolls, and they all had names. Treet wavered between amusement and alarm over her obsession with her children. If she continued along this vein, he figured he'd have to lock *her* in the dungeon when she rocked into her teenage years.

He made a mental note to ask Hadleigh if he should be worried.

Giving the salad another toss, he declared it ready and placed it in the center of the table. The spaghetti sauce simmered on the stove, and the noodles were draining. On another counter, buttered French bread lay waiting to go in the oven when their guests arrived.

Guests.

Treet paused in the act of sprinkling garlic powder over the buttered bread as he contemplated the word. With a devilish grin, he changed his mind and returned the bottle to the spice rack above the stove. Just in case he saw the opportunity to steal a kiss, he didn't want anything to deter him—and garlic would definitely do that. Besides, some kids didn't care for garlic, and he didn't want to risk displeasing Samantha.

Samantha.

Wow.

Treet clutched the rim of the counter as the full realization of the coming visit hit him like a ton of bricks.

Sam. His daughter.

He was about to meet her, see her, touch her, for the first time.

Well, maybe not touch her, if Hadleigh knew her daughter, and he suspected she knew her very well. According to Hadleigh, Samantha's fists were lethal weapons, and he hoped to have use of his family jewels for some time to come.

Emotional hugs were probably out of the question.

His chuckle came out a little shaky, and like the sharp tack she was, Caroline, who had been studiously applying bibs to babies, heard and noticed.

"Daddy? What's wrong? You laughed."

"Yeah."

"What's funny?"

"Nothing, sweetheart." Everything. But funny in a bizarre way that she could never understand.

"Oh."

He knew she was confused, but he couldn't very well explain what had made him chuckle. So he improvised. "I was wondering if we should warn them about Bo Bo." Bo Bo was a very large tarpan turtle that had the run of the house. Sometimes it was weeks before he came out of hiding to lumber around in plain view. When he did decide to grace them with his presence, he parked his shell under the kitchen table until someone noticed and fed him.

And Treet couldn't recall the last time he'd seen the turtle. Bo Bo had been a part of their lives for such a long time, he was like an eccentric member of the family. Or a piece of the furniture. He'd bought the turtle at a pet store when he was just a kid, and Bo Bo had grown much bigger than he had expected.

"Why? Doesn't Sam like turtles?"

"I don't know. Some people are afraid of critters."

"Bo Bo wouldn't hurt anybody, Daddy!" Caroline giggled as if the suggestion were the silliest thing she'd ever heard.

Before they could come to a decision about Bo Bo, the buzzer sounded on the intercom. Treet froze; Caroline let out a squeal of excitement.

Antsy, Treet's handyman and gatekeeper, announced their visitors over the crackly speaker. "They're here, boss. Should I send them up to the house?"

With a muffled curse, Treet stomped to the intercom and jabbed the button down. "I told you to let them in when they arrived. In fact, I described the vehicle *and* Miss Charmaine and her daughter." This was Brutal's doing, Treet thought with a growl of frustration. His bodyguard was still determined to protect him from the man-eating woman.

"Sorry, boss."

The intercom went dead.

This was it. Nervously, Treet finger-combed his hair back into place and removed his apron, stuffing the spaghetti-splattered garment beneath the sink. He motioned Caroline over and checked her dress for food stains, smoothed her neat cap of straight brown hair, and rubbed a spot of tomato sauce from the corner of her mouth. Finally he nodded with satisfaction. She looked neat and well cared for. Hadleigh should have no complaints.

He shook his head at his silly thoughts as he took Caroline's hand and prepared to meet his very special guests.

It wasn't the biggest mansion in Beverly Hills, but it was twenty times bigger than Hadleigh's apartment. Or thirty. Maybe even fifty.

Those Baby Blues

The grounds leading up to the house boasted big, stately oak trees and spectacular fountains. Everything appeared well cared for, yet the viewer was left with the impression that a touch of wildness lurked among the trees and bushes.

Awed to the point of speechlessness, Hadleigh parked the Intrepid in front of the single-story, sprawling mansion and rested her arms on the steering wheel. It was a modern house, designed for the modern family, full of slants and interesting angles and solar windows. An open porch ran half the length of the house, its slanted roof in keeping with the symmetric design.

That's where the formality ended.

There was a child's three-wheeler blocking the sidewalk leading to the porch, its plastic wheels scarred from use and the vinyl seat bleached by the sun. As Hadleigh stepped out of the car, she also noticed a fresh mound of dirt in the yard, surrounded by a child's digging tools and a bucket.

The moment Samantha spotted the toys, she headed in that direction. Hadleigh snatched her hand up and tugged her back before she got out of range. "Oh, no, you don't. We're going to eat dinner first."

Pouting, Samantha allowed Hadleigh to lead her to the front door. "I was just gonna get her stuff for her."

"She probably doesn't want it in the house. It's dirty."

"You let me bring *my* stuff in."

Hadleigh stooped and adjusted the straps of Samantha's velvet blue jumper, tightened a braid, and wiped a smudge from her cheek. Then she rose and smoothed a hand over her own hair. She'd opted for a casual dress, no hose, and sandals.

If Treet answered the door wearing a suit, she was going to kill him.

"This is a big apartment," Samantha observed.

"It's not an apartment, honey. It's a house."

"It's a big house."

"Yes, it is."

"I bet a bunch of people live here."

Instead of answering, Hadleigh concentrated on slowing her heart rate and controlling her breathing. She didn't think there was anything she could do about her trembling legs. What would she feel when she saw Caroline? What if she felt nothing? What if Caroline hated her on sight? What if Sam and Caroline hated each other?

Taking a deep breath, she reached out and banged the brass knocker, although she was fairly certain Treet knew they had arrived.

"I hope they have a dog," Samantha said, hopping restlessly from foot to foot. "If they don't, I'm not staying."

"Don't start," Hadleigh warned. "Besides, how would you leave? You can't drive yet."

"I could walk."

"I don't *think* so."

"I could."

"Samantha, this is a bad time to start an argument."

"Why?"

"Because we're about to eat dinner, and it's bad for the digestion." Where in the hell were they? Hadleigh wondered. Her stomach pitched and rolled in nervous anticipation. It would be a miracle if she managed to eat a single bite of food.

She was about to meet Caroline, the baby she'd carried for nine months, the baby she'd strained and sweated giving birth to.

"I'm not eating if they don't have a dog," Samantha muttered.

"Samantha Leigh!" Exasperated, Hadleigh knelt and took Samantha by the shoulders, intending to explain how rude it would be not to eat.

The door opened. Treet and Caroline stood hand in hand on the threshold, both looking about as jittery as she felt.

Slowly, Hadleigh rose, her gaze quickly sliding from Treet to focus on the little girl at his side. The sinking sun behind them glanced off Caroline's cap of rich dark hair cut in a traditional pageboy style. Framed by thick, dark lashes, her eyes were a darker, richer brown than Jim's. So dark, in fact, that Hadleigh couldn't see where her pupils began. They were huge dark orbs in her delicate little face.

She was a doll come to life.

Caroline seemed unaware of Hadleigh's scrutiny; her eyes were on Samantha. Without hesitation, she reached for Samantha's free hand. "Come on, Sam, I'm going to let you feed Gertrude."

"Is Gertrude a dog?" Samantha demanded, but she allowed Caroline to pull her across the threshold.

"No, silly goose, it's a doll. She's hungry, too, and when she's hungry, she starts crying really loud. You have to feed her to shut her up."

Trembling inside, Hadleigh held her breath, waiting for Sam's reaction. She expected a tantrum, but prayed for a miracle. To her astonishment, Sam didn't pout or argue—or worse, throw one of her famous tantrums.

She shrugged and said, "Okay."

The two girls disappeared in a flash, leaving Treet and Hadleigh standing in the doorway, staring at each other in stunned silence. Hadleigh couldn't have been more shocked if a spaceship had landed in the front yard and beamed the girls up through a column of bright light.

Her voice was shaky as she said, "That was uncanny."

"Not exactly what I expected," Treet agreed, sounding just as shaken.

"Bizarre."

"As if they already knew each other."

"Yeah." Hadleigh crossed her arms over her chest, rubbing a rash of goose bumps along her arms. "I would have bet good money that Samantha was on the verge of a tantrum."

"Why?" Treet sounded amused at the possibility.

Hadleigh wasn't. "She—she said she wasn't going to eat if you didn't have a dog."

Treet's rumbling laughter vibrated through her, stirring emotions she'd rather have kept a lid on.

Finally, he got his laughter under control. "I take it she likes animals?"

"That would be a huge understatement," Hadleigh muttered.

"Then she'll like Caroline's petting zoo."

It was Hadleigh's turn to laugh. "You're kidding."

"No, I'm not. It's out back."

Abruptly, Hadleigh sobered. "You're not kidding." When he shook his head, Hadleigh covered her face with her hands and groaned. Getting Samantha through the door would be nothing compared to getting her *out* the door once she found out about the petting zoo. *A petting zoo?* What kind of kid had her very own petting zoo?

She was beginning to wonder if coming here was such a good idea after all.

Chapter Eight

Treet had managed to look at Samantha all of thirty seconds before his overexcited daughter had hauled her into the house, but it was enough to shake him to the core.

Glancing into Samantha's eyes had been like looking into a mirror. The dark, auburn, waist-length braids she'd obviously gotten from Cheyenne, along with the freckles Cheyenne had hated, but the eyes were his free and clear.

The last trace of doubt dropped away, leaving Treet churning with conflicting emotions. Samantha *was* his daughter, and now that he'd met her, she would always be his daughter.

He knew then, quite suddenly and surely, that he couldn't let her go now that he'd found her. Somehow, he'd find a way to keep Caroline *and* Samantha in his life.

The woman standing on his porch was the key, and right now she looked as if she'd like nothing better than to snatch Samantha up and flee. What had he said?

"Do—do you have any other surprises I should know about?"

Ah. The petting zoo had come as an unpleasant shock, Treet realized. He should have waited, should have considered that what was ordinary to him might be a bit overwhelming to someone else.

He found himself doing something he rarely did— explaining. "The animals belonged to an old friend of mine. He trained exotic animals for the film industry, and last year he decided to retire. I bought his animals and set up the zoo for Caroline." He watched closely as the color began to return to her face. The stricken look had faded, but not the wariness. "The zoo is open to the Children's Hospital on Saturdays and Sundays."

"Oh. That's nice of you. What—what kind of animals do you have?"

Instead of answering, Treet slipped his hand in hers and pulled her across the threshold in much the same way Caroline had done Samantha. Her hand was soft, warm, and slightly damp. They'd both had a hell of a shock, despite the fact they'd known about it in advance. "Follow me to the kitchen and I'll tell you more. I need to pop the French bread in the oven."

"You cook?"

She sounded so surprised it made Treet chuckle. "Occasionally. I gave Trudy the night off." He led her into the spacious, state-of-the-art kitchen and indicated a stool at the breakfast bar. He could hear the girls chattering as Caroline led Sam from room to room, probably introducing Sam to her "family," he mused.

"I thought Trudy was the nanny."

"Nanny, cook, and housekeeper." Treet turned on the oven and slid the pan of French bread inside. He set the timer before turning around to look at her. "She's been after me to hire someone to help her, but I haven't gotten around to it yet." When she frowned, he added, "Everyone pitches in. There's myself, Brutal, and two groundsmen who also serve as extra body-guards when I need them."

"They help with the housework?" she asked skeptically.

Treet smiled. "Yep. Don't worry, they get paid enough."

"I'm sure they do."

His smiled widened. Casually, so as not to alarm her, he sauntered over and seated himself on the bar stool next to hers. Their knees were inches from touching—hers barely concealed by the soft, feminine dress she wore. Everything about this woman seemed refreshingly feminine. "You don't think much of my lifestyle, do you?"

Primly, she said, "I don't *know* enough about your lifestyle to make a judgment."

Treet wondered whether he should take a chance on alienating her by challenging her obvious lie. She might not know much about it, but she *was* judging him. He opted for another explanation, surprising himself once again. "You can't imagine how hard it is to find domestic help I can trust." He was heartened to see her pretty, bow-shaped lips smile.

"You're not the president, Treet."

"No, I'm not." He flashed her a rueful grin. "But sometimes I think he has more freedom than I do. I don't think he has to worry about getting torn limb from limb every time he goes outside his house."

"Because he has a whole passel of Secret Service men," Hadleigh said. "Couldn't you hire—"

But Treet stopped her well-meaning suggestion with a shake of his head. "I've gone that route, and believe me, less is more. The more bodyguards I have with me, the more people notice and recognize me."

"It must be tough."

Her sincere sympathy warmed him. "Stardom has its drawbacks—and its perks. Because of Caroline, I have to be extra careful who I hire."

She shifted on the stool, drawing his interested gaze to her smooth, tanned knee. "I've never thought about it that way, I guess."

"Most people don't. They think it's all glamour—wild parties, orgies, and drugs." Her guilty blush made him chuckle. "Am I right?" he teased.

She nodded.

"Take Mel Gibson, for an example."

"I guess you . . . know . . . Mel Gibson personally?" she asked faintly.

Treet felt a surprisingly strong rush of jealousy at her awed tone. "We've gone fishing a couple of times."

"Mel Gibson *fishes?*"

"We *are* human, Hadleigh," he chided, reaching over to close her mouth. He pointed to a jagged scar along his forefinger. "Mel hooked me with a bass lure; I had to have four stitches."

"Ouch."

"Believe me, the stitches were nothing compared to getting that lure out. As I was saying, Mel's been married to the same woman for a long, long time."

"So he's an exception to the rule—"

"Are your parents still married?" Treet interrupted, determined to win this argument.

"No."

"Neither are mine. My mother is a retired schoolteacher, and my dad is a mechanic. Divorce happens to all types of people. The only difference is that when it happens to movie stars, it's splashed across the headlines."

The oven timer sounded. Treet reluctantly left Hadleigh mulling over divorce statistics while he finished putting dinner on the table. As he rinsed the drained spaghetti, he caught a movement from the corner of his eye.

He nearly dropped the steaming pan when he realized Samantha stood at his side, regarding him quizzically. He finished pouring the spaghetti into the colander, then carefully dried his hands on a towel before turning to confront her.

"Caroline says you have a turtle."

Treet's heartbeat tripled. His palms began to sweat. She was an angel, he thought, staring into her direct blue gaze. He couldn't wait to get to know her.

Recalling Hadleigh's advice, Treet refrained from dropping to his knees and gathering her close. Instead, he took a deep breath and forced himself to sound casual. "We do. His name is Bo Bo."

"We can't find him. I think she lied."

"Sam!" Hadleigh admonished sternly.

Carefully, so that Sam couldn't see him, Treet put his hand behind his back and held up a warning finger. "Well, let me see. Did you look under Caroline's bed?"

Sam nodded.

"How about in the sunroom?"

Again, Sam nodded.

"The showers?"

"Yep."

"Tell you what." The urge was too great; Treet hunkered down so that he was eye level with Sam. "After we eat dinner, we'll all go on a turtle hunt. You and Caroline against me and your mom. Whoever finds Bo Bo gets to serve dessert."

Sam frowned. "I want to find him now, and I don't know how to surf dessert."

"It's chocolate cake. All you have to do is cut it."

"Mommy won't let me have a knife."

"This knife isn't sharp, and I'll help."

Treet held his breath as Samantha hesitated. He figured the best advantage he had was the fact that she didn't know him. "Deal?"

"Okay."

Behind him, Hadleigh let out a relieved sigh. Pleased as punch, Treet rose and clapped his hands together. "Let's eat!"

* * *

It was downright spooky watching Sam and Treet together, Hadleigh thought as she wound spaghetti noodles around her fork. Treet possessed the same persuasive abilities as Sam, only he'd darn near perfected his.

Since dinner had begun among much chattering and noisy cutlery clanging, Hadleigh tried not to stare at Caroline, or at least let Caroline catch her staring. She didn't want Caroline to feel uncomfortable, or to become suspicious.

That left Treet and Samantha, and that was just as wrenching, just as emotional, and just as frightening. She glanced up, catching Treet's shell-shocked gaze, and felt slightly better when she realized he was experiencing something similar.

He winked at her as if to assure her. Instead of assurance, the action only succeeded in increasing her anxiety by sending an alarming jolt of heat zinging along her nerve endings. Hadleigh hastily grabbed for her water, silently chiding her uncontrollable response.

"I'm finished," Sam announced halfway through the meal.

"Then sit there quietly until everyone else finishes," Hadleigh instructed.

Sam opened her mouth to argue, but Caroline distracted her in a diplomatic way Hadleigh was fast recognizing as a trait in her newly discovered daughter. She watched with growing interest as Caroline slid from her chair and padded to the sink. Grunting as she stretched her little arms to reach the faucet, she ran water over her cloth napkin, then brought it to Sam.

"Here you go. Gerty has food all over her mouth, so you can clean her up while we finish eating."

Caroline, apparently, was a peacemaker.

Ten minutes later, Treet gave the girls their instructions. "You two look in the sunroom, music room, living room, den, and dining room."

"Where will you look, Daddy?" Caroline asked.

"Hadleigh and I will look in the bedrooms, my office, and the closets."

A thrill of alarm speared Hadleigh's belly. The bedrooms? The closets? She shot him a suspicious look, but he appeared not to notice. Just how many bedrooms did this house have?

"If you find Bo Bo, just shout."

"I'll shout *real* loud," Sam assured him. He laughed and yanked one of her braids.

"Good. Now get going."

The two girls squealed and ran off hand in hand. Their voices faded as they disappeared from sight. Hadleigh swallowed nervously, indicating the cluttered table, hoping to stall him. "Shouldn't we clear the table first?"

"That would give the girls a head start," Treet pointed out, poker-faced. "You might as well know now that I hate to lose."

"I had already figured that one out on my own," Hadleigh muttered dryly.

His expression pure innocence, Treet held out his hand. "Shall we, partner?"

Filled with trepidation and a shameful excitement she couldn't deny, Hadleigh placed her hand in his.

Bizarre as it sounded, she was going on a turtle hunt with Treet Miller.

The rooms Treet had assigned to the girls were on the opposite side of the house from the area he and Hadleigh were to search.

He knew he should be ashamed, but he wasn't; he was enjoying himself too much. Just holding hands with Hadleigh was enough stimulation to roust his libido to raging life, and the possibility of luring her into his bedroom made his mouth go dry with anticipation.

Hmm. Getting her into the dark linen closet might prove interesting, too. It would be just like old times.

Humming lightly, he led Hadleigh to his office. "We'll look in here first." Her relieved look made him chuckle.

Together, they searched the room. Finding it empty, they went from bedroom to bedroom—three guest rooms in all—until they came to his room at the end of the hall. Caroline's room was across the hall from his.

Hadleigh lingered in the doorway. Pretending not to notice her reluctance, Treet searched the room by himself. He rose from looking under the bed. "Nothing under there but a black sock and an empty shoe box. Caroline's room is next."

This time Hadleigh came into the room with him, but spent most of her time looking around. Treet swallowed a lump at the soft, dazed look in her eyes.

"Does she always keep her room this neat?" she asked in a hushed tone, smoothing the Scooby Doo comforter on the bed.

"Heavens no. Trudy cleaned it yesterday, and I straightened it today. Normally it's a mess."

"Samantha isn't happy unless every bare inch of floor is covered in toys and clothes."

Treet looked under Caroline's bed, inadvertently catching an arousing view of Hadleigh's shapely legs as he bent over. She was standing right beside him—if he was so inclined, he could move a little closer under the pretense of searching, and see what color panties she wore.

If she wore any at all.

Hmm. Maybe he'd better think of something else, or she'd be noticing something else that was making a swift rise in his jeans. Hastily, he got to his feet and ushered her from the room. "We've searched everywhere but the linen closet."

The linen closet was a short distance down the hall from his room. He turned the light on and began to search the lower shelves, stacked with blankets and pillows. He was pleased to note that Hadleigh was doing the same on the opposite side of the closet, where Trudy kept the vacuum cleaner and various other cleaning equipment.

"How big is this turtle?" Hadleigh asked, gingerly moving a broom aside to look in a shadowy corner.

"He's about the size of a small pizza, with a greenish gold shell."

"That's a big turtle."

111

"I've had him since I was a teenager."

"I didn't realize they could live that long."

Treet pretended to be hurt by her remark, although he was fairly certain she hadn't realized how he might take it. "I'm not *that* old," he growled, turning around just in time to see the closet door swing shut.

He heard whispering on the other side; then something bumped against the door. He and Hadleigh exchanged a puzzled look as he moved to the door and tried to open it.

It wouldn't budge. "Caroline?"

There was the muffled sound of girlish giggles, then silence.

Hadleigh frowned. "Sam? Is that you?"

"I think they've locked us in," Treet pointed out, more amused than alarmed. "Déjà vu, wouldn't you say?"

But Hadleigh seemed far from amused. She pounded on the door. "Samantha Leigh, open this door right this instant!"

Seeing that she was genuinely upset, Treet nudged her aside. "Caroline? Open the door, honey. It was a funny joke, but we'd like to come out now."

"I'm sure Sam's behind this," Hadleigh muttered, blowing out an exasperated sigh. "Sam! Open this door or you will do without TV for a month!"

"Caroline's perfectly capable of plotting something like this, so don't be so quick to blame Sam."

"It's all your fault, Treet."

Surprised by her sudden attack, Treet held up his hands. "My fault? How is this my fault?"

"You had to go and bribe her with the knife. Sam doesn't like to lose any more than you do."

"How was I supposed to know she's knife happy?"

"She's not knife happy! It's the thought of doing something grown-ups do that got her attention. It was a bribe, pure and simple."

Growing a little angry himself, Treet said, "And your threat strategy works better, I suppose?"

For an answer, Hadleigh simply folded her arms and glared at him. Finally, she said, "If I didn't know better, I'd think you put them up to this."

"For what purpose?" Treet demanded.

"To get me into the closet, alone."

"Hadleigh, you're missing the obvious. I already had you in the closet, and the lock is on the inside."

"So how did they lock us in?"

"I'm guessing, but I think they propped a chair under the knob."

"They're four years old, Treet. They wouldn't know to do that."

"Caroline would. She goes with me on location, remember? I remember one scene where I lock my wife in the closet the exact same way after finding out she's planning to leave me."

Hadleigh's eyes rounded in shock. "Surely you don't allow her to sit in on—"

"Brutal takes her out for ice cream if the scenes get too rough," Treet informed her defensively.

"I didn't mean to imply—"

"You could have fooled *me.*"

113

Clamping her lips together, Hadleigh pounded on the door again. "Sam, will you please open the door for Mommy? I—I need to go to the bathroom."

Silence.

"Sam? Caroline?"

"I think they left, but I'm sure they'll be back."

"If they don't forget about us. They're four years old."

"It's Brutal's night to patrol the grounds. He checks in every two hours. When I don't answer the intercom, he'll come running with guns blazing."

"Oh, that's comforting."

Treet sighed. "It was just an expression."

"So what do we do in the meantime?"

He started to wiggle his eyebrows suggestively, but one glance at her stony face and he thought better of it. "Guess we just make ourselves comfortable until the girls give up the game or Brutal makes an appearance." Treet began pulling blankets and pillows from the shelves, making a pile on the carpeted floor. When he was finished, he collapsed against the soft bed, patting the space beside him and hoping to put her at ease.

When she regarded him warily, Treet flashed her an innocent smile. "I'm not going to pounce on you, Hadleigh, so come here and make yourself comfortable."

"I think I'll stand."

"Suit yourself."

She began to pace the small space between the door and Treet's makeshift chair. "What if they set something on fire?" she asked, nibbling her nail.

"I have sprinklers in every room of the house."

"Of course."

"There you go with the censure again. Fire prevention isn't just for the wealthy and decadent."

"I'm not being censorious. I was merely agreeing with you, so stop putting words in my mouth."

"Sassy woman."

"And stop calling me that. I'm only sassy around *you.*"

"I'll take that as a compliment."

"You would. Has anyone ever told you that you're conceited?"

She paced too close after that remark. Treet snagged her ankle and toppled her onto the pile of pillows and blankets. With a deft twist of his body, he thrust her onto her back and placed an arm on either side, trapping her beneath him.

"How's *this* for conceit?" he growled softly, his gaze fixed on her parted lips. "I think you're frightened of being in here with me because you're afraid of the way I make you feel."

"No. I—"

Treet kissed her until they were both breathless. He pulled away an inch, staring into her alarmed eyes. "Why do you insist on fighting such a good thing?" His voice became a sex-roughened rumble. "If I make you half as crazy as you make me . . ."

"I explained it to you before, Treet," she whispered, moistening her lips. "I don't think it's a good idea for us to complicate an already complicated situation."

"How about if we just kiss?"

"I've heard that line before."

"It's not a line, it's a promise. I'll leave it entirely up to you to go further than kissing."

"That's not fair."

Treet lifted a brow. "So you admit it wouldn't be easy?"

"No, I don't admit anything!" She gave a halfhearted chuckle. "Treet, you're impossible."

"I'll take that as a yes," he whispered, lowering his hungry mouth to hers again.

Chapter Nine

Treet Miller's sex appeal was enormous.

Enormous enough to make Hadleigh panic. The equally enormous bulge pressing into her hipbone didn't help matters, but it did, however, confirm a naughty rumor she'd once read in a magazine about a certain part of Treet's anatomy.

Lordy, Lordy.

As his million-dollar mouth settled persuasively on hers, Hadleigh's second absurd thought was that she was glad there hadn't been garlic on the French bread. She wondered if omitting the garlic had been an oversight, or a *fore*sight on Treet's part. *Silly! Maybe Caroline just doesn't like garlic,* she chided silently as her fingers crept up to tangle in his silky soft hair. Or maybe he was afraid Samantha wouldn't like garlic.

This was nothing but a kiss. She had prodded Treet's conquering instincts into play, nothing more, nothing less. So maybe, Hadleigh mused while her tongue dodged his persistent one, the smartest thing to do would be to go along, as undoubtably most women did.

If she didn't run, maybe Treet wouldn't feel compelled to chase. And if she began to chase, perhaps Treet would do the standard thing and run.

In a bold move that would have astonished her closest friends had they been observing—heaven forbid—Hadleigh moaned and pressed her body closer, openly acknowledging his rock-hard arousal. She began to kiss him back as if she were loving it.

Which, in fact, she was.

Nope, no need to fake a moan or pretend to be aroused. In fact, she began to pray that her plan worked, and worked fast, or her heart would be in real danger.

What had she gotten herself in to? She didn't want this to stop; she wanted it to go on forever.

Just the kissing part, because she seriously doubted her overloaded system could handle much more.

His mouth was custom-made for kissing, she decided, straining closer despite the warning bells clanging loud and clear inside her head. His hair was made for her fingers, the texture stimulating her skin, the masculine scent teasing her nostrils.

It was some foggy moments later before Hadleigh fully realized that her plan had backfired, and that she was in the process of getting far more than she had bargained for.

Treet wasn't retreating. He was advancing, and he was advancing very well.

She should have known there was nothing standard about Treet Miller. He hadn't gotten on the cover of *Star* magazine by being standard.

When Treet broke the kiss, Hadleigh saw her chance to get out of a potentially disastrous situation.

Treet had other ideas. Before she could speak, he placed his warm hand on her knee, then slowly trailed it upward, gathering the silky folds of her dress along the way. His movements were seductive and arousing.

Hadleigh sucked in a sharp breath, feeling liquid pool in regions that hadn't felt so wet in quite a while as his hand inched closer to her thigh. She kept her eyes closed tightly—knowing beyond doubt that this was her only defense against Treet.

Looking into his eyes would seal her fate.

She felt his breath fan her neck just seconds before his lips seared her heated flesh. Treet's mouth moved down, slowly trailing a path of fire to her breast. At the same instant, his hand against her thigh began to tighten.

In one smooth, startling move, he shifted her bottom, slid his hand along her leg to her inner knee, and brought her leg up.

Now she cradled his burning erection, felt the heat of it against the very sensitive part of her that tingled and throbbed. Speaking of throbbing . . . Hadleigh could feel him throbbing against her.

"Lordy," she whispered, her voice catching in another sharp gasp when he began to rock against her in a sweet, mind-blowing rhythm that had her clutching his shoulders.

His mouth returned to hers, ending her chance to protest—as *if*—his lips hotter than ever, his tongue demanding a duel. The low, deep moan that emerged from his throat thrilled Hadleigh to the bone. He continued to rock gently against her, creating a glorious friction between them.

Her explosion came so quickly she was left stunned and gasping, her fingers gripping his shoulders as if she feared she would drown if she let go. She bit her tongue to keep a betraying moan locked in her throat, praying desperately that he wouldn't realize what had happened—what *he'd* done.

Oh, God. She couldn't believe she'd—she'd *climaxed* in a matter of moments, with nothing more than a kiss and the friction of his erection against her! When she was married to Jim, more often than not she'd gone to sleep unsatisfied after their bouts of lovemaking. She'd always blamed herself . . . and eventually Jim had blamed her as well.

But with Treet . . . merciful heavens!

Heat swept into her face. She was absolutely mortified.

Suddenly, Treet grew still. In the silence that followed, their harsh breathing seemed magnified in the small space.

His husky chuckle came as a shock. "We'd better slow down before . . . well, before I embarrass myself."

Hadleigh opened her eyes, reluctantly meeting his rueful, aroused gaze. She still clutched his shoulders.

With an effort, she relaxed her grip and forced a smile, relieved to see that he apparently didn't realize that she had already embarrassed herself. "Yeah, I guess we *are* acting like teenagers." If only he knew!

"Yes. It's good between us, isn't it?" He chuckled again before she could respond. "At least, I think it would be if we weren't lying on a linen closet floor."

"Don't forget the girls." She stiffened as he ran an inquisitive finger around the elastic of her panties. His lids drooped seductively.

"Honey, you can be certain I haven't forgotten the girls. Otherwise . . . you wouldn't be wearing these."

His sheer conceit should have angered her, or at the most disgusted her. Instead, Hadleigh found herself laughing helplessly. He was just too cheeky to take seriously, she decided.

"Boss? You in there?"

Brutal's muffled voice from the other side of the closet door came as a relief to Hadleigh. She quickly squirmed away from Treet and covered her legs. He glanced at her, his eyebrows raised.

"Yeah, I'm here."

"She with you?" Brutal asked.

Treet closed his eyes, his jaw hardening for an instant. When he opened them again, Hadleigh saw nothing but amusement and more than a little exasperation.

"Yes, *Miss Charmaine* is with me. Did you find the girls?"

"They're looking for Bo Bo," Brutal responded.

Hadleigh heard the sound of a chair scraping, then the rattling of the doorknob. Brutal appeared in the doorway, his gaze landing briefly on her before he focused on his boss. He stared at him hard as if to assure himself that Treet was unharmed.

"Caroline lock you in here?"

"She had help," Hadleigh said quickly. She accepted Treet's hand and got to her feet. Brushing at her crumpled dress, she added with renewed irritation, "In fact, I wouldn't be a bit surprised if this wasn't Sam's idea."

"Don't be so hard on her."

Treet's rebuke skittered across her sensitive nerves like nails on a chalkboard. "Don't underestimate Sam, Treet. I wouldn't trade her—" She stopped abruptly, swallowed hard, and started again. "I love her, but I know her faults."

"Aren't you underestimating Caroline by assuming this wasn't her idea?" Treet challenged, folding his arms across his chest. Brutal remained in the doorway, his interested gaze bouncing from one to the other.

"I wasn't underestimating Caroline, just stating a fact. Sam is notorious for pulling stunts like this."

"I don't think they meant any harm."

"Nevertheless, she needs to be taught that she can't go around locking people in closets. Someone might get hurt."

Or seduced.

"Maybe she does it to get attention."

Hadleigh bristled at Treet's implication. "Believe you me, she gets plenty of attention."

"I didn't mean—"

"Anyone want a drink?" Brutal inserted loudly.

"No, thank you." Hadleigh thrust her chin out, ignoring Treet, although she felt him watching her. "I don't drink and drive." Deliberately, she looked at Treet as she added, "And I don't ignore my child. Since you're so convinced that Caroline played a part in this little game of lock up Mommy and Daddy, maybe you should ask yourself why she did it."

"I've already explained to you why Caroline did it."

Lifting a disbelieving brow, Hadleigh said, "Because she watched *Behind Closed Doors*?"

"Ah-ha! You *do* watch my movies."

She itched to wipe that smug grin from his face. "I never said that I didn't."

The patter of little feet coming along the hall effectively ended their ridiculous argument. Looking startled, Brutal stepped hastily aside as Caroline barreled past him and into Treet's arms.

"Daddy!" she wailed, tears streaming down her face. "Tell Sam she doesn't die!"

Bewildered, Treet lifted his sobbing daughter into his arms until she was eye level. "What, sweetie? Daddy didn't understand you."

Knuckling her eyes, Caroline hiccuped and stammered, "Sam said—said that Sleeping Beauty dies, Daddy! Tell her she doesn't neither die!"

As the reason for Caroline's distress sank in, Hadleigh closed her eyes and groaned. They flew open at the sound of Sam's stubborn voice. She was standing in the doorway beside Brutal, seemingly oblivious to his hulking presence.

123

"She does, too. Just ask my mommy. She reads it to me every night, and Sleeping Beauty pricks her finger and goes to sleep forever and ever."

Suddenly, Samantha turned to study Brutal, a tiny frown marring her brow as she looked him up and down in her usual, candid way. "You're chocolate," she announced matter-of-factly. "Like my chocolate bunny rabbit I got from the Easter bunny, only bigger. A *lot* bigger."

Hadleigh silently prayed for the closet floor to open up and swallow her.

Caroline had stopped crying, but the sadness in her eyes remained. Each time Hadleigh looked at her delicate little face, she winced.

Samantha, on the other hand, had grown solemn and quiet, apparently realizing, finally, just how much she had upset her new friend.

The two girls sat on the sofa in Treet's living room. Hadleigh and Treet sat across from them on the love seat, and Brutal stood in front of the cold fireplace as if carved from stone, legs akimbo, arms crossed over his massive chest.

Hadleigh had a strong suspicion that he blamed *her* for Sam's impulsive nature. It was apparent he didn't blame Sam, for his impassive gaze softened each time he glanced her way.

"Do you want to read, or shall I?"

Treet's question jarred Hadleigh back to awareness. She looked at the book in his hand and shook her head. "You read it." She'd already informed Treet that Sam

124

always fell asleep by the time she got to the part in the story where the handsome Prince kissed Sleeping Beauty awake, which had left Sam with the impression that Sleeping Beauty remained asleep forever. According to Treet, Caroline wasn't quite that far along in the book.

It startled Hadleigh to realize that although the girls seemed totally different, in some ways they were much the same.

"Should I start where Caroline usually falls asleep?" Treet inquired of his audience.

"No, Daddy! Start at the beginning where the ugly old witch comes to see the baby princess."

"Yes!" Sam added her plea to Caroline's.

With a dubious look at the angels on the sofa, Treet turned to the front of the dog-eared book and began to read *Sleeping Beauty.*

Hadleigh hadn't bargained on what Treet's voice would do to *her* peace of mind. As she listened to the low, captivating sound of his baritone as it rose and fell with varying emotion, she began to relive those all-too-brief moments in the linen closet.

Her reaction to him reinforced the sense of danger she felt around Treet. That he was a heartbreaker, she had no doubt, although she was wise enough to realize that much of the heartbreaking Treet did he probably never even knew about. Still . . . there was that other percentage that he probably did know about.

He was adored by millions. Lusted after by hundreds of thousands of women. She suspected he could have any woman he wanted with a flash of his sizzling baby blues. Heck, he could probably *buy* any woman he wanted.

So what was he doing in the linen closet with her, acting as if he'd never been with a woman before? As if she were the only woman in the world he'd ever felt an attraction for? She knew she wasn't ugly, and her figure wasn't half bad, but she was not Nicole Kidman, and she was definitely a far cry from the sultry, husky-voiced Demi Moore. Hadleigh had watched him seduce and be seduced by both leading ladies on-screen. And that was just to name a few.

What about off-screen? she wondered, surprised and appalled to realize she was jealous at the thought of Treet kissing *them* the way he kissed her. Stroking *them* the way he'd stroked her. She had no claim on Treet Miller. Why, the very idea was ludicrous.

Or . . . was it?

Fighting a self-conscious blush, she shot him a speculative look from beneath the concealment of her lashes, watching his beautifully shaped mouth move as he read. So, what was the attraction she held for him? Was she right on target when she'd suggested he was pursuing her because she wasn't falling at his feet?

Her gaze fell on Samantha, who was staring at Treet as if she, too, was mesmerized by the sound of his voice. The sight of her awestruck daughter prompted another thought. A not-so-nice one. Could Samantha be the true reason for Treet's interest in her? Hadleigh had to admit it would make things mighty convenient for both of them if she and Treet got together as a couple. They could have their cake and eat it too, as the saying went.

At that moment, Treet paused in his reading to look at his captivated audience. As he shifted his loving gaze from Caroline to Samantha, Hadleigh noted his expression didn't change. It hadn't taken him long to fall in love with his real daughter.

At least Hadleigh understood. Each and every time she looked at Caroline, her heart lurched queerly. She'd only known her biological daughter for a few hours, but already she found herself dreading the moment when she would have to leave her.

Yet she wasn't about to let her heart deceive her into thinking she was falling in love with Treet, just so that she could spend more time with Caroline. And if this was Treet's ultimate quest—whether consciously or subconsciously—she would quickly set him straight on the matter. The last thing Hadleigh wanted was to put Samantha through a messy divorce when Treet came to his senses later on and realized he'd made a mistake.

Hadleigh smothered a moan, realizing she'd gone so far in her daydreaming she'd actually thought of marriage to Treet. Yes, it was definitely time to get Treet alone and lay down a few ground rules if they were to continue on this course.

A movement from the sofa caught her eye. She looked up just in time to see Caroline slip her chubby little hand into Samantha's. Samantha scooted closer, giving Caroline a smile filled with love and mischief. Hadleigh's heart melted at the sight.

From the looks of things, this bizarre ship they were on wasn't slowing down.

*　　*　　*

"Treet."

Treet paused in his reading as Hadleigh spoke his name. He decided he liked the sound of it rolling from her tongue. A sweet little tongue it was, too.

Bracing himself to appear casual—when he felt anything but casual with her—he focused his rather fuzzy gaze on her. His vision cleared, leaving him an uncluttered view of her moist lips, sultry green eyes, and flirty lashes.

The woman was fit for a king. Or a prince.

"Hmm?" The syllable came out a little husky, since he couldn't help remembering that less than an hour ago he'd been having the time of his life kissing her senseless. That wasn't all he'd been doing, but there were children present—best he not think about *that* right now.

He followed the direction of her gaze to where the girls sat on the sofa.

Correction: where the girls *slept* on the sofa. Heads and hands together, they looked like two little cherubs.

Or two little Sleeping Beauties.

With a rueful shake of his head, Treet closed the book. "I give up. I'm convinced Caroline will never know the ending of this book."

"I know what you mean," Hadleigh said with a soft little laugh that made his insides turn to mush. "I've tried nudging Samantha awake when she starts to doze, but it doesn't work. She sleeps as hard as she plays."

"Sounds like me." He hadn't meant the words to sound suggestive, but he could tell by her sudden blush that she'd taken them that way. Good. He liked her thinking that way. It meant that she wasn't as cool as she'd like him to believe.

"We should be going."

Treet jumped to his feet. "I'll carry Samantha for you." Brutal had gathered a sleeping Caroline into his massive arms and was disappearing down the hall in the direction of Caroline's bedroom. Treet reached the couch at the same instant as Hadleigh. Their heads nearly collided as they both reached for Sam.

"I can get her," Hadleigh said. "I'm used to carrying her."

For a long moment, Treet held her gaze, not bothering to hide his yearning. "Please, let me. It might be my only chance of getting this close to her." He stifled a relieved sigh when she reluctantly moved away. Very, very gently, he gathered Samantha into his arms. She was a little heavier than Caroline, he thought, gazing into her flushed, sleeping face.

"I think she likes you," Hadleigh whispered, smoothing a stray tendril of auburn hair from Sam's brow.

Treet shot her a hopeful look. "You think so? How can you tell?"

"I haven't seen her give you any of her 'looks.' "

"Looks? What kind of look?"

Hadleigh's lips twitched. "Go-to-hell looks."

"She wouldn't by any chance get that from her mother, would she?" Treet teased as he led the way to the front door. When Hadleigh opened it, he stepped onto the lighted porch. He'd been having so much fun, he hadn't even noticed that it had grown dark.

With the efficiency born of experience, Treet settled Sam into her child's safety seat and buckled her securely. He closed the car door as quietly as he could, despite Hadleigh's insistence that Sam wouldn't awaken.

Then he snatched Hadleigh around the waist, leaned against the car, and pulled her between his spread thighs. Her soft little gasp of surprise made him smile. She braced her hands on his chest, but she didn't resist.

"And what about Mom?" he drawled seriously. "Do you think she likes me, too?"

"Who *doesn't* like you?"

Her flippant answer failed to satisfy Treet. He lowered his hands to her bottom and pulled her firmly against his growing arousal. "Forget about everybody else. I'm asking *you.*" The driveway light overhead illuminated her wary expression.

"We've been over this more than once, Treet. We owe it to the girls to keep things simple between us."

Treet leaned his head forward until their mouths were mere inches apart. His gaze settled on her parted lips as he said, "I don't think it gets any simpler than this."

"Sex might be simple for you, but it isn't for me."

"I think this is more than just sex," Treet returned stubbornly, inching his mouth closer.

"And I thought this was about Samantha and Caroline, not us."

"Why can't it be both?" Treet thought his question quite logical. Apparently Hadleigh didn't.

"It isn't fair to the girls. If we get involved, then we won't be concentrating on them."

"Have you always been so single-minded?"

"When it comes to Sam, yes. And now I have Caroline to consider. . . ."

She looked so worried all of a sudden that Treet wanted to kiss her frown away. But of course he didn't. "Why are you worried? We've got everything under control."

"Do we?"

Well, she did have a point, Treet mused, shifting to ease the tightness in his groin.

"Have you considered the possibility that this is happening because I'm conveniently convenient?" she continued, pulling free of his hold.

Disappointed, he watched the sway of her hips as she rounded the hood of the car and opened the driver's door. She paused before getting in, eyeing him over the car. "I think we should forget about this—this chemistry between us and concentrate on the girls. Good night, Treet."

Galvanized into action by her farewell, Treet stepped away from the car. "I'll call you tomorrow."

"Okay. Give Caroline a good-night kiss for me."

"I will."

He watched her drive away, thinking about what she'd said. Perhaps he *was* coming on too strong. Maybe what she needed was a little old-fashioned wooing—both mother *and* daughter.

Treet thoughtfully rubbed his jaw, his unseeing gaze on the dwindling tail lights of Hadleigh's car.

Chapter Ten

"We can't come over tonight," Hadleigh told Treet the next day when he called. "It's girls night."

"Girls night," he repeated with just enough amusement in his voice to cause a ripple of awareness inside Hadleigh.

She gripped the phone tighter and willed her heart to stop its silly acrobatics. "Yes. We all get together and talk girl talk. I'd—I'd forgotten." And she had, to her shame and her friends' disgust.

"And you can't get out of it?"

He'd never know how long and hard she'd tried. She made a face at the bowl of popcorn on the coffee table and the pitcher of margaritas on the bar. She knew what tonight's discussion would be about. "No. I'm having enough trouble convincing my friends that I'm not starstruck without adding fuel to the fire by canceling our sacred night."

After a short silence, Treet said softly, "I'm glad you're not starstruck."

"Me too."

"Well, you don't have to be *that* adamant," he protested, making her chuckle. "If you keep playing hard to get, I might end up wishing you *were* just a little starstruck. At least I'd have something of an edge."

"You don't mean that."

"No, I don't." He interjected enough reluctance to make her smile. "Have fun."

"We usually do." Hadleigh had a strong, sinking feeling this night would be an exception. Instead of fun, she'd be on trial with Judge Doreen, Judge Barbi, and Judge Karen presiding.

The doorbell pealed, making her jump. *Speaking of the devils,* she thought. "Treet, I have to go. The girls are here."

"I'll send Brutal over with my car tomorrow evening at six."

"No—I'll drive over." She held her breath, expecting him to argue. Apparently he thought better of it.

"All right. See you then."

"Bye."

Feeling ridiculously guilty, Hadleigh hastily hung up the phone and raced to the door. Doreen and Barbi nearly fell across the threshold when she opened it, leaving her with the impression that they'd had their ears to the door.

"Hi!" Doreen said breathlessly. "We're right on time."

"Yeah. Can't wait to get started. I brought chocolate." Holding up a six-pack of Hersheys with almonds, Barbi cast a bright-eyed glance over Hadleigh's shoulder into the empty living room. "Where's Karen?"

"Taking Sam to her mother's house," Hadleigh said, waving them inside. She shut the door and turned to follow her friends into the living room.

Barbi took her customary seat in the recliner, and Doreen sank onto one end of the sofa. She kicked off her shoes and curled her feet under her legs, letting out a lusty sigh.

Hadleigh took the love seat. "Have a hard day?" she asked Doreen.

Doreen nodded, reaching for the bowl of popcorn. She settled the bowl on her lap and began to pick out the kernels with the most butter. "Nasty accident on the bridge," she mumbled around a mouthful.

"Stop hogging the good ones." Barbi reached for the bowl, but Doreen grinned and held it out of reach.

"Get your own."

Karen arrived a few moments later. She followed Hadleigh into the kitchen and helped her pour the margaritas into tall, frosted glasses that Hadleigh had placed in the freezer earlier. When they were all settled again, Barbi wasted no time getting to the point.

"Spill it, Hadleigh. We've all been going crazy wondering what happened last night."

Karen took a man-sized gulp of her frosted margarita before adding, "That's putting it mildly."

"Amen," Doreen breathed. "I've had trouble concentrating all day, and that's a little dangerous in my line of work."

It was on the tip of Hadleigh's tongue to inform Doreen that she wasn't responsible for her lack of concentration, but three pairs of avid eyes stopped her. She had to admit she would be just as curious if their situations were reversed.

Taking a deep breath, Hadleigh began, "Well, she's absolutely adorable. Sweet and well mannered. Dark hair, dark eyes . . . like a little gypsy." She took a sip of her drink, her eyes misting in remembrance. "She wears her hair in that cute pageboy style that's coming back into fashion. She's crazy about dolls." Hadleigh's voice dropped a note. "She looks a little like Jim, and a little like me."

It grew so quiet in the room, Hadleigh could hear her bedside clock ticking.

Finally, Karen asked, "How did he react when he saw Sam?"

Hadleigh ran her finger around the salt-encrusted top of her glass, then sucked the salt from her skin before answering. "I think he felt the same way I did: stunned, scared, and emotionally charged."

"You *think* he felt the same way?"

Leave it to Doreen to leap on that single word, Hadleigh thought. "I'm not psychic, Dory, but yes, I think he felt the same way."

"He's an actor—"

She cut Barbi off before she could finish. "Yes, he is. And very talented, as we all know. But he wasn't acting."

135

"How did Sam react to *him?*" Doreen asked.

They all leaned forward as if in anticipation of Hadleigh's words. Hadleigh bit her lip to keep from smiling at their comical expressions. She knew them all very well. Doreen was single and childless, but Hadleigh knew she was starting to yearn for a family. Barbi was a divorcee, and childless. Karen was married to an airline pilot and they had one child, Jason, a boy, ten years old.

To Sam, they were all wonderful "aunties," who had a penchant for spoiling her rotten at Christmas and birthdays, and Jason was her hero.

Right now Hadleigh was more prone to think of the aunties as major pains in the butt. "I think she likes him." Her announcement met with varying degrees of disbelief.

"You're joking." Barbi sat back with a smug smile. "She kicked him, didn't she?"

"Yeah, now, *that* I could believe," Doreen added.

Karen laughed outright. "Come on, Hadleigh! Give us credit for a little intelligence here. Sam doesn't like *any* man around you. She's proved it a dozen times."

Hadleigh decided it was time to shake up her friends with a few facts. "Sam and Caroline locked Treet and me in his linen closet."

All three women gasped.

"So if your theory is right and Sam hates men, why would she lock me in the closet with one?"

"Are you sure it was Sam's idea?" Barbi asked.

To this, Hadleigh cocked a sarcastic eyebrow. "What do *you* think? Although putting the chair beneath the doorknob—"

"They put a *chair* beneath the doorknob?" Doreen squeaked. "Hadleigh, they're four years old!"

"I know, I know. Treet takes Caroline on the set with him, so he thinks she might have gotten the idea from—"

"*Behind Closed Doors!*" Karen finished with a girlish squeal. "I *loved* that movie." With characteristic energy, Karen popped to her feet. "I think we all need another drink!"

"Count me in."

"Me too. Hadleigh?"

Hadleigh shook her head. She already had a slight headache from the first one. The doorbell rang before Karen made it to the kitchen bar.

"I'll get it!" she called over her shoulder, her tone puzzled. "Did someone order a pizza?"

"Not me."

"Me either."

They grew quiet, listening as Karen opened the door. Hadleigh couldn't think of a single soul it could be. All her friends were here, and Treet knew she was entertaining tonight.

"Hadleigh . . . ?"

At Karen's surprised exclamation, Hadleigh rose from her chair and went to the door. Her brow rose in question on seeing a stranger. He was young, perhaps in his late teens.

"Hadleigh Charmaine?"

Hadleigh unconsciously clutched her throat. "That's me."

"I've got a special delivery for you." Smiling, he held out a beautiful red rose, its petals sparkling with dewdrops. When she automatically took it, he said, "No need to tip—Mr. Miller took care of that." With a quick salute, he turned and headed for the elevator across the hall.

So the mystery was solved, Hadleigh mused, shutting the door.

"There's a note," Karen said. She freed the slip of paper from the stem of the rose and handed it to Hadleigh.

Conscious of her friends watching her, Hadleigh silently read the note: *To my closet buddy.* She smiled at the corny message. It was just like Treet to take a romantic gesture and twist it into something humorous.

Suddenly, Hadleigh realized the room had gone completely silent. She looked up, glancing from one to the other, easily reading their expressions. Barbi looked expectant; Doreen looked both envious and resigned.

Karen, as usual, made no bones about voicing her opinion. "Romantic, but suspect. Why would he send you a single rose when he could afford dozens?"

As if she'd pulled the stopper, everyone began talking at once. Hadleigh remained silent; she knew she wouldn't be heard anyway. Slowly, she brought the beautiful flower to her nose and inhaled the rich, sweet scent, closing her eyes. As Karen had pointed out, Treet could have sent a dozen—or even five dozen—roses, but he had somehow known she would appreciate the simple gesture of a single rose.

Doreen, Barbi, and Karen continued their heated conversation as if she weren't in the room.

"Maybe he's on the up-and-up," Doreen surprised everyone by saying. "Maybe Hadleigh's right. Maybe we're all judging him too quickly."

"Ha! *Now* who's got stars in her eyes?" Karen demanded triumphantly. The others had given her a hard time over her breathless reaction to meeting Treet Miller the first time.

"Hey! *I'm* not the one who owns all his movies," Doreen retaliated. "Believe me, I'm not starstruck over that ruthless—"

"And you, Barbi!" Karen interrupted. "Still got that poster of him on your office wall?"

"That was a freebie," Barbi snapped, red-faced with embarrassment.

"Wait!" Hadleigh shouted the word. Shocked, they fell silent. Fighting to keep her voice level, Hadleigh said, "I think you've all forgotten that you're talking about Samantha's father." She angled her chin out. "And you've all forgotten that I'm a grown woman and this is *my* life." When Barbi would have spoken, Hadleigh quickly held up a hand. "I'm not finished. Now, I know you all are concerned about my well-being—and Samantha's—but you're carrying this too far. Ultimately, it will be my decision whether Sam and I continue to see Treet and Caroline."

"I think it's a bad idea," Barbi stated.

"Me too." As if to strengthen their position, Karen went to stand beside Barbi. They both looked expectantly at Doreen.

Doreen shrugged, then sighed. "To tell the truth, I don't know what I believe. I've never met the guy." Her voice softened as she continued. "I *do* know that I hate to see you get hurt, Hadleigh. Just be careful."

"Yeah," Barbi muttered, "be careful. This guy packs a punch with the ladies." She slanted a mischievous glance at Karen, breaking the tension with her teasing remark. "Just ask Karen if you don't believe me."

"Go to hell, Barbi," Karen growled. "I can't wait to see *your* reaction when you meet him!"

But Hadleigh didn't have to be told; she knew first-hand what a punch Treet packed with the ladies. She'd fast discovered she was no exception to the rule.

And that was what bothered her.

Was she just another overzealous fan? Like other women, she'd daydreamed about Treet Miller, fantasized about what it would be like to have those famous baby blues focused on her, to feel that sensuous, beautiful mouth moving against her own.

But she'd never dreamed it would actually happen.

Having her best friends openly drooling over him didn't help matters. She hadn't known she was the jealous type until recently . . . with Treet. If she was jealous of her friends, how would she react when she and Treet were in a crowd of beautiful women? Worse yet, how could she hope to compete?

What the hell was she thinking? She'd made it clear to Treet they could be nothing more than friends. She had no business fantasizing about a relationship with Treet Miller, no matter how convincing and charming he was. Chances were she'd never make a public appearance with Treet, so her worries were groundless.

In fact, the entire conversation they were having was a ridiculous waste of energy. She and Treet were connected through their daughters, nothing more and nothing less. She would not—could not—let it go beyond that.

"You don't have to worry, girls." She said the words softly, but with great determination. "I'm not going to get involved with Treet Miller on a personal level. I've already decided, so you see, your worries are groundless."

"So you admit that it would be a mistake."

Hadleigh bit back an exasperated snarl at Karen's taunt. "No, I don't. It's just something I've decided *on my own,*" she emphasized. "Treet and I are from different worlds. I wouldn't be comfortable in his, and he wouldn't be comfortable in mine." She would have elaborated, but the doorbell interrupted her.

She went to answer it, fully expecting another corny delivery from the crazy movie star.

What she wasn't expecting when she opened the door was to find Treet lounging against the frame, wearing faded, button-fly jeans and a T-shirt that had seen better days. A shadowed jaw added to his dangerous, disreputable appearance.

He was the ultimate fantasy man: gorgeous, sexy, sinful, and wholly male.

Her stunned gaze traveled from his lazy smile to the boxes he held in one hand, and the six-pack of beer he held in the other.

"Mind if I crash the party? I brought pizza and beer. Hope you like Canadian bacon and mushroom. Oh, and I brought a deck of cards."

He brushed past her before Hadleigh could respond. Slowly she turned to follow him into the room, belatedly remembering that she wasn't alone.

Damn it.

"Ah, these must be Sam's 'aunts,' " Treet drawled, flashing his bone-melting smile in the direction of the openmouthed women. His gaze lingered on Karen's pale face. One brow rose in recognition. "Karen, isn't it? We met in the hospital cafeteria."

Karen's mouth closed, then opened again as if she was trying to speak and couldn't. Her eyes drifted backward, and to the utter amazement of the others, she began to slump to the floor.

Doreen instinctively leaped to catch her before she hit the carpet, her training as a paramedic kicking in. Barbi remained rooted in place, her gaze glued to Treet, seemingly oblivious to Karen's reaction.

Treet turned, casting Hadleigh a sheepish, endearing look that sent a telltale weakness to her knees. "Guess I should have called first."

Hadleigh folded her arms and glowered at him.

Three hours later, Treet allowed Hadleigh to push him in the direction of the front door. He was pleased as punch when the other women protested his leaving.

"It's still early, and I've got a good hand for once!" Doreen complained in a disgusted voice. She pitched her cards onto the table and leaned back in her chair, a fierce scowl on her face.

Barbi covered a yawn. "I, for one, have to get up in the morning, so I should be going too." She glanced at Karen, who was busy counting her substantial stack of quarters. Karen had been on a winning streak the past hour and was obviously quite proud of herself. "Can you give me a ride, O great one?"

"I'd be delighted," Karen said without glancing up from her task. She had finally recovered from the shock of seeing Treet again, and now seemed hardly aware of his presence.

He took that as a very good sign.

At the door, Treet turned to Hadleigh. She looked flushed, with a peculiar sparkle in her eyes he couldn't decipher. He fought the urge to steal a kiss from that soft, provocative mouth, reminding himself that now was not the time or place. "I had a good time," he said, keeping his voice low. It was the truth—he'd had a great time, especially after they'd all figured out he was just an ordinary guy.

The best part was spending time with Hadleigh, watching her trying to be subtle about watching him, sneaking winks and playing footsies beneath the table while the others were preoccupied with their cards. Her friends were great, too, each unique in her own way.

"Yeah, you were a real hit with the ladies," Hadleigh said without enthusiasm.

His brow rose at the bite in her voice. "Jealous?"

She snorted. "Hardly. Need I remind you that you were *not* invited? I specifically said 'girls night,' and you are definitely not a girl."

"Thanks for noticing." He grinned when she blushed. "Sorry about crashing the party. I couldn't help myself."

"Are you always this impulsive?"

Treet gave it some thought, studying her flushed face intently. Finally he shook his head. "Not usually *this* impulsive. I think I have you to thank for that."

"I'm sure Brutal doesn't consider it an asset," she said dryly. She reached around him and opened the door, her lips pursed in a determined line. "Good night, Treet."

"Good night, Hadleigh." Quickly, he leaned forward and brushed his mouth lightly across those pretty pursed lips, confident the others couldn't see him. "Sweet dreams," he whispered in her ear.

She gave him a push and closed the door firmly behind him.

"Man, you got it bad, and I mean *bad,* boss."

Treet turned to find Brutal watching him with something akin to pity. He scowled at the bodyguard. "I *like* her, Brutal. There's a vast difference between *like* and *love.*"

"Sure, man. Sure."

The elevator doors slid open. Brutal glanced inside before motioning for Treet to enter. As the elevator began to descend, the bodyguard resumed his lecture.

"You really think those women are gonna keep quiet about this?"

"They're Hadleigh's friends," Treet reminded him patiently. "Yes, I think they'll keep quiet, and what if they don't? Fame has its price. I knew that when I went into acting."

"Everything has a price, boss."

Treet slanted him a suspicious look. "What's that supposed to mean?"

Brutal shrugged. "Just that you might find yourself paying a high price for being . . . *friends* with this woman."

"This *woman* is Caroline's mother. And she barely tolerates me." Something he hoped to change in the near future.

The bodyguard laughed outright. "Man, you *are* living in a fantasy world. Maybe you should take a vacation."

"As a matter of fact, I plan to do just that. I'm taking the girls and Hadleigh to Montana for a few weeks."

"The hell you are."

"The hell I'm not."

"Todd ain't gonna like this," Brutal growled.

"My agent will get over it."

"I'm goin' with you."

"I was hoping you'd say that."

Chapter Eleven

"I found some Dramamine in the med kit."

Hadleigh took the pill and the bottled water from Treet, her worried gaze on Samantha, who was looking greener by the minute. "I don't get it. She's flown before and she didn't get air sick."

They were in the plane bathroom, with Samantha clutching the compact toilet as if her life depended on it. Beneath her supporting arm, Hadleigh could feel Sam's little belly spasm pitifully each time she retched into the commode. When the spell had passed, Hadleigh halved the pill and urged Samantha to wash it down with a sip of water.

Sam listlessly obeyed—a sure sign she was sick. "I don't feel good, Mommy."

Those Baby Blues

"I know, sweetheart." Her heart aching, Hadleigh smoothed Sam's damp brow. "But the medicine will help." She glanced at Treet, noticing that he looked a little pale as well. Behind him in the narrow doorway, Caroline watched the scene. It was easy to read the confusion and fear in her large, solemn eyes.

"The medicine might make her sleepy," Treet said, reaching out as if to touch Sam's head. He drew back with a sigh, curling his arm around Caroline's shoulders and drawing her against him for a reassuring hug.

"Anything has to be better than this." Hadleigh wet a cloth and wiped Sam's face. Finally, after about five minutes with no further retching, Hadleigh asked, "Do you feel well enough to leave the bathroom, sweetie?" When Samantha nodded, Hadleigh gathered her up and headed in the direction of the luxurious cabin.

The private jet hit an air pocket, causing her to stumble. Treet was there in a flash, steadying her with his firm hands at her waist. "Do you think we should take her to a hospital?"

He sounded anxious, and so serious Hadleigh couldn't resist a smile. "No, she's just air sick. The Dramamine should help."

Caroline tugged at Hadleigh's elbow. "What's wrong with Sam? Is she going to die?"

Stifling a laugh, Hadleigh struggled to keep a straight face. If Sam didn't get well soon, she suspected she'd have an all-out panic on her hands. "No, darling. She's not going to die. She's just going to sleep a little while; then she'll feel all better."

147

"Then she can play with me?"

Hadleigh's heart turned over at the sight of Caroline's earnest, worried face. "Then she can play with you," she agreed.

Sam stirred in her arms. Her eyelids had begun to droop, and her eyes had taken on a glassy sheen. "I threw up on his plane."

"I know, sweetie. He doesn't mind."

"I made a big mess."

"Trudy cleaned it up," Hadleigh assured her.

"Trudy's nice," Sam mumbled, finally giving up the fight to stay awake.

With Samantha in her arms, Hadleigh sank onto the plush couch and let out a shaky sigh. She hated to see her baby sick.

Treet sat on the couch opposite her. Caroline, with her gaze locked on Samantha's flushed, sleeping face, climbed into her daddy's lap and buried her cheek against his shoulder.

Hadleigh watched as Caroline struggled not to follow Sam's footsteps into la-la land. Her eyelids drifted shut, then snapped open, over and over again, making Hadleigh smile. Finally, her little body went lax against Treet. He automatically tightened his hold.

"She asleep?" he whispered above Caroline's head.

Hadleigh nodded, not trusting herself to speak around the sudden lump in her throat.

"Wanna switch? I hate to waste an opportunity like this."

"Okay." Yep, her voice was noticeably husky. She gently laid Samantha along the sofa beside her as Treet

148

rose with his burden. He placed Caroline on her lap, then scooped Samantha into his arms, returning to the couch.

When they were both settled again, Hadleigh gazed down at Caroline. "She's lighter than Samantha."

"Yeah, I noticed that. Must be all that salad she eats."

"I can't get Samantha to touch anything green."

"I noticed that, too."

Without realizing it, they were both speaking barely above a whisper. Hadleigh softly traced the shape of Caroline's ear. "How much did Sam weigh when she was born?"

"Seven pounds. How about Caroline?"

"Seven pounds, twelve ounces. Felt more like ten pounds, thirteen ounces," Hadleigh added with a rueful chuckle.

"By the way, Brutal found Bo Bo."

Her head jerked up. "The turtle?"

"You know another Bo Bo?" he teased. "Brutal took him with him to the ranch."

"Sam will be tickled to finally get to meet him." She grimaced. "After two visits to Caroline's petting zoo, she's never going to settle for a gerbil."

"Do you think Cheyenne made the switch?"

The unexpected question startled Hadleigh. She glanced up, catching a flash of pain in Treet's eyes before he masked it. She wet her lips, hesitating to voice a suspicion she couldn't prove.

"Just your opinion, ma'am," he drawled, apparently sensing her hesitation. "You aren't under oath."

He was smiling, but Hadleigh noted the smile didn't quite reach his eyes. "The thought crossed my mind when I found out—" Her alarmed gaze skipped from one sleeping child to the other; she'd learned the hard way not to underestimate Samantha. She relaxed when she heard the faint sound of Sam snoring. "She—she had said she was going to make sure you didn't get the baby." Taking a deep breath, Hadleigh shifted Caroline in her arms to get a more secure grip. "She claimed you were threatening to take the baby from her, that you tricked her into getting pregnant."

Moments ticked by, and with each of them, Hadleigh's tension grew. She waited for him to deny it. Prayed that he would and feared that he wouldn't. And why should he? He wasn't obligated to explain anything to her.

The sigh he expelled sounded angry. "Why would she do something so devious if she wasn't going to gloat to me about it? Where's the satisfaction in silent revenge? Or is that a woman thing?"

He hadn't meant to attack her personally, Hadleigh knew, but she felt the prick nonetheless. "Don't judge us all by the likes of Cheyenne. Maybe she just chickened out."

Treet lifted a silken braid and wound it around his finger. He wore an expression of awe as he stared at Sam's auburn hair, his look a complete contradiction to the bitterness in his voice. "Or maybe she just planned to wait until Caroline graduated from high school before she told me."

"Would it have mattered?" Hadleigh challenged.

"No."

No hesitation there. "Then what difference does it make? Why waste your energy on being angry with her? What's done is done."

"You're very forgiving."

"No, I'm not. I just try to look at the bright side. She didn't leave me childless. In fact, if I *could* go back and change things, I'm not sure I would." She could tell by his expression that he understood. She explained anyway. "Because if it meant I wouldn't have these memories with Sam, I—"

"Yeah, I see your point. Still, it's going to be difficult now that we've—now that we've—"

"I know," she inserted quietly. That he had trouble saying the words reminded her of just how serious the situation was. "We're smart people, Treet, and if we keep being smart, we can turn this fiasco to our advantage." She hesitated a heartbeat, then asked, "How do you think Cheyenne will feel when she learns that her long-term revenge plan is out of the bag?"

Treet's eyes narrowed, as if he was thinking about something unpleasant. "If she knows what's good for her, she'll stay away from me and mine. We could both sue her ass—" He broke off as Sam stirred restlessly in his arms.

He had little warning as she suddenly sat up, blinked at him, and stated, "You're not my mommy. I'm gonna be sick again."

And then she was—all over Treet's chest and lap.

To his credit, he didn't leap up or throw her off his lap. He just held tight as she retched helplessly.

Hadleigh winced at his pained expression. "It was *your* idea to switch," she reminded him. When he simply stared at her, she quickly shifted Caroline to the sofa. "I'll get Trudy. I think she's in the cockpit."

The moment Hadleigh disappeared from sight, Treet cursed himself for not telling her about his brief conversation with Cheyenne before they'd left for the airport. Apparently the hospital had called Cheyenne before they notified him. Cheyenne had given herself away the moment she opened her lying mouth, trying to assure Treet that she had known nothing about the mix-up at the hospital.

That was when he'd realized that Cheyenne *had* masterminded the switch. Cheyenne was pretty, but she wasn't very bright.

"Are you mad, Mr. Miller?"

"No." Forcing his black thoughts to the back of his mind, Treet found a part of his T-shirt that wasn't soiled and carefully wiped Sam's chin. He tried to breathe through his mouth.

"You look mad," Samantha persisted.

"This isn't my mad look. It's my gosh-this-stinks look."

Sam giggled, completing the meltdown in Treet's heart. "It *does* stink. I'm sorry. I hate to puke. It gets all in my nose and—"

"I get the picture," Treet interrupted hastily, wishing Trudy would hurry. His stomach was trying to rebel, and he didn't know how much longer he could keep it steady. It wasn't the first time he'd been puked on, but he'd never been very good at dealing with it. Usually when others got sick, he got sick right along with them. Kept them company, so to speak.

To his relief, Hadleigh and Trudy came running in. With her usual efficiency, Trudy lifted Sam from his lap and whisked her to the washroom.

That left Hadleigh to help *him*. The manly man in him wanted to shoo her away; the weak stomach in him accepted her help with gratitude and more than a little desperation. "If you could just grab the ends of my T-shirt and lift it slowly over my head—I think I can hold the worst of it away from my face." If he emptied his stomach in front of Hadleigh, he'd have to consider jumping from the plane.

And then there was Brutal. He would never let Treet live it down.

"Okay. Are you ready?"

He clenched his teeth and nodded, for the moment ignoring the hint of amusement in her voice. "Easy. Go slow, and stop when I tell you to."

"I've got it."

Together they managed to get the T-shirt off without dumping the contents of Sam's upset stomach. Hadleigh carefully wadded the soiled shirt and stuffed it into a plastic bag, tying it securely.

"What should I do with it?"

"Throw it from the plane?" Treet suggested. He looked up in time to see her lips twitch. "And what the hell is so funny?"

"You. *You're* funny. Treet Miller, brought to his knees by a little baby puke."

"I'm not on my knees, in case you didn't notice. And it *wasn't* baby puke. Baby puke I can handle." Which was a bald-faced lie, and if Brutal had been there, he would have called him on it. "What she launched on me was a full-course meal."

Grinning openly now, Hadleigh said, "Well, whose idea was it to introduce Sam to peel-'em and eat-'em shrimp, hmm?"

"She loved them."

"Yeah, all two dozen of them. Or was it three dozen? Then there were the crab cakes. I still can't get over how much she liked them, but the oysters were the biggest surprise."

Treet's stomach muscles clenched in protest. He groaned and gave up. "Okay, okay! Let it be known that I cried uncle first. Just *please* change the subject."

"All right, but first can you answer one question? Just this one itty-bitty question? I'm dying of curiosity."

Suspicious, Treet squinted at her too-innocent face from his position on the sofa. "What?"

"Were those little black nuggets in the ice cream chocolate chips, or walnuts?"

Driving a cherry-red minivan that looked as if it had just rolled off the assembly line, Brutal picked them up at the private airport in the small, rural town of Burlington, Montana, just before sunset. Trudy climbed into the front with Brutal, Hadleigh and Treet appropriated the second seat, and the girls were secured in the back in the built-in child safety seats.

The moment the door slid shut, Sam made her announcement. "I puked on Mr. Miller."

Everyone looked at Treet. Caroline giggled and pointed, then clamped her hand to her mouth. Brutal's eyes narrowed. "Boss, did you get sick too?"

"No," Treet muttered. Louder, he said, "No, I did not get sick."

"I did," Sam repeated almost proudly. "And Mr. Miller didn't get mad at me."

"Sam?"

"Huh?"

"Would you please stop calling me Mr. Miller?"

Sam frowned. "Okay. Do I just call you Miller without the mister?"

"How about just calling me Treet?"

"No, 'cause that's a silly name."

"Sam!" Hadleigh admonished, twisting to glare at her daughter. "Don't be rude."

Treet came to her rescue. "You're right, darling, it *is* a silly name. I've always thought so."

"Then why don't you change it?" Sam asked seriously.

"Because my agent seems to think it's catchy."

Hadleigh looked at him in surprise. "Treet's not your real name?" When he shook his head, she prompted, "Then what is?"

"I'll tell you later," he whispered.

"I'll hold you to that."

"Hmm. Now, *that's* something to look forward to."

Blushing, Hadleigh turned her face to the window. Once again he'd managed to add a double entendre to her words. He was a devil in disguise, and she was reckless and crazy to agree to this trip. Reckless and stupid to think she could keep him at bay, because the plain, shocking truth was she didn't to keep him at bay. She wanted him not to be *the* Treet Miller, or even the father of her child—the child she'd believed was her own. She wanted him to be an ordinary man so that she could enjoy flirting with him, and not be thinking constantly that she shouldn't be for this reason or that.

And there were plenty of *this*s and *that*s.

"Scared?" Treet taunted in her ear.

Hadleigh jumped and shot him a dark look. "I don't know what you're talking about."

His sultry gaze dropped to her mouth. He stared at it so long her nipples peaked. Damn him.

"I think you do."

"It's not nice to whisper," Sam informed him sternly. "Mommy says so. Isn't that right, Mommy?"

"That's right, sweetheart." Hadleigh smiled smugly at Treet's disgruntled expression.

"You never said that to me, Daddy."

Hadleigh's smile grew at Caroline's scolding tone. Treet's eyes narrowed. His expression clearly promised retribution. Her smile slipped. She truly had to stop taunting him before she got herself into real trouble, because she suspected Treet's brand of retribution would be the best kind of torture.

Such as kissing her senseless.

Or touching her in secret, sensitive places until she cried for mercy.

Lordy, he could just stare at her for a while and she'd get hot. Hadleigh turned her face away and closed her eyes for a brief moment. What was she doing here? What had she been thinking?

Sam.

Caroline.

They were the reasons she was here, sitting beside one of the most eligible bachelors in the country, on her way to a Montana ranch that probably belonged to Robert Redford, or Gene Hackman.

Unbelievable.

Her thoughts roamed back to their conversation on the plane when she'd told him what Cheyenne had said after Sam's birth. Treet hadn't denied Cheyenne's accusations, which could mean he was either guilty of her charges, or he had just assumed Hadleigh hadn't believed the model. Hadleigh would have felt a lot better about things if he had laughed or outright denied the rumors.

Was Treet the ruthless, manipulative monster Cheyenne had described? Should she be afraid he would try to take Sam from her, as her friends feared? Treet certainly had the means and the money, and the motive as well. Surely it wasn't standard practice for a man to be so accepting of another man's child? Not in her experience, anyway. Yet what if those other rumors were true? What if he'd known all along that Caroline wasn't his, yet he loved her anyway? If those rumors *were* true, then it hadn't come as a shock to discover he hadn't fathered Caroline.

157

But it must have come as a shock to discover that he *did* have a child of his blood, after all.

Samantha.

Her daughter, if not in blood then in heart and soul. She'd warned him he wouldn't get her, and he'd promptly claimed he wouldn't give up Caroline.

That didn't necessarily mean he wouldn't try to gain both daughters, did it? Hadn't she thought—briefly— that in a perfect world *she* could have both daughters?

"I could get used to this," Treet said, startling her out of chaotic thoughts.

She turned quickly to look at him. "Get used to what?"

He jerked his head in the direction of the backseat. The girls were dozing, hands linked as if even in sleep they couldn't bear to be apart. "That. Having the two of them together. I can't believe how close they've already become. It'll be hard to separate them."

His hushed words chilled Hadleigh, coming so close on the heels of her disturbing thoughts about Treet's motives. As if she weren't paranoid enough!

Chapter Twelve

Montana.

Big Sky Country.

As they neared the ranch in the eastern part of the state, Hadleigh could certainly see how the mountainous state came by its nickname. It was the same sky she viewed each and every day in California, yet it wasn't. This sky looked bigger. Enormous. Huge.

And she soon found out it wasn't the only thing big in Montana. "You call this a ranch?" Hadleigh asked, staring at the sprawling cluster of structures with a mixture of trepidation and awe. "It looks more like a resort!" The mysterious ridge of mountains rising in the far distance intensified the postcard effect.

"Yeah, Clint said it was more than he needed, but the deal was too good to pass up." With a casual move,

159

Treet flung his arm over the backseat and leaned into her, sharing the same view through the window.

"C—Clint?" Hadleigh swallowed hard. No, she wouldn't ask. She didn't want to know. She was intimidated by the sheer size of the ranch itself without knowing she might be sitting on a couch where Clint Eastwood parked his famous behind, or sleeping in a bed where he'd slept.

No, she would *not* ask.

Damn. She *had* to. "Are we talking about Clint Eastwood?"

Treet laughed at her expression. "No. Clint Loveless. He's a producer—friend of mine."

"Never heard of him." Thank God. Hadleigh let out a sigh of relief. "For a moment there I thought you were going to say Clint *Eastwood*."

One gorgeous dark brow rose mockingly. "You a fan of his?" he teased.

"Aren't you?" Her tone dared him to say one bad word about Clint.

"Yep. He's my idol. You'd like him. He's a homebody like me. Typical all-around good guy. Kinda old, though."

"There's nothing *typical* about Clint Eastwood," Hadleigh argued, trying to keep a straight face. She had learned to recognize the glint of jealousy in his eyes when she talked about another movie star. And there was a definite glint now. "Or old, for that matter. He could be a hundred and still make me swoon."

"He's gay."

"He is not!"

Treet's burst of laughter roused the girls.

"Are we there yet, Daddy?"

"Yes, sweetheart. We're here."

"Mommy, I gotta pee," Sam said, sounding sleepy and grumpy. "Do they have a bathroom?"

"I'm sure they do." Probably a half dozen or so, Hadleigh thought, trying to figure out which of the four doors was the main entrance. A rustic porch fashioned from rough-hewn logs ran half the length of the house—which to Hadleigh looked at least a quarter of a mile long. She caught a brief glimpse of an Olympic-size swimming pool sparkling beneath the sun. To the right of the house was a corral filled with beautiful horses, a few gangly colts, and a black and white cow. Beyond the corral was a huge red barn, picture perfect, complete with hay spilling from an open window at the top.

She resisted the urge to pinch herself. She felt as if someone had plopped her right smack dab in the middle of a postcard; the spread was a charming mixture of past and present.

As the van rolled to a stop in front of door number three, Treet idly fluffed the damp hair at the nape of her neck. "What do you think?"

"I'm speechless." She shook her head in wonder, trying to appear causal about dislodging his hand. "I don't know how anyone can own a place like this and ever leave it." Behind her, the girls were squealing with excitement; they'd spotted the horses.

"I'll take them to the fence," Trudy volunteered. Brutal popped the hatchback and soon the foursome went

161

trooping across the yard to the corral, leaving Hadleigh and Treet alone to exit the van.

Treet caught her chin with his finger and turned her head. Hadleigh found herself drowning in his fantastic blue eyes, made all the more brilliant by the sun shining through the glass. Tension popped and sizzled between them. She wanted to move away—jump out of the van—but she couldn't.

"Will you be comfortable here?" he asked softly, seriously.

"I think Sam will love it." Her evasive answer earned a frown.

"I know Sam will . . . and so will Caroline. I'm asking about *you.*"

"This isn't about—" His finger on her lips shushed her.

"Yes, this *is* about you, too. And me. We're all in this together. If you aren't relaxed, the girls will pick up on it, am I right?"

She managed a nod.

"So I'm asking you again, will you be comfortable here?"

"I honestly don't know." She shrugged, then grimaced, gesturing toward the house. "This is someone else's home."

"Clint manages to visit once or twice a year, mostly just for the weekend. He has a couple that takes care of the place. They live in the guest house out back."

"So you're saying—"

"He doesn't feel as if this is his home any more than we do."

"But still, his personal stuff—"

"He bought it furnished, and hasn't had time to make it personal. In fact, he's talked about selling it."

She took a deep breath. "Has anyone ever told you that it's impolite to interrupt?"

"Yes, Brutal tells me all the time." His naughty smile was infectious as he leaned over her and opened the door. "Ladies first."

Butterflies dipped and whirled in her stomach. She stepped from the van, telling herself that she was smart, that she wouldn't let the atmosphere affect her judgment. Treet was just a man, not a king, and Montana was just a state like any other. It just *seemed* like a place out of time, and the beautiful home she was about to enter was just a glorified log house, not a castle.

Okay. A glorified log *mansion,* maybe.

When she turned back to Treet, she found him juggling suitcases and bags. Here was proof when she needed it the most; the movie star with the million-dollar smile was up to his fantastic blue eyes in luggage. Good-ole ordinary domestic activity.

She let out a shaky breath and smiled. "Need some help?"

Instead of answering, Treet looked beyond her, smothering a curse. "What the hell is *he* doing here?"

Hadleigh followed his gaze to a tall, well-dressed man striding toward them from door number one. His hair, long and black, hung loose around his broad shoulders. A diamond sparkled in his right ear, and more sparkled on his fingers. Hadleigh judged him to be in his early forties.

He looked determined.

"That's my agent, Todd Hall." Treet's scowled deepened. "I told him I was on vacation, damn it."

"I know what you told me," Todd said as he reached them. "But this couldn't wait."

"And you couldn't have used the phone?"

"No." Todd didn't elaborate.

Treet literally growled, thrusting luggage into Todd's hands. "Then you can help me carry this stuff inside." He paused to lift a sarcastic brow. "You *can* wait until we get inside, can't you?"

Todd flushed. "Yeah, of course." His gaze flickered over Hadleigh, who stood in uncomfortable silence. "You must be Hadleigh Charmaine."

"Yes."

"I'm Todd Hall, Treet's agent." He juggled the bright purple backpack Sam had insisted on packing with toys and various other essentials and managed to stick out his hand.

Hadleigh shook it, wondering if she should tell him that he had something sticky on his hand. She suspected he'd gotten it from Sam's bag. After deciphering the irritation in his quizzical gaze, she kept silent.

"Let's go inside before I drop this stuff," Treet grumbled.

"I—I'll join the girls."

Treet flashed her an apologetic look that would have melted a wicked witch's hardened heart. "I'll join you in a moment."

*   *   *

"You followed me to Montana—arriving before me, I might add—just to show me a *script?*" Without glancing at it, Treet pitched the neatly bound script onto an end table and glared at his agent. "I can't believe you."

"Treet, this isn't just *any* script. This is Academy Award material."

"You've said that before." Treet waved an impatient hand. "Anyway, I don't care about an Academy Award."

"Since when?"

Treet hesitated. They were standing in the rustic family room of the ranch house, the room's impressive, high-beamed ceilings and wide-open space reminding Treet anyone could walk in. He would have taken Todd to a more private room—but he hadn't had time to check out the place. "You know that I have a personal crisis on my hands." In his mind it wasn't a crisis, but he didn't have the time or the inclination to try to explain this to his agent. He doubted Todd would have cared. Todd was in the business of making money, not helping his clients solve their personal problems.

"All I'm asking is that you read it and let me know. The studio wants an answer—preferably tomorrow—and if they don't get it soon they'll cast someone else."

"Maybe they should." Treet meant it. Right now acting was the last thing on his mind. Something else Todd would find hard to believe. No one knew his ambitions better than his agent.

Todd shook his head and looked away, as if he'd decided Treet had lost his mind. "They want *you*. Look, I understand that you've got things to work out with . . .

Miss Charmaine, but hear me out. Read the damned script and *then* tell me you don't give a damn. I'm betting you'll change your mind. It's fantastic."

"I'm not making any promises," Treet said.

"Guess I'll have to take my chances." Todd pointed at the script. "Just don't forget that time is important. They want to start filming next month."

Treet let out a bark of disbelieving laughter. "You've got to be kidding."

"No, I'm not."

"Who's the leading lady?"

"Julia Roberts."

Despite himself, Treet was impressed. Julia Roberts was one of the hottest stars around at the moment, and in great demand. His gaze strayed to the script before he sighed and looked away. Damn it, he'd planned this trip to get to know his daughter—and her mother.

Sensing that he was weakening, Todd said, "You won't be with them every moment, will you? Surely you can find time after everyone goes to bed to read over the script?"

Treet had other ideas about what he wanted to do after the girls went to sleep, but he'd best keep those plans to himself. "I'll give it my best shot. *If* I find myself at loose ends, then I'll read it."

"Good." Todd pumped his hand and grinned as if he'd won a major victory. "I have faith in you, man. Call me tomorrow. I'll have my phone with me at all times."

"I'm sure you will. Now get the hell out of here so I can enjoy my vacation."

Todd made it to the wide arched doorway leading into the foyer before he stopped and looked back at Treet. "Oh, yeah. I forgot to tell you that I got a call from your ex-girlfriend."

"Cheyenne?" Treet scowled. What the hell was she up to now? "What did she want?"

"She asked me if I knew what you had decided to do about the mix-up."

"I hope that you told her that it was none of her damned business," Treet said softly, with an underlying layer of steel. He'd hate to lose Todd, but if he discovered the agent couldn't keep his mouth shut about his personal life, he'd have no choice but to sever their relationship. He valued what few secrets he had.

Todd grinned. "I did better than that. I told her that you and Miss Charmaine were thinking of becoming one big happy family."

Treet groaned. "You didn't."

"I did." Todd shrugged, looking defensive. "I thought you'd be pleased."

"I won't be pleased if Cheyenne decides to blab what she knows to the damned papers," Treet growled. He felt like strangling Todd. Dropping such an outrageous hint to Cheyenne was like waving a red flag in front of a bull. "From now on, don't do me any favors, okay?"

"Fine. I won't."

The slamming of the front door a moment later told its own story; he'd ticked his agent off—royally. Treet sighed, thinking it wasn't the first time, and probably wouldn't be the last.

* * *

"Bunk beds! Yay! Look, Caroline, we get to share a room!" In her excitement, Samantha grabbed Caroline and danced in a circle, dragging the less exuberant Caroline along. "This is gonna be fun!"

Hadleigh stood in the doorway of the bedroom, smiling. She sensed rather than heard Treet slip up behind her. She tensed, half expecting him to put his arms around her waist. It would have been a "Treet" thing to do. Without turning, she whispered, "You sent Brutal ahead to fix this room up for them, didn't you?"

"Yeah. I figured they'd like sharing a room."

The room was a dream come true for a child—or in this case, children. Along with the bunk beds, there was a walk-in closet, a huge pine toy box overflowing with games and dolls, two dressers, two chest of drawers, a desk, an entertainment center with a television, DVD player, and stereo. Her gaze landed on the stack of Disney movies by the TV. The only one that looked new was *Sleeping Beauty*.

Her brow rose. She tilted her head to look at him. "Do you really think they'll stay awake through the whole movie?"

Treet's vivid blue eyes gleamed with a devilish light. "We're going to watch it with them—armed to the hilt with super soakers." He curled warm fingers around her arm, sending a jolt of lightning into her belly. "Come on. I'll show you your room."

They hadn't gone far when Treet paused and opened a door to his left. Hadleigh followed him inside.

The room was lovely, with a matching chest and dresser, and an old-fashioned four-poster bed covered with a beautiful blue velvet quilted comforter. A quick peek in the bathroom revealed—to her delight—a deep, claw-footed tub.

With a helpless shrug, she turned to Treet. "It's lovely."

"I'm glad you like it. This is your vacation—"

"No." She couldn't let him say it again. "This isn't a vacation. We're here to get to know our daughters, and to figure out what we're going to do about the—the—"

"Situation?" he supplied. "I agree, but why can't you enjoy yourself while you're here? Is it a crime to be comfortable? To have fun?"

They were interrupted by Caroline's startling bellow.

"I'm telling my daddy!"

Immediately following Caroline's shouted declaration came Sam's equally loud, "And I'm telling my mom!"

Hadleigh met Treet's startled gaze. "Their first fight?"

"Sounds that way. We'd better referee."

"You'd make a good diplomat," Hadleigh told Treet later that night as they tucked the girls into bed. The *same* bed—the coveted bottom bunk.

They had discovered that both girls were afraid of heights.

"Ah, shucks," Treet drawled. "I'm just doin' my job, ma'am."

"You do it well." And she meant it. Okay, so she believed in not spoiling children, and Treet seemed to lean toward giving them the moon. Who was to say she was right and he was wrong? Caroline was a sweet, sensitive person despite Treet's spoiling of her. Perhaps together they could give them balance.

Together.

Was she, then, considering sharing Sam with Treet? How could she not, when he looked at Sam with such love and yearning? And Caroline . . . sweet, wonderful Caroline. Hadleigh couldn't imagine life without her, now. The little dark-eyed girl already had a firm grip on her heart.

Sam loved Caroline—it was plain to see. And she seemed to like Treet, as well, which was a shock.

Hadleigh gave the covers one last tuck, kissed their soft, flushed cheeks, and stood. They lay side by side, with Caroline's favorite dolls, Amber and Gertrude, squashed between them. Sam slept on her back with one arm flung upward on the pillow; Caroline slept on her side, knees bent, hands tucked beneath her cheek.

Treet tapped the book he held in his hand, then sighed dramatically. "Another failed mission to educate them on Sleeping Beauty," he said. "But tomorrow night we watch the movie—*all* of us. Are you with me?"

Slanting her hand against her forehead in a mock salute, Hadleigh said, "Yes, sir. I'm with you all the way, sir." *Bad choice of words.* "Just waiting for you to issue my weapon," she added hurriedly.

He laughed, his warm gaze heating her blood. "You want to have a nightcap with me?"

She was tempted, oh, Lordy, was she tempted, but she was also determined to keep things platonic between them. For the girls' sake. Oh, hell. For *her* sake as well. It would be too easy to lose her head over Treet.

Not to mention her heart.

"I'd love to, but I have work to do; then I'm going to hit the mattress. I'm beat."

He didn't bother hiding his disappointment. "Good night, then."

"Good night, Treet."

They walked to the door, Hadleigh behind Treet. She reached out to flick the light switch at the same instant Treet did the same. Their fingers tangled. She swiftly drew them away.

Treet turned off the light, then snaked his hand around her neck. His lips covered hers for a brief, soul-shattering kiss. "Scaredy-cat," he whispered huskily.

Before she could refute his very accurate description, he released her and walked away.

Chapter Thirteen

What had he expected?

Alone in the family room, Treet shifted a log with the tip of the poker, squinting against the bright shower of sparks that shot upward through the chimney. It was not yet eleven P.M. and he was restless and not the least bit sleepy.

He couldn't stop thinking about the two new girls in his life.

Samantha, with her bright, mischievous eyes, and Hadleigh, with her determined air and toe-curling smile. Each captivating in her own unique way. Without even trying, Samantha had stolen his heart.

He suspected that with little effort, Hadleigh could as well.

It was the *effort* part that was causing the trouble. She'd told him in no uncertain terms that she wasn't about to get intimately involved with him. Never mind that her eyes seemed to darken to jade when he looked at her, or that he could feel her quiver each time he touched her.

God, he could still taste her mouth, a hint of cherry from the lip balm he'd watched her roll across her luscious lips just before they landed on the private airstrip in Burlington. The kiss had been brief, but searing. Arousing. Making him hunger for more. Making him ache in a way that he hadn't ached in a long time.

Perhaps he could sneak into her room for a quick peek, see if she was still working, or if she'd quit and gone to bed. He could claim he couldn't sleep—which wasn't a lie—and persuade her to join him in front of the fire.

Treet chuckled ruefully. Perhaps Brutal was right; maybe he *had* gone too long without feminine company—other than Caroline's, that is. It wasn't as if he hadn't had the opportunities. In his line of work, opportunities were ubiquitous.

Yet Hadleigh was the one he wanted to be with. Hadleigh was the one he wanted to kiss. Hell, Hadleigh was the one he wanted to make love to! In front of the fire. Outside beneath the big Montana moon. In her big four-poster bed.

In fact, the kitchen table looked sturdy enough to hold them, too. He had a sneaky suspicion making love to Hadleigh would be unforgettable.

He'd most definitely like to test his theory.

But Hadleigh was fighting it, fighting the attraction she didn't try to deny. She believed they would be making a mistake in getting involved.

Treet didn't agree, but he knew something that Hadleigh didn't, and probably wouldn't believe. He didn't just lust after Hadleigh; he truly enjoyed her company, her personality, and a whole lot more.

What a couple they would make.

The sudden thought startled Treet, and reminded him of what his agent had told Cheyenne, about him and Hadleigh becoming one big happy family. He hunkered before the fire and stared at the flames. It *did* have a nice ring to it, and there was no denying the fact that they would all benefit from the union. Caroline and Samantha could be together all the time, and he and Hadleigh would have both daughters.

He sighed, remembering the one flaw in his daydream; Hadleigh didn't seem to be that crazy about him. She was an honest, decent, levelheaded woman. He couldn't see her agreeing to marry him just so they could all be together. He knew she was attracted to him, but he also suspected attraction wouldn't be enough for Hadleigh. She was an old-fashioned girl— if he knew nothing else about her, he'd figured that much out. No, with Hadleigh it would be all or nothing, and the fact that he was a famous movie star didn't matter one whit to her. She wasn't easily influenced, which was one of the things that he admired most about her.

Not that he had given up on trying to bring her around to his way of thinking; he was all for their getting to know each other on a more personal, intimate level.

Treet rose from his position by the fireplace, stuck his hands in his jeans pockets, and mused on how he was going to pass the time until he expended this restless energy that always seemed to hit him in the late evening hours. His gaze landed on the script lying where he'd pitched it on the end table. He guessed it wouldn't kill him to read it, if only to pacify Todd, who really was a good agent.

He picked up the script and sat in one of the matching brown leather recliners by the fire.

Ten minutes later Treet was deeply engrossed in the story. His excitement grew with each page he turned. Todd hadn't been exaggerating. The script *was* fantastic, the characters well fleshed and memorable, the plot nothing short of brilliant.

As Treet continued to read, an idea began to emerge. The more he considered it, the more excited he became.

If he took the part, he'd need to start getting a feel for the character, and the sooner the better. Todd had said the production company wanted to start filming next month, and Treet wasn't a slouch when it came to learning his lines before a shoot.

But he needed someone to stand in for the leading lady. Grinning to himself, he backtracked to the love scene in the first act. A little too mild for what he had in mind, but that could be changed using his imagination and the computer he'd found in Clint's well-equipped office.

There was the little matter of convincing Hadleigh to stand in for the leading lady, but with a bit of luck and a lot of guile, he just might succeed. Feeling naughty and more excited by the moment, Treet carried the script with him to the office.

Once inside, he pushed the power button on the computer. As an afterthought, he retraced his steps and locked the door.

Hadleigh awoke the next morning with a start. She lay still, staring at the unfamiliar ceiling until she remembered where she was. With a contented sigh, she closed her eyes, allowing herself the luxury of remembering the dream she'd been having about Treet, which involved soft, fragrant hay, and a lot of shocking, naked flesh.

Hers and his.

Eventually she noticed the silence, and silence in conjunction with Samantha usually meant trouble. The last time Hadleigh awakened to silence, she'd found Samantha in the kitchen making pancakes.

It had taken her an hour to clean up the mess, and another half hour cleaning up Samantha.

Logic reminded Hadleigh that she wasn't alone and neither was Samantha, but habits were hard to break. She got dressed in record time, slipping on a pair of jeans and a black sweater before padding down the hall in her bare feet.

The girls' room was empty.

She continued on, finally hearing the faint sound of someone humming. The sound led her to the kitchen, a huge, cheery room filled with old-fashioned country charm. Copper pots hung from the ceiling above an oak kitchen island; potted plants sprawled in the window-sill above the sink. The air was scented with cinnamon and coffee.

Trudy stood at the sink with her back to Hadleigh, peeling apples and humming to herself.

"I overslept," Hadleigh stated, wincing as Trudy let out a startled gasp. "Sorry, I didn't mean to scare you. Where is everyone?"

"Riding pony." Trudy flashed her an apologetic smile. "English not so good, but better every day."

Hadleigh helped herself to a cup of coffee, gratefully sipping the hot brew. "I don't usually sleep this late."

"Mr. Miller, he said let you sleep." Trudy shrugged, still smiling. "He pay me good, no argue. You want breakfast?"

She shook her head. "No, thanks, Trudy." Sliding onto a stool at the breakfast bar, Hadleigh hesitated, then plunged on. "By the way, I don't expect you to look after Samantha while we're here. I know you have enough to do without having to take care of another child. Also, I'm going to help you with the housework and the cooking."

But Trudy was laughing and shaking her head before Hadleigh had finished her speech. "I have help. Mrs. . . . Mrs. *Spencer* help me." The woman beamed, obviously happy to have pronounced *Spencer* right. "She live here—she help out." Intercepting Hadleigh's stubborn

177

glance, she added, "I like to cook, clean, care for kids. Mr. Miller good to me. Sam good kid. Caroline good kid. You have fun, don't worry so much."

"Trudy's a wise woman. You should listen to her."

At the sound of Treet's voice so close to her ear, Hadleigh stiffened. Hazy, erotic memories of the dream she'd had rose to mind. Her face heated. She pretended a great interest in her coffee as she mumbled, "Good morning."

"Good morning."

She slanted a quick glance at him, then quickly resumed her study of her coffee. "Did the girls get you up at the crack of dawn?" she asked.

"Just Caroline. We both woke Sam by tickling her nose with a feather. She's not exactly a morning person, I gather."

His low, amused chuckle slithered down her spine like warm molasses. "No, she isn't." She cleared her throat. "Where are they now?"

"Riding a pony. Brutal's leading them around the corral." Taking her arm, he led her to the window. Trudy moved aside, slicing apples into a bowl. "There—see? They're having a blast."

Hadleigh could see that they were, riding double on a fat brown and white pony. She caught her breath as Treet moved his face closer to hers.

"Do you ride?"

"Not very well," she admitted.

"We'll have to change that. Do you swim?"

She turned to look at him, trying not to think about how close her mouth was to his. "Yes, but isn't it too cold—"

"The pool's heated." His gaze dropped to stare at her mouth. His voice dropped as well. "You look beautiful in the morning."

Her breath caught. "Flattery will get you nowhere."

He laughed. "You're supposed to say, 'Flattery will get you *every*where.'"

"I'm sorry to disappoint you," she retorted.

"You could never disappoint me."

"I guess in your profession there isn't a line that you *don't* know."

That silenced him for a moment. Finally, he smiled, flashing incredibly white teeth. Hadleigh swallowed very, very slowly, so that he wouldn't realize just how much he affected her.

The man was simply too gorgeous for words and too charismatic for his—or her—own good.

"I guess it would be a waste of breath to try to convince you that it wasn't a 'line,' so I won't even try. Eventually you'll realize that I mean what I say."

His words held both a delicious promise and a disturbing, erotic threat.

They spent the first day horseback riding through a sea of golden prairie grass that shifted and swayed in the mild breeze. They saw prairie dogs and rabbits, and once, in the distance, a breath-stealing glimpse of a black bear and her two cubs before they scrambled for cover in the woods.

Afterward they played water polo in the heated pool, pausing at lunchtime to gobble down Trudy's delicious homemade pizza on the patio. Before lunch was over,

Hadleigh and Treet had buckled beneath the onslaught of Sam's and Caroline's pleas to return to the pool for another hour.

One hour turned into two, then three.

Finally, Hadleigh insisted they go inside before they all turned into prunes. Besides, she desperately needed a hot shower and a break from the constant, disturbing contact with Treet in the pool. She didn't think *all* of them were coincidences or accidents, the rat.

As she stood beneath the invigorating, hot spray, Hadleigh wondered how much longer she could continue resisting Treet. The reasons for keeping her distance were becoming harder and harder to remember. Hadleigh glanced down at her still rigid nipples and cursed beneath her breath. Just thinking about him . . .

Chuckling ruefully, Hadleigh reached for the towel and stepped out of the shower.

"Would you fix my hair like Sam's?"

Hadleigh let out a startled shriek, clutching the towel to her breasts. Caroline sat on the closed commode, regarding her with large, solemn brown eyes. Her hair was twisted inside a towel, and she wore flannel pajamas printed with various poses of the popular cartoon character, Scooby Doo.

Recovering from her near fatal heart attack, Hadleigh perched herself on the edge of the bathtub. "Well, your hair is a lot shorter than Sam's, and finer. More like mine." Caroline would never guess in a million years why that was so.

Caroline's expression fell. "So you can't fix it?"

"I can try, but in a different way. Ever heard of a French braid?" When Caroline shook her head, Hadleigh said, "How about if I show you; then if you don't like it we can take it down."

"Okay, Haddy."

With her heart in her throat and her chest aching, Hadleigh watched Caroline slip from the commode and out the door. She'd called her Haddy. Not that she cared, as long as Caroline called her *something* besides Miss Charmaine—which she had painstakingly pronounced as *Charming*.

Haddy. Hadleigh bit her lip. How would Caroline react if, or when, she found out that Haddy was her mother? Did Caroline even know about Cheyenne? She and Treet hadn't discussed the past much, so she had no idea what Caroline knew about her mother.

She'd have to ask him.

Tucking her towel securely around her, Hadleigh emerged from the steaming bathroom to find Caroline sitting in front of the dresser, waiting patiently.

Hadleigh's stomach bottomed out at the sight. She was nervous, she realized. Nervous about being alone with her real daughter. Treet would laugh if he knew, call her a scaredy-cat.

Which she supposed she was.

Slowly she approached the dresser, meeting Caroline's big-eyed, darling gaze in the mirror. She picked up the brush and removed the towel from Caroline's head, tossing it aside. "Where's Sam?" she asked casually as she gently drew the brush through Caroline's hair.

"Helping my daddy make popcorn for the movie."

"Oh." Hadleigh hoped she didn't sound as shocked as she felt. Sam . . . helping Treet while *she* helped Caroline. What was going on?

"We made a deal," Caroline added. "She's never had a daddy, and I've never had a mom, so we're pretending."

Startled by her admission, Hadleigh dropped the brush. She bent over to retrieve it, wondering if the conversation could get more bizarre.

"Just for tonight, though. Is that okay, Haddy?"

"It's great—I mean, that's fine with me if it's okay with you." She swallowed to ease the dryness in her throat. Her heart was pounding wildly. "Was this your idea, or Sam's?"

Caroline frowned as if she was trying to remember. "I think it was mine, because I miss having a mom. But don't tell Daddy because it might hurt his feelings. Sam said she didn't miss having a daddy, but she said my daddy's okay."

"She did, did she?" Hadleigh murmured. Her fingers shook as she began to twist and braid Caroline's hair. What she wouldn't give to have been a fly on the wall when the two busy little munchkins had this conversation!

"Yeah. She also said that she liked *my* daddy because he didn't pretend to be nice to her just so he could kiss you."

A gasp escaped before she could stop it. Cheeks burning, she avoided Caroline's curious gaze. "Hmm." Okay, she couldn't resist; if Caroline knew, then *she* had to know. "Did Sam say why it bothered her for a man to kiss me?"

Without hesitation, Caroline said, "She don't want you to leave her."

Hadleigh nearly dropped the brush again. She closed her eyes for a moment, then forced herself to resume braiding Caroline's superfine hair. It was no mean task. "Why in the world would Sam think I would leave her just because a man kissed me?"

Caroline shrugged. "Maybe it's because Emanuel's mom left *him* when her boyfriend kissed her."

More confused than ever, Hadleigh said, "I don't understand." She knew Emanuel was a little boy in Sam's preschool class, but after that she was stumped.

"Well, Sam said Emanuel's daddy got mad, and the next morning when Emanuel woke up, his mom was gone."

"Oh." Oh boy. Now she understood. All too clearly. She would have to sit down with Sam and have a long, long talk with her. No wonder Sam was insecure when she went on a date! Sam's fears were not only misguided, but she was also totally confused about a lot of other things. Understandable since she was only four years old. Still, Hadleigh felt a twinge of hurt that Sam hadn't come to her. She could have explained to Sam that *she* wasn't married, and that it was perfectly okay for another man to kiss her—provided Hadleigh didn't object.

"I've never seen my mom. Daddy says she wasn't ready to be a mommy, so she gave me to him."

Well, now Hadleigh knew what Treet had told Caroline about her mother—and was impressed to discover he'd been as straightforward as he could. Detecting the underlying sadness in Caroline's matter-of-fact statement, Hadleigh chose her words with care. "I'm sure your mom tried, darling. Some people just aren't cut out to have children." She didn't owe Cheyenne diddly-squat, but Hadleigh would try to move heaven and earth if it meant she could ease Caroline's pain even the tiniest bit.

"That's what Daddy said." Caroline's wistful sigh wrenched at Hadleigh's heart. "But I wish she could have stayed."

After having this enlightening conversation with Caroline, Hadleigh felt an increased hope that when the time came to tell Caroline the truth—*if* it came—the child might take it better than Hadleigh had first thought. She obviously missed having a mother.

But Hadleigh also knew Caroline wouldn't be very happy to find out her darling daddy wasn't really her daddy at all. Then there was the disquieting revelation that Sam didn't share Caroline's yearning for the other parent.

What a mess.

"Watch out—the bag's hot," Treet cautioned, keeping an eagle eye on Sam as she opened the microwave door and gingerly retrieved the bag of popcorn.

"I know."

He grinned at her scornful response. "Did we burn this one too?"

After a close inspection of the steaming bag, Sam dropped it into the trash with the other three bags. Disgusted, she said, "Yep. Want me to try another one?"

"Might as well. We've got five packages left; then it's plain chips or nothing."

"I don't like this microwave," Sam said, placing the flat package in the center of the turntable and slamming the door with enough force to rock the appliance.

"Try two minutes, thirty seconds this time."

"Okay, but I don't think it's gonna work. This microwave sucks."

"Tsk, tsk, such language." But Treet's gentle reprimand lacked the necessary heat to impress Sam. He watched, enthralled, as she carefully studied the panel of numbers before punching in the correct time. Her quick mind both astonished and pleased him beyond measure.

Standing back, Sam folded her arms and glared at the microwave, as if she could stare it into submission. "You'd better work this time, buster."

Treet smothered a laugh. His errant daughter reminded him so much of himself when he was a child that he couldn't help feeling proud. She was spirited and refreshingly candid. While these two traits might exasperate Hadleigh, they delighted Treet just as much as Caroline's cautious, aged-beyond-her-years attitude.

When Sam had entered the kitchen offering to help prepare the snack tray, Treet had wanted to do a joyful jig. He viewed her appearance without Caroline or Hadleigh as a major step forward.

He filled two glasses with milk, and another two with ice-cold Coke, then set them on the tray. Striving for casualness, he asked, "So your mom's fixing Caroline's hair?"

"Yep." Samantha leaned forward, her eyes narrowed as she peered through the amber-tinted door of the microwave. The popping noises had begun to slow. "I loaned her my mom for the night."

Treet knocked over a glass of milk, muffling a curse as the cold liquid spread quickly across the counter. He grabbed a dish towel and attempted to stop the flood before it disappeared beneath the glass canister set. Maybe he hadn't heard her right. "You—you *loaned* her your mom?"

"Yep." With a cry worthy of a Viking warrior, Samantha jabbed her finger into the release button on the microwave door. The door popped open. She snatched the swollen bag of popcorn out and examined it beneath the kitchen light with the single-mindedness of a surgeon. "She misses having a mom, but I don't miss having a daddy, 'cept I don't mind helping you so I told her okay. Moms are better at fixing hair, you know."

He nearly choked over that sexist remark coming from such an innocent little mouth. So his little girls had traded parents for the night, had they? Interesting. Very interesting. He couldn't wait to hear Hadleigh's reaction.

Chapter Fourteen

The moment Treet saw Hadleigh's shell-shocked face, he knew that he wasn't the only one privy to their daughters' parent-switching plan.

It didn't lessen his shock, however, when Sam crawled onto the sofa beside him, and Caroline plopped down on his other side next to Hadleigh.

Treet exchanged an ironic glance with Hadleigh as the previews on the video started rolling.

Caroline reached up and tilted his face down. "Do you like my hair, Daddy?"

He looked her over, feigning a shocked expression that made her giggle. "Is that *you*, Caroline? My sweet little baby girl? I thought you were someone else!"

"No, Daddy, it's me! I just got my hair fixed different. Haddy did it."

"I see." He studied the slightly askew French braid a moment before he announced seriously, "You look fantastic. Like a little grown woman."

His daughter leaned forward and shot Sam a smug look that totally mystified him. "See, I told you!"

"So?" Sam retorted. "She just barely did get it all up. Your hair's too short."

"No, it's not."

"Yes, it is."

"No, it's not! Yours is too long."

"Is not."

"Is too."

In perfect sync, Treet and Hadleigh covered the girls' mouths with their hands. "Enough," Treet said, trying to contain his laughter. "The movie's started."

"Are you going to warn them?" Hadleigh asked, tongue in cheek.

Treet affected an evil grin. "No. That would take all the fun out of it."

Caroline looked from one to the other, as did Sam. "Warn us about what, Daddy? Tell us!"

"Yeah, tell us!" Sam added, beginning to look alarmed.

"Well, let's just say that you two had better stay awake and watch the *whole* movie."

Both girls fell silent. It was Sam who finally asked in a comically subdued voice, "What will happen to us if we fall asleep?"

With a flourish, Treet pulled out a cheap water gun from where he'd hidden it in his waistband. *"This* is what will happen."

"Daddy!" Caroline cried, rising to her knees to wrest the gun from him. "Don't you dare squirt me with that!"

"You rat!" Sam yelled, pummeling him mercilessly—and painlessly—in the chest.

Treet laughed at their puny efforts, finally crying uncle. His amused gaze met Hadleigh's soft, luminous one. He stilled. She was watching their antics with a tenderness that formed a lump in his throat.

What a woman.

Eventually, the girls calmed down and began to watch the movie. Treet pretended to watch it with them. It was impossible to concentrate on something as mundane as a child's movie when Hadleigh sat so near.

He could smell the enticing scent of her light perfume, and the faint smell of the herbal shampoo she'd used.

He could hear her breathing, slowly, shallowly, as if she wasn't quite as settled and relaxed as she'd like him to think.

Brutal had taken Trudy to the movies in town, so it was just the four of them alone in the big house. Was she as affected as he was by the cozy setting? With little effort, he could imagine that she was his wife, and that Caroline and Samantha were their children—*together*. Did the sensible Hadleigh Charmaine ever harbor such fantasies? he wondered.

Treet decided to test his theory. Slowly, he inched his arm along the back of the sofa until his hand came to rest near the nape of her neck. Holding his breath, he brushed her skin with the tips of his fingers.

She turned quickly, shooting him a dark, warning look.

He gave her one of his best, slow, sexy, on-camera smiles.

She frowned and leaned forward slightly, breaking the contact with his fingers.

So she wanted to play hardball, did she? Undaunted, Treet reached for her neck again, curling his fingers around the base of her skull. When she didn't immediately move, he began to massage her skull with slow, light strokes.

This time her rejection was more direct. She glanced pointedly down at Caroline, then at Sam before giving her head a quick shake.

With a sigh he settled his arm along the sofa again, leaving her alone for the time being. After all, the night was young.

It had been a long, activity-filled day.

At least, that was what Hadleigh told herself when she awoke with a guilty start sometime later.

The VCR had kicked into automatic rewind, signaling the end of the movie. It was the whirring noise it made that had awakened her, she realized.

Groggy from sleep, she lifted her head from the sofa arm and rubbed her eyes, fully expecting to encounter Treet's lazy, devilish grin when she looked around.

Not so.

Samantha, Caroline, and Treet were all huddled together on the sofa. Treet had an arm around each girl in an unconsciously protective gesture.

And they were sound asleep—all of them.

Easing from the sofa, Hadleigh gathered the half-eaten bowl of popcorn and the tray with their empty glasses. Still smiling, she headed to the kitchen, determined to do her part in easing Trudy's workload. Afterward, she would wake Treet and together they would carry the girls to bed.

As if they were a couple—a family like any other.

You're treading on dangerous ground with that kind of thinking, girlfriend. Hadleigh's smile faded at the grim reminder. They were far from being a family. Heck, they hardly knew each other!

Hadleigh heard the soft, muted sound of voices before she reached the kitchen. Brutal and Trudy must have returned from town, she mused. She would have kept on going, but something in Brutal's tone slowed her steps. She paused in the hall, debating whether she should tiptoe back the way she'd come, or blunder on.

"She knows what she's doing, leading him on this way."

Leading him on? Hadleigh's jaw dropped. Was Brutal talking about *her?*

Trudy's voice was muffled and indistinct, much to Hadleigh's frustration, but Brutal's voice carried loud and clear.

"She's using that little girl as a lure, too."

Another muffled response, which Hadleigh wouldn't have heard anyway over her gasp of outrage.

"How do I know? Because I've worked for the boss for the past ten years, and in all that time, I ain't never seen a woman resist him, especially when he's inter-

191

ested in her—and Treet is definitely interested. So she's got to be pretending, and the little game she's playing seems to be working. He just don't realize that she ain't gonna give him what *he* wants until he gives her what *she* wants."

And what would that be, pray tell? Hadleigh had to physically stop herself from charging forward and finding out for herself.

"Maybe . . . wrong."

It was Trudy, and those were the only two words Hadleigh could make out. Brutal's energetic response filled in the blanks.

"Then why else would she be playing hard to get?"

Why else indeed! Hadleigh scowled at the hall wall. So Brutal believed that she had hidden motives behind her resistance to Treet. Of all the blasted conceit—

"He's got money, looks, and fame. Ain't many women can resist that combination."

Wanna bet?

"I say she's holding out for marriage."

Hadleigh nearly dropped the tray at Brutal's bald statement. But the bodyguard wasn't finished. . . .

"She wouldn't be the first . . . and she sure won't be the last."

Brutal's bitter tone chilled her to the bone. She'd had no idea the man believed her capable of being so devious. Not a clue. He was always polite to her in manner and tone—at least he had been the past week. Okay, so he wasn't overly friendly, but she'd just assumed his aloofness was part of his character.

Hadleigh managed a humorless smile. Brutal would probably never believe it, but if not for their daughters, she most likely would have thrown caution to the wind and jumped in headfirst—into Treet's bed, that was. It wasn't every day she encountered a man who could float her boat the way Treet apparently could.

But then, if not for their daughters, odds were she would never have met him.

"He's acting crazy, too. Did you know he turned down a chance to work with Simon Callister?

The Simon Callister? The *movie director* Simon Callister? Hadleigh let out a silent breath of awe. Simon Callister was the equivalent of Steven Spielberg.

"You know he's got it bad when he loses interest in acting. She'll ruin him before all's said and done."

Lordy, if only she possessed the power Brutal seemed to think she did! Not that she did . . . or would ever think that she did . . . or would ever misuse that power if she did have it. In fact, it was downright flattering to hear someone suggest such a silly, ridiculous possibility. Imagine, *her* having power over someone like Treet.

She wondered if Treet was aware that his bodyguard was prone to dramatics. Big ones. Laughable ones.

Taking a deep breath, Hadleigh rattled the tray as she closed the gap between the hall and the kitchen entrance. She couldn't stand to hear anymore without laughing out loud. The silly man was *so* wrong. Way, way off base. She wasn't out to lure Treet to the altar, and she damned sure wasn't out to wreck his career! In fact, she couldn't think of a single thing she wanted from Treet.

Not a single thing.

Okay, so there were a few things, but thinking about *those* things made her face heat, so she wasn't going to think about them. Besides, those things had nothing to do with money or fame.

Pasting a bright smile on her face, she moved into the light. "Oh, you're back. How was the movie?" She nearly smiled at Brutal's startled, guilty look.

"James Bond," Trudy said, beaming at her.

The woman was always beaming. Hadleigh suspected she didn't possess a mean bone in her body. Maybe some of her goodness would rub off on Brutal, Hadleigh thought hopefully.

"Yeah, it was great." Brutal cleared his throat and looked everywhere but her face. "So, how was *your* movie?"

"I wouldn't know." Hadleigh unloaded her tray on the kitchen counter by the sink and began rinsing out glasses before she put them in the dishwasher, giving Brutal enough time to let his imagination soar. "I slept through it, and so did Sam, Caroline, and Treet."

Trudy giggled. It was a wonderful, lighthearted giggle. Hadleigh giggled right along with her. "You should see them—they're all huddled together on the sofa."

But Brutal didn't crack a smile. Instead, he frowned. "That ain't like the boss to nod off this early. Hope he ain't getting sick."

Hadleigh hoped he wasn't either, because she was fairly certain Brutal would find a way to blame her for that, too. Struggling for an innocent look, she said,

"Maybe he's just tired from all that good, *clean* fun he had today."

If Brutal noticed her emphasis on the word *clean*, he gave no clue. She watched him as he slid his big frame from the stool and stretched. Muscles bulged in his arms and chest. "I think I'll take a turn around the grounds, then lock up for the night."

Curiosity prompted Hadleigh's question. "You really think that's necessary way out here? Nobody knows we're here, do they?"

He met her gaze head-on with a faint look of scorn. "Treet could be on the moon and they'd find him."

"They?"

"The media. His fans."

"Oh."

How could she forget, even for a moment? But she had, and for more than a moment, too. All day long, in fact. And who could blame her? Throughout the day, they'd played with the girls and talked and laughed like a normal fam—like normal people. Treet had scraped his elbow on the side of the pool and laughed it off. He'd eaten pizza with the same dive-in-and-get-it-while-it's-hot gusto as the rest of them had, ignoring the tomato sauce dripping from his chin.

He'd popped popcorn and burned four bags before he got it right, according to Sam. Best of all, he'd fallen asleep holding two little girls in his arms.

Just like a normal, run-of-the-mill kinda guy.

But Treet Miller was anything but normal, and she knew it.

So how had she forgotten?

*   *   *

Eavesdropping wasn't normally Hadleigh's style, but the opportunities just kept popping up.

The second time happened late the next morning. She walked in on Treet having a phone conversation with Todd Hall, or so she gathered from Treet's irritated tone and the content of his answers. He had his back to her, one hand braced upon the fireplace and his sneakered foot propped on the hearth. Just as she was about to let him know of her presence, he spoke into the phone again.

"I can't do that to the girls, Todd. I persuaded Hadleigh to take off work and come out here with us. It wouldn't be right." He paused, his back rigid with tension. Then: "You've got to be kidding! Rehearse here? And who would act as leading lady? Brutal? Trudy? Caroline? I don't *think* so."

Hadleigh cleared her throat. When he didn't appear to hear her, she began backing slowly out of the room.

"I can't ask Hadleigh."

Another long, suspenseful pause. Hadleigh stopped in midstep, holding her breath. Ask Hadleigh what? she wanted to know. And she wanted to know badly. And whatever it was, why couldn't he?

Treet let out an explosive breath. "I just can't. We're not here to work; we're here to spend *quality* time with Caroline and Samantha. I mean it, Todd. I'm passing this one up. You'll just have to live with it."

The phone crashed into the cradle, making Hadleigh jump. She pivoted and headed for the door, silently praying she'd manage to disappear before he spotted her and realized she'd overheard his private conversation with his agent.

"Hadleigh. Wait."

Damn. Hadleigh slowly turned to face him, hoping her face wasn't as red as it felt. She decided to make the best of it by coming clean. "I, um, couldn't help overhearing your conversation." When he simply stared at her, she licked her lips and continued. "You—you don't have to turn down the job on our account. Samantha and I aren't going anywhere."

His brow rose. A smiled tugged at the corners of his sexy mouth. "Are you offering to help?"

"H—help?" she squeaked, wondering what the heck she was getting herself into. "How could *I* help?" She couldn't seem to stop staring at his mouth. It was so extraordinary . . . beautiful. Sensual.

"By standing in for the leading lady. Hadleigh?"

She gave a start, struggling to remember what he'd said. Oh. Oh, God! "The leading lady? You want *me* to stand in for the leading lady?"

"Why not? It's just a rehearsal . . . and it would be just you and me."

And that was supposed to make her feel more relaxed? "I would probably just embarrass myself," she said, her words tumbling out in a rush. "I can't act. In fact, I've never acted . . . well, there was that one time in the high school play, but I only had two lines, and—"

"Hadleigh."

She stopped rambling and looked at him. "What?"

"Is that a yes, or a no?"

How *could* she say no to that sexy, grinning, devil-ishly handsome face? How did *any* woman say no to Treet Miller? "Yes. I'll help you . . . as long as you don't expect too much." She wished she could catch her breath. Losing it was becoming a habit when she found herself alone with him.

Slowly, he sauntered toward her. She held her ground, but every instinct in her urged her to turn tail and run. When Treet turned on the charm, he was downright lethal.

He reached her, brushing a stray strand of hair from her chin, his fingers both amazingly tender and hope-lessly arousing. "I've got a feeling you'll be more than adequate for my needs."

They *were* talking about acting, weren't they? Had-leigh suspected *she* was, but Treet wasn't. At least, not any longer. She made a halfhearted stab at pretending she didn't know that he'd skillfully twisted her words. "Well, I hope I don't disappoint you." *Or myself,* she added silently.

His voice became a hypnotic whisper as he said, "I think you underestimate your . . . abilities, Hadleigh."

She swallowed hard. "So, who's the leading lady?"

"Julia Roberts."

Hadleigh's stomach dropped. "I'll make a fool out of myself." And she would; she just knew it. "Can't you call her, see if she'll fly out and rehearse with you?"

Treet shook his head. "Todd said she was on location in Alaska, and won't be finished for two more weeks." He affected a pleading expression that made Hadleigh

Join the Love Spell Romance Book Club
and **GET 2 FREE* BOOKS NOW—**
An $11.98 value!
Mail the Free* Book Certificate
Today!

Yes! I want to subscribe to the Love Spell Romance Book Club.

Please send me my **2 FREE* BOOKS**. I have enclosed $2.00 for shipping/handling. Every other month I'll receive the four newest Love Spell Romance selections to preview for 10 days. If I decide to keep them, I will pay the Special Members Only discounted price of just $4.49 each, a total of $17.96, plus $2.00 shipping/handling ($23.55 US in Canada). This is a **SAVINGS OF $6.00** off the bookstore price. There is no minimum number of books I must buy and I may cancel the program at any time. In any case, the **2 FREE* BOOKS** are mine to keep.

*In Canada, add $5.00 shipping and handling per order
for the first shipment. For all future shipments to Canada,
the cost of membership is $23.55 US, which
includes shipping and handling.
(All payments must be made in US dollars.)

NAME: _____

ADDRESS: _____

CITY: _____ **STATE:** _____

COUNTRY: _____ **ZIP:** _____

TELEPHONE: _____

E-MAIL: _____

SIGNATURE: _____

If under 18, Parent or Guardian must sign. Terms, prices, and conditions subject to change. Subscription subject
to acceptance. Dorchester Publishing reserves the right to reject any order or cancel any subscription.

want to laugh, it was so obviously contrived. "You're my only hope."

"I can't act, Treet." She couldn't stress the fact enough.

"I'll teach you."

I'll teach you. The simple words evoked a trembling deep in the pit of her belly. She found herself nodding. "Okay, but—" Before she could finish, Treet enveloped her in a rib-crushing hug.

"Thank you. You won't regret it, I promise."

She hoped not, but was very afraid that she would.

Treet was almost ashamed at how easily he had manipulated Hadleigh into his naughty plans.

Almost, but not quite. He *knew* she was attracted to him; he also knew how stubborn she could be in resisting the attraction, and was equally determined to change her mind.

He couldn't wait to get started.

Time seemed to crawl at a snail's pace. Lunch consisted of soup and sandwiches, and conversation centered on a litter of motherless kittens Caroline and Samantha had found in the barn and insisted on bringing into the house. All five kittens were now purring happily in a box in the laundry room. His gaze drifted for the umpteenth time to Hadleigh. She wore a casual tank top and shorts, and her hair shone soft and silky beneath the overheard chandelier. She looked so natural and sexy and glorious that Treet had a hard time keeping his eyes off her.

She caught him watching her and smiled. "So, what's the movie about?"

Taking his time answering, Treet finished chewing and swallowing the delicious rice pudding Trudy had prepared for dessert. He noticed that Caroline was methodically picking out the raisins and piling them beside her bowl.

"It's a comedy," he said, deliberately leaving out the "romantic" part. No need to set off alarm bells at this early stage. She'd know soon enough, like in the first scene. "It's called *In the Scheme of Things*," he added with a shrug. "Todd seems to think it's a blockbuster."

"And what does Treet think?"

"I think he might be right." The pile of raisins beside his daughter's bowl had grown, and after a quick glance at Sam, he soon knew why. She'd been adding to Caroline's pile when she wasn't looking.

Sam caught him watching her and grinned sheepishly. Treet winked and grinned back. He'd never believed in forcing kids to eat foods they didn't like. He didn't know Hadleigh's views on the subject, but didn't intend to find out by ratting on Sam.

"Shouldn't I read the script before we begin?"

Treet focused on Hadleigh. "I think it might be easier on you if you don't. This way you can concentrate on what's happening at the moment, instead of thinking about what comes next." He held his breath until she nodded, then carefully let it out in a sigh of relief. He hadn't finished doctoring the script.

"I bow to your expertise."

"What's that word, Daddy, and what does it mean?"

"It means when someone knows a lot about something."

"Oh. You mean, like you know a lot about acting?" Caroline persisted.

Sam's eyes widened. "You're an actor, like in the movies?"

Under his mock-glowering look, Hadleigh blushed. She shrugged her dainty, reddened shoulders. "What can I say? The only thing she watches is the Animal Planet channel, and I guess I, um, forget to tell her."

"Tell me what, Mommy?" Sam demanded.

"That Treet is a movie star."

"You mean like Steve, the crocodile hunter?"

Hadleigh chuckled. "Bigger than that."

"You mean like Clint Eastwood?"

At Sam's question, Treet cleared his throat and gazed pointedly at Hadleigh, who had the grace to look sheepish.

"I, um, have a few of his movies, and sometimes Sam watches them with me."

"When she lets me stay up late with her," Sam added with an air of importance. "Mostly just on the weekends."

Caroline picked up the unspoken challenge, and the subject of Treet's occupation was dropped. "I don't have a bedtime, do I, Daddy?"

"Of course not." Just as Caroline stuck her tongue out in Sam's direction, he added, "You're always asleep by nine o'clock, so there's no need."

"Daddy!"

Treet laughed at her outraged expression. "Well, it's true! Believe me, I've *tried* to keep you awake. It doesn't do any good."

"Now Sam's gonna call me a baby."

"No, she won't," Hadleigh said with a warning glance in her daughter's direction.

Eyes glinting with mischief, Sam opened her mouth. Hadleigh reached over and shoved a spoonful of rice pudding inside.

Raisins and all.

Chapter Fifteen

"Here, try this. It'll help get you in the mood."

Alarmed, Hadleigh stared at the drink he held out. "What's in it?" It wasn't the question she meant to ask. What she should be asking is what the hell he meant by "get in the mood." She was here to help him rehearse—nothing more, nothing less.

She narrowed her eyes in suspicion.

He held her gaze a beat or two before grinning. "Just kidding." He planted the glass in her hand. "It's tangerine and kiwi juice."

Relieved, she took the drink. "Good, because I don't think it's a good idea for me to—"

"And a tiny splash of tequila," he added, his grin pure sin.

Instead of arguing, she took a tiny sip. If she tasted a smidgen of alcohol, she wasn't going to drink it.

She didn't. In fact, the tropical drink was wonderfully sweet and tangy. "Okay, just this one." Her hand trembled, making the ice cubes tinkle against the glass.

A dark brow shot upward, disappearing into a lazy lock of hair across his forehead. "You're nervous," he said.

"You think?"

"Smart mouth."

"That's me." Hadleigh took a deep breath, wishing she could relax and have fun. This was the opportunity of a lifetime—to actually rehearse with a movie star.

A movie star who made mud pies with his daughter and read bedtime stories like nobody's business.

The reminder helped . . . until she remembered how aroused she became just listening to him read those innocent bedtime stories.

"At least give me a brief summary of what the script is about," she said abruptly, taking another fortifying drink of the fruity beverage.

"All right. Zoey Kraft—that would be you—is in advertising. Her boyfriend of five years is her boss. His name is Frank Dorsey, and he's also in advertising. Owns his own business. He and his competitor, Russell Linuchi—that would be me—have both bid on a new perfume ad for a major company called Unique, to be presented in two weeks. Frank wants to know what Russell is planning, and Zoey volunteers to go undercover as Russell's new secretary to get the scoop."

"Why?"

"Because she's hoping to make Frank jealous. Frank is a businessman, and although he claims to love Zoey, he hasn't been very good at showing it lately. Zoey knows about the rivalry between Russell and Frank and hopes to push Frank into proposing to her by embellishing her dates with Russell to Frank. Before long she doesn't *have* to embellish them."

Hadleigh was enthralled. "You're pretty good at this."

"Thanks. What Zoey doesn't count on is her instant attraction to playboy Russell Linuchi, and his determination about getting what he wants. She has trouble resisting him."

"Hmm." Hadleigh, who had relaxed a bit, immediately tensed again. The situation sounded too familiar. "Tell me more about Russell."

"He's Italian, and a confirmed bachelor. He loves women, and women love him. The reason he goes through so many secretaries is that he gets involved with them."

"And he fires them when he's finished."

Treet shrugged. "He's not a nice guy . . . at first. But then Zoey comes along."

"Challenging him."

"*Intriguing* him," Treet corrected. "Changing him," he added more seriously.

"So Russell falls for Zoey—or *thinks* he does. The plot thickens. Tell me more."

"Frank doesn't react the way Zoey planned, and her attraction for Russell grows. Since she seems determined not to sleep with him, Russell changes his strategy and begins to romance Zoey—something she's missed with Frank."

"Zoey falls in love, and in the end she can't betray Russell," Hadleigh guessed.

"Right. But Russell, who is falling in love with Zoey, finds out she's a spy before she can tell him the truth. He believes everything she's said and done with him is an act. . . ."

"Go on," Hadleigh prompted when he paused.

Treet smiled and shook his head. "What, and spoil the ending for you?"

"You can't leave me hanging!" Hadleigh's dismay wasn't feigned. When he remained stubbornly quiet, Hadleigh tried a different tactic. "Okay, so it's a good plot—although not exactly original—and I can see how it could be comedic."

"But?"

"But what sets this movie apart from any other?"

"The sizzling sexual tension between Russell and Zoey."

"Oh." Hadleigh swallowed hard as she absorbed his shocking words. The sudden, strong urge to run hit her. She actually took a few stumbling steps backward.

Then she stopped, torn between the absurdity of her suspicion, and the tiny—and she meant tiny—possibility that she was right.

He'd set her up.

No, he couldn't have.

He could *not* have invented an entire movie script just to—to—

Ridiculous. Enormously conceited of her. No man went to that kind of trouble just to get close to a woman. Treet could have just about any woman, although he had assured her he wanted no other. She wasn't foolish or immature enough to believe him.

Of course not.

She held her ground and pushed her cowardice aside. "So let's get started." She thought she heard a muffled sigh escape him, but when she shot him a sharp glance, she decided she must have been mistaken. He was frowning thoughtfully at the script in his hands.

"I've made you a copy of the first scene, and highlighted your lines. You don't have to worry about actions—unless the urge hits you. I'll tell you what to do."

"Every man's dream," she murmured sarcastically.

"You got that right," he murmured back, his eyes warm with amusement. "Okay, in the first scene, Zoey applies for the job as secretary. She knows that Russell is a womanizer, and knows that she has to look attractive enough for him to want to hire her. She's basically planning to lead him in circles."

"What's she wearing?" Hadleigh wasn't sure what prompted the question, but judging by Treet's startled look, she'd surprised him as well as herself.

"She's wearing a white blouse and a short black skirt. High heels—black—and black hose. She enters the office with a flirty walk that instantly gets Russell's attention."

Hadleigh's mouth went dry. "Should I try it?"

Treet shrugged. Who was he to argue? "Sure, if you're game." He pulled a chair in front of the fire, then led Hadleigh a few yards away before returning to his chair. "Pretend this is my office, and you're coming through the door."

This is where it gets fun, Hadleigh thought. Her stomach fluttered with nervous excitement as she silently read Zoey's lines, highlighted in pink. One line, one simple little line. Surely she could do it?

Taking a deep breath, Hadleigh pretended to open a door and step through. She sauntered toward Treet, swinging her hips seductively. "Hi. I'm Zoey Kraft, and I'm here to apply for the secretarial position," she said in a throaty voice.

She could tell by the slight widening of Treet's eyes that she'd surprised him again. But he didn't comment. Instead, he took his time looking her over, his slow, sexy appraisal making her heartbeat faster.

Just a rehearsal, girl. Calm down.

When he rose from his chair and circled his imaginary desk to stand before her, Hadleigh caught her breath. Perhaps just as the real Zoey might have done when faced with such pure male appreciation. She hoped that if Treet noticed her reaction, he'd believe that she was merely playing the part.

He made a slow, thorough circle around her, as if she were a love slave on the auction block. She forced herself to remain still when what she really wanted to do was fidget.

Finally he faced her again. Without taking his eyes from hers, Treet reached out and unbuttoned the top three buttons of Hadleigh's shirt, folding back the lapels until her cleavage was exposed. The faint scrape

208

of his knuckles against her skin made her knees go weak.

She was wearing pleated khaki shorts that hit her about midthigh instead of the short skirt Zoey would be wearing, but after Treet finished ogling her, she felt completely naked. *Not Treet, but Russell.*

"*Now* you look like a secretary," he said. Or Russell said. Without looking at the script, she couldn't be sure that was an actual line. She had to assume it was.

Treet glanced pointedly at the script she held. She quickly read the next highlighted line. "Does this mean I get the job?" she asked, injecting a hopeful note into her voice.

Again Treet looked surprised. He quickly masked it, returning to his playful, I'm-so-sexy attitude. "Yeah, babe . . . if you pass the Russell Linuchi test."

Hadleigh was proud to speak the next line without looking again. Not that it was very long. "The test? What—what test would that be, Mr. Linuchi?" Stumbling over her words fit the part perfectly. Only she hadn't been acting.

"I'm going to kiss you. Stand perfectly still. When I'm finished, you shrug and say, 'Not bad.' "

"Russell doesn't actually tell me—her—that he's going to kiss her, does he?"

"No, he doesn't."

"Ready?"

She managed a convincing shrug. "Go ahead." She saw a flash of his white teeth before his mouth met hers. He'd told her to stand still, but it wasn't easy. Her body wanted to lean into him, feel him against her. Her arms wanted to circle his neck and pull him in, deepen the kiss.

In her opinion, Treet was more intoxicating than liquor.

Just when she didn't think she could "act" any longer, he broke the kiss. She licked her lips, scrambling for her line. "Um, not bad." When he remained silent, she consulted the script in her hand, aware that her cheeks were burning. "But you could use a little practice."

"Then we'll practice—over dinner tonight."

"So I've got the job?"

"Maybe. I hate to make decisions on an empty stomach."

Hadleigh couldn't resist. She shook her head. "Russell really is a jerk, isn't he?"

Treet laughed at her chagrined expression. "Yes, babe, he is. That's what makes it so great when he really *does* fall in love. He doesn't know what's hit him until he's in bed with Laura and can't get it up."

"Who's Laura?"

"One of his girlfriends." Treet's lips twitched. "One of three."

"You're kidding."

"No. He's a regular all-around stud."

Stud was an understatement. Oversexed came closer to the truth. "Three girlfriends and they don't have a clue about each other?"

"He never invites them to his condo. Claims he lives with his invalid mother. Imagine his surprise when he finds out Zoey really does live with her invalid mother."

"I don't think I like Russell," Hadleigh blurted out.

"You're not supposed to like him. In fact, you really can't stand him at first—"

"I can't imagine ever liking him."

"Oh, but you will. You will. Russell can be quite romantic when he wants to."

Suddenly, Treet cupped her head and brought her in for another sizzling kiss. He broke away just long enough to whisper, "On second thought, I've got ten minutes to blow."

"Does he really say that?" Hadleigh whispered, more than a little breathless.

"Yes, he does. Then he kisses her again and again. Zoey tries her best to keep an image of Frank in her head, but after a few minutes, she begins to really get into kissing him back."

"Do—do we have to do that? Can't we just skip—"

But Treet was shaking his head, his mouth still temptingly close to hers. "I have to get to know Russell inside and out. Acting out his every move is the only way."

Since Hadleigh knew next to nothing about acting, she couldn't argue. Besides, she really didn't want to— did she? She was helping Treet. Who was she kidding? This was nothing more than a license to be naughty!

"Treet," she whispered as he nibbled at the corners of her mouth. His hand against the nape of her neck sent delicious shivers down her spine. "I don't think I can do—"

"Zoey, Zoey. Relax. We're just getting to know each other better."

Hadleigh, lost in the sensations he was creating, stiffened at the sound of another woman's name on his lips—until she remembered that she was supposed to be another woman. Silently chiding herself, she angled her chin down so that she could see the script. Treet—er, Russell—continued to feather her face with sizzling kisses, steadily working his way to her neck. Her voice was husky as she read her next line. "We'll have plenty of time to get to know each other later, won't we?" Her gaze dropped down to the next line of the script. Her eyes widened with incredulity. "Surely he doesn't—"

Strong, warm hands suddenly cupped her bottom and pulled her flush against his arousal. And he was most definitely aroused, which immediately prompted the squeaky, breathless question, "Do you always get—get—"

"No," Treet said, his voice muffled against her neck. "Like you, I'm having trouble concentrating on the part. It would help if you stuck to your lines and stopped reminding me that you're not really Julia Roberts."

Not in a million years could Hadleigh have kept from laughing at his outrageous remark. "Yeah, right!"

He lifted his head and looked at her. "Are you attracted to the president?"

"I've never met him."

"Well, I've never met Julia Roberts. Just because she's a star doesn't mean I'm automatically attracted to her."

He had a point, a legitimate one, too, but Hadleigh still found it hard to accept the compliment at face value. He was a movie star, Julia Roberts was a movie star—not to mention gorgeous. Despite the mind-blowing proof pressing warmly against her belly, she simply could not believe it. He'd probably been thinking about Julia Roberts, she decided.

"And I wasn't thinking about anyone but you."

Hadleigh's jaw dropped at his uncanny perception.

"So get that out of your head."

He sighed, and the sound melted her heart. It couldn't be easy being who he was. Okay, she would give him that much. With extreme concentration, she forced her breathing back to normal and reminded herself Treet was simply playing a part, just as she was. She was Zoey Kraft, a woman in love with a man who ignored her, in the arms of a man who needed to be soundly slapped.

A man who was clutching her buttocks as if he would never let her go. An aroused man who claimed that *she* was the reason for his state of . . . excitement. A man who even sounded a little disgusted with himself for not keeping his mind on his business.

Okay. She could do this. She really could. If Treet could do it, then she could do it. Taking a deep breath, she glanced at her next line. "So, Mr. Linuchi, I see the rumors about you are true." Lordy, she'd thought the same thing about Treet the first—no, second—time they were alone in a closet.

"Ha-ha. You ain't seen nothing yet, honey. It gets much bigger." He let out a low, sexy growl and nipped at her neck.

213

Hadleigh swallowed a giggle—not Zoey's, her own. "Oh, you *are* a big boy," she practically purred, lifting the script up behind his back so that she could read over his shoulder. Good thing he had a firm grip on her butt—her bones had turned to liquid. She'd bet Julia Roberts had better control!

But then, Julia had yet to find herself in Treet's arms.

The thought made her frown. She quickly pushed it from her mind, glancing at Treet's next move just in time to brace herself.

He brought one hand up to cup her breast, squeezing gently. "Are these real?" he breathed.

"Well," Hadleigh—Zoey—managed to sputter around a gasp, "that's for me to know and you to find out."

"When?" Treet—Russell—demanded, rubbing her nipple with his thumb.

Seriously, Hadleigh thought, nearly buckling against him, did he have to be so literal? Couldn't he just pretend? Injecting an admirable note of coyness into her voice, Hadleigh said, "If I told you, it would spoil the surprise, now, wouldn't it? Let's just say that I'm worth the wait."

She was totally fooled by his sudden crestfallen expression. He looked exactly like a naughty, thwarted boy. Damn, he was good. But then, she knew that, didn't she?

"I have to wait? How long?"

Improvising, Hadleigh used her free hand to tiptoe her fingers along his arm. She glanced at him, then quickly lowered her eyes. "Oh, I don't know. I'm the kind of girl that really likes to get to know a guy before I get down and dirty." Her finger landed on his lips. She lowered her voice to a sultry whisper. "And believe me, I can get down and dirty."

It was a long, measuring moment before Treet spoke. If she didn't know better, she might think he'd forgotten his lines.

"Can I at least get a sample?"

After consulting the script, Hadleigh shook her head and sighed. She uncurled his hand from her breast, and stepped out of his hold. "I'm sorry, Mr. Linuchi. If we're going to have dinner later, then I definitely want to keep my appointment with my hairstylist. Where shall I meet you?"

He made a grab for her, but she danced out of reach. She nearly choked on laughter at his leering expression. It was so *not* like the man she knew. She could almost believe he *was* Russell Linuchi.

"I think this is where your phone rings," she told him. Her breast still tingled from his touch. Thank God the scene had come to an end.

Like someone coming out of a daze, Treet blinked and shook his head. He smiled, his warm gaze lingering on her exposed cleavage. "Now that wasn't so bad, was it?"

Hadleigh self-consciously folded her arms over her chest. "No. I just hope the director knows what he's doing. It won't be easy redeeming Russell."

"If it was easy, then it wouldn't be a good script." Treet stretched his arms above his head, drawing her attention to the rippling muscles in his chest.

She swallowed hard. "There's just something not quite right with this scene, though. Somehow, I don't think Zoey would let a complete stranger maul her like that."

"Don't forget, Zoey wasn't as repulsed by his touch as she thought she would be. Besides, she has to get the job."

"Don't tell me she sleeps with him?"

He lifted an amused brow at her shocked question. "No, she doesn't sleep with him. At least not right away. But to keep his interest, she has to do a lot of teasing and promising." His voice suddenly dropped, sending shivers down her spine. "You were great, by the way. Ever thought about acting?"

"Thanks, and no, I haven't. And I'm not interested. I'll leave that to experts like yourself."

"Was that a compliment?" As he spoke, he began to close the distance between them.

Hadleigh resisted the urge to inch back. He looked so purposeful . . . intent. "Yeah, I guess it was. But then you don't need me to tell you how great you are." She caught her breath as he stopped in front of her.

And held it as he began to fasten the buttons of her shirt. Whether deliberate or by accident, he managed to touch a lot of her skin in the process.

"Maybe I do need you to tell me," he said seriously. "Your opinion matters a lot to me."

There was a sudden tension between them. Her lips parted. "I can't imagine why."

"Can't you?" He pulled her slowly toward him. "Are you ever going to face what's happening to us?"

"Lust is nothing new to either of us." It was new to her, but he didn't have to know that. "Besides, Treet, you know how I feel about getting . . . involved. The girls—"

"What if we fall in love?"

What if *she* fell in love and he didn't? Now that was the all-important question Hadleigh didn't want to find out. She decided to be as honest as she could. "What if you *did* think you were in love? How could you be sure it wasn't because of Sam?"

He frowned, apparently confused. "What does our falling in love have to do with Sam?"

Hadleigh hesitated, then plunged recklessly ahead. "Falling in love with me would mean you could have Caroline *and* Sam."

He looked totally shocked by her words. But then, she had seen for herself just how convincing Treet could be. Only moments ago he was a leering creep of a playboy whose only thought was how quickly he could get his potential new secretary out of her clothes. He'd been so good at it she had *wanted* to get naked with him.

Not that he had to be good to get her to that point. Hell, a look, a touch, a tiny kiss and she was putty in his hands.

Finally, he recovered enough to throw her words back at her. "You would have the same advantage, or haven't you thought of that?"

"That's just it. How can either of us trust ourselves at this point in time? I don't want to leave Caroline now that I've met her, and you don't want to part with

Sam. Am I right?" She didn't bother waiting for him to nod; it was obvious he adored Sam. "It would be too convenient for us to fall in love. It would be just as sad to find out later that we were only fooling ourselves."

The frown was back. "This is all conjecture. You're saying we should fight this amazingly strong attraction, and our own instincts, just in case we're conjuring them up because of subconscious motives we aren't even aware of?" He shook his head, a wry smile on his sexy mouth. "You're something else, you know that?"

"But I could be right." And that was the scary part. She was a coward, and didn't want to find out that she *was* right.

Treet's expression turned bleak. "So because of these remote possibilities, you're willing to ignore everything between us? You *are* a scaredy-cat."

Her chin rose. "Maybe I am, but that's not all of my concerns. We can't ignore the fact that you're who you are."

"So we're on that subject again. Who I am doesn't matter to me, and it shouldn't matter to you. What does matter is that when I'm with you, I'm happier than I've been in a long time. When I kiss you, I'm mindless. When I touch you, I burn. When I'm standing next to you, all I can think about is how wonderful and sexy you smell, and how your eyes glitter like jewels—and that's *my* line, thank you. When I'm not with you, I'm thinking about you and anticipating the next time I see you."

Stunned by his passionate outburst, Hadleigh could only stare wordlessly at his chiseled, beautiful features.

His words frightened her, petrified her. Shaking her head, she backed away. "I can't talk about this anymore. You don't realize what you're saying. I'm going to bed. Good night, Treet."

He caught up with her before she reached the doorway, grabbing her arm to halt her flight. "Wait."

It was a plea she couldn't ignore. So she waited, keeping her gaze from his face. She had no willpower when she looked at him.

"I'm sorry for pushing you. I didn't mean—what I mean to say is, I hope I didn't scare you away. Will you still help me rehearse if I promise to be good?" He let go of her arm, but she didn't run.

"I don't know if it's a good idea." For lots and lots of reasons.

"Then I'll call Todd tomorrow and let him know that I've decided not to take the part."

It was a threat, plain and simple. She closed her eyes and muttered a curse beneath her breath. Instinct warned her that she was making a mistake, but she heard herself saying the words anyway. "Okay. I'll help you."

Chapter Sixteen

Hadleigh awoke to a sudden pressure on her chest and the sound of a girlish giggle. *Sam,* she thought, keeping her eyes closed and pretending to be asleep. It was a game she and Sam played often.

"Mommy?" Sam whispered. "Are you awake?"

"No," Hadleigh whispered back, barely moving her lips. Because of the pressure on her chest, she could easily picture Sam leaning over her, staring into her face.

"I found Bo Bo."

It took a moment for Hadleigh to recall who Bo Bo was. When she did, she smiled. "Oh, the turtle." She'd forgotten about the turtle, which wasn't surprising. Treet could make a girl forget her own name. A turtle didn't stand a chance—especially a turtle that had a penchant for hiding. "Where did you find him?"

"Under your bed."

"So where is he now?"

"On your chest, silly!"

Hadleigh's eyes popped open. She stared straight into the reptilian eyes of the monstrous turtle a full thirty seconds before she managed to squeak, "Sam, get this—this *thing* off me!"

With an impish giggle, Sam removed the turtle and set him on the floor. "Go on now, Bo Bo. Mommy doesn't like you."

Flustered—and who wouldn't be?—Hadleigh sat up, peering over the edge of the bed to watch as the turtle began his ponderous journey to the door. She wasn't imagining things, and Treet hadn't lied; the turtle *was* the size of a small pizza.

She put a hand over her thundering heart and shot Sam a stern look. "Sam, promise me that you will never do that to me again."

Sam pouted, but agreed. "Okay, I promise." She perked up immediately. "I came to tell you that Treet wants me and Caroline to go to town with him, and he wants to know if you wanna come too."

Without hesitation, Hadleigh shook her head. After last night she wasn't even certain she could face Treet, let alone spend the day with him.

"Well, Caroline doesn't want to go, neither."

"You mean 'either.' Why not?" Hadleigh flung the covers aside and blew a strand of hair out of her eyes, her heartbeat finally returning to normal. Bo Bo had made it to the door, and was now lumbering across the threshold.

"She doesn't like the way people stare at her daddy. She says it scares her." Sam sucked her bottom lip between her teeth. "She said if you don't go, she's gonna stay with you. Will it hurt your feelings, Mommy, if I go with Treet?"

"What's the occasion?"

It took Sam a moment to figure out the meaning of the question. Finally, she said, "If that means what I think it means, then we're gonna go get cat food and cat litter, and a nice bed for the kittens. Oh, and Trudy says she needs nilla favors."

Hadleigh smiled. "You mean, vanilla flavoring?"

Sam nodded vigorously. "She's gonna make cookies."

Thinking this was the perfect opportunity to go fishing, Hadleigh asked, "Sam . . . you do like Treet, don't you? You're not just pretending so that Caroline can spend time with me while you spend time with Treet?"

With perfect seriousness, Sam said, "He's okay. Can I go?"

Hadleigh couldn't find a logical reason to say no, and Sam appeared to be genuinely excited about the trip. "Okay, but you'd better be good. Mind your manners, too."

As usual when getting her way, Sam beamed happily. "I will, and I promised Caroline I wouldn't let anyone hurt her daddy."

"My fierce warrior," Hadleigh teased, laughing when Sam glared at her. She threw a pillow at her and Sam threw it back, missing the bed by a couple of yards. "I'm sure Brutal will be there to guard Treet, so you can relax and have fun."

Sam snorted. "That big ole baby? He doesn't scare anybody!"

Long after her daughter had disappeared, Hadleigh continued to chuckle over Sam's declaration as she made the bed and brushed her teeth. Brutal's ego would be crushed to hear Sam's scornful description of him.

She chose a pair of faded, comfortable jeans and a plain T-shirt, wondering if Caroline and Sam were simply "trading" parents again, or if Caroline truly was afraid to go out in public with her daddy. What a sad thought! Did Treet know about Caroline's fears? Had something terrible happened to make her fearful?

Well, she'd just have to find out for herself, Hadleigh decided, slipping on a pair of sandals and running a brush through her hair. Hoping she'd given Treet enough time to leave, she went in search of Caroline.

She found her with the kittens, attempting to coax them to drink milk from a saucer. "Aren't you hungry?" Caroline crooned, gently pushing a whiskered face into the milk.

Hadleigh, standing behind her, grinned as the distraught kitten let out a loud meow and struggled to save himself from drowning. "Caroline."

Caroline glanced around, flashing Hadleigh a sunny smile that went straight to her heart. "Oh, hi, Haddy. I'm glad you didn't go with them to town." Her big brown eyes suddenly clouded. "I don't like the way peo-

ple stare at Daddy, and sometimes they chase him."
With the innocence of a four-year-old, she added, "I
don't think they like my daddy."

"Oh, sweetheart!" Hadleigh sank to her knees and
gently freed the kitten, putting it back in the box with
its siblings. She pulled Caroline closer. "Surely your
daddy has talked to you about this? People *love* your
daddy because he's famous. That's why they act strange
when they see him."

Her new daughter didn't look convinced. "They
scream and shout at him, and wave their fists around
in the air like this." Caroline lifted her arm and pumped
her fist up and down, screwing her face into a comical
imitation of what she had apparently witnessed. The
expression looked like anger on Caroline; Hadleigh suspected that on a fan, it would resemble incredible excitement, perhaps even a crazed excitement.

An understandable mistake for a young child to
make.

"You should have told your daddy how you felt,"
Hadleigh chided gently. "Then he would have explained why people react the way they do when they
see him."

"*You* didn't act that way," Caroline pointed out.

Swallowing a chuckle, Hadleigh shook her head.
"No, I didn't, but that's because I know your daddy,
and I know he's just a regular guy." A regular guy with
heart-stopping buns, incredible blue eyes, and a mouth
that was out of this world. She could have gone on and
on, but this wasn't the time or place to recall Treet's
considerable assets.

"So they like him?"

Hadleigh nodded.

"And they don't want to hurt him?" This time Caroline sounded a little more hopeful.

"No, they don't want to hurt him, although sometimes people get carried away and . . ." She bit down hard on her wayward tongue. No sense confusing Caroline at this early age with shades of gray.

The child stared solemnly into Hadleigh's eyes as she whispered, "Then I wished I had went with them. I think I hurt Daddy's feelings when I told him I didn't want to go."

Caroline looked so grown-up in her regret that Hadleigh decided she had to do something. She straightened and smiled down at her. "Why don't we see if Mr. Spencer will give us a lift into town? I don't think it's too late to join them, do you?" Maybe now that she had explained, Caroline would see her daddy's devoted followers in a new light.

Burlington, Montana, wasn't a big town, but since it boasted the only Super Dollar Mart within a fifty-mile radius, Saturday was generally the town's busiest shopping day of the week. Local restaurants were crowded with hungry shoppers; the streets were packed with an odd assortment of farm trucks, Park Avenues, and economy-sized cars.

And inside Super Dollar Mart, the manager, Enis Redmond, had a situation on his hands.

Five minutes, Treet thought with understandable irritation as he watched the terrified manager bolt his office door against the unruly crowd of women and children. Five lousy minutes inside the store and he'd been recognized by a blue-haired lady who looked at least a hundred and five.

She hadn't possessed the lungs of an elderly woman, Treet recalled, trying to find a smidgen of humor in their familiar situation.

Mr. Redmond stood with his back pressed against his office door—which shook from the force of the women fighting to get inside—his thinning hair sticking up, his glasses fogged from his agitated breathing.

He glanced wildly from Sam's wide-eyed, fiercely frowning face, to Treet's and Brutal's resigned expressions. Gathering himself, he tested the lock again and carefully moved away from the door.

"I'm honored by your visit, Mr. Miller," he began in a high-pitched voice. "But did you have to pick *this* Saturday?"

Treet merely lifted a brow, waiting for the shaken man to explain. He gave Sam's hand a reassuring squeeze. She squeezed it back as if to give *him* comfort.

Reminding himself that this was the price of fame didn't quell his irritation much.

"It's . . . we're having a half-price sale on lingerie."

"We just wanted to buy a litter box, mister," Sam said staunchly, moving closer to Treet. "And some cat food for our kitties."

Brutal crossed his arms, his face impassive. "I'll need help getting them out of here." He picked up the phone from the desk. "You'll need to call the local police. Tell them you've got a riot on your hands."

"A—a riot?" Mr. Redmond squeaked. He tugged at his tie, then pulled out a handkerchief and mopped his face. "But we're having a sale . . ." His voice faded, then gathered strength again. "You'll have to excuse me, I've never been in this situation before."

Taking in the manager's unhealthy pallor, Treet experienced a surge of familiar guilt. He hated causing a scene, but it invariably happened wherever he went. "I'm sorry, Mr. Redmond. I thought—well, I was hoping to get in and out before I was recognized."

Mr. Redmond nodded. "I'm sure you meant no harm. I'd better call the police," he muttered, taking the phone from Brutal. "That crowd is probably using this opportunity to steal me blind."

Treet felt Sam tugging on his hand. He looked down at her, into big blue eyes shining with fierce determination. His heart did a triple somersault; his hand tightened around hers.

"Don't worry, Treet," she whispered loudly. "I'm not gonna let them hurt ya. I promised Caroline I wouldn't."

Before Treet could respond to her strange declaration, the manager hung up the phone and turned to them. "The sheriff said he'd be right over."

"How many men is he bringing?" Brutal asked.

"Let me see . . . I think he's got four men, maybe five. Bruce broke his leg a while ago, and I don't know if he's back to work—"

"That won't be enough." Brutal jerked his head in the direction of the shaking door. Shouts and screams—interspersed with colorful curses—could be heard through the thick wood. "How many do you think are out there?"

The manager ran a distracted, nervous hand through what little hair he possessed. "Oh, I'd say thirty, maybe forty. The whole town probably knows by now."

Brutal groaned and shook his head.

"There sure is a lot of people at this store," Caroline said the moment she and Hadleigh entered through the big glass doors at the front.

"Yes, there certainly—" Hadleigh stopped dead, mouth agape at the thick crowd of women and children huddled at the back of the store. They were shouting and jumping up and down, jostling each other as if they were a pack of dogs fighting over a bone.

It didn't take her long to understand what they were shouting, and it took even less time to figure out what must have gotten them in this agitated state.

"Damn," Hadleigh muttered beneath her breath. But Caroline apparently heard her.

"My daddy says that sometimes when he's mad. Are you mad, Haddy?" She craned her neck, trying to see over the cash registers. "Do you see Daddy and Sam anywhere? What are they doing over there? Is someone hurt?" Her breath caught. "Is it my daddy, Haddy? Is he hurt?"

"No, sweetheart. I'm sure your daddy is fine." Hadleigh didn't feel that sure, and her anxiety escalated when she remembered that Sam was with Treet, which meant—

She tugged on Caroline's hand, leading her to the edge of the crowd. Next to them, a toddler bounced and bobbed on his mother's hip. Hadleigh tapped the mother on the shoulder. "What's going on?" she shouted.

The woman barely glanced at Hadleigh before jealously closing the slight gap between herself and her neighbor. "Treet Miller's in there!" she yelled over her shoulder.

"Where?" Hadleigh's second question earned a hostile, irritated glare from the excited mother.

"In the manager's office!" Her smile was fanatical. "But he's gotta come out sometime!"

Getting a stronger grip on Caroline's hand, Hadleigh tried to make a path. "Let us through!"

"No way, sister!"

"Are you nuts?"

"I was here first!" another woman hissed at Hadleigh, shoving her back.

Stunned, Hadleigh caught her balance before she plowed into Caroline, whom she had thrust protectively behind her. "Now wait a damned minute—" she began, her temper fraying.

But it was Caroline's scream that finally got everyone's attention. The women might have been starcrazed, but they were first and foremost mothers, daughters, grandmothers, and nurturers at heart.

The sound of Caroline's scream broke through their temporary insanity. One by one, they grew quiet. Heads turned in Caroline's direction, angling this way and that, trying to see whose child had screamed with such ferocity, and why.

Caroline glared at them, red-faced and panting. Tears streamed down her cheeks, and her bottom lip quivered. "I want to see my daddy!" she shouted. "So you'd better get out of our way, or I'll—I'll—" She stopped, clearly lost at this point. But she'd gotten their attention, however briefly.

It was a startled moment before someone in the crowd asked, "Who's your daddy, sweetheart? Are you lost?"

"She doesn't look familiar," another one said. "I don't know who she belongs too."

"She's a doll, whoever she is."

Caroline took a deep, shaky breath, and Hadleigh took one with her. She suspected what Caroline was about to say, and she wasn't at all sure it was a good idea.

Pointing her finger in the general direction of the office door, Caroline said clearly and distinctly, "My daddy's in there, and I want to see him."

The woman with the toddler attached to her hip threw back her head and laughed. Hadleigh decided that violence must be contagious, because she sure felt like belting her one.

"Honey, unless your daddy's Treet Miller, he's not in there."

"My daddy *is* Treet Miller," Caroline shouted, stamping her foot.

Hadleigh knew the signs of a tantrum only too well, and Caroline appeared to be on the verge of one. It was time to clear a path, she decided, and if she had to knock a few senseless heads together . . . well, so be it.

"All right, ladies. You heard her. She wants her daddy, so I suggest you let us by." They made it past the first row of women before someone grabbed Hadleigh's sleeve.

"And just who are *you?*" a snarling voice demanded.

"None of your business," Hadleigh snarled right back, jerking free.

After that, the crowd grudgingly let them through. They reached the door without a scratch. Hadleigh turned to glare at the grumbling crowd, clutching Caroline protectively to her.

For a long moment, she scanned the flushed, excited faces of the women. She could feel Caroline trembling, no doubt traumatized anew.

Damn it!

She didn't know where she found the courage, or the words, but they seemed to flow without hesitation, spoken in a strong, angry tone that carried across the mumbling crowd. "You are all mostly grown women, I see, but you're acting like children. It's because of scenes like this that Caroline is afraid to go anywhere with her father. She believes you want to hurt him."

A surprised murmur swept over the crowd.

Hadleigh nodded. "Yes, she does, and who could blame her? You're screaming and shouting and pushing one another—recklessly endangering your own children! What if one of them gets trampled? And for what? A glimpse of a movie star, if you're lucky?"

One brave soul spoke up. "We just want an autograph!"

Another cried, "Yeah, easy for *you* to say! You obviously get to see more of him than *we* do!"

"It's your own fault!" Hadleigh shouted above the sudden babbling that followed the women's outburst. They grew quiet again. "Can you deny that his very life would be in danger if he came out right now? That you all wouldn't start fighting and pushing again?"

Over the heads of the crowd, Hadleigh spotted the police coming into the store. Another woman saw them and gave the alarm.

"Hey, it's the cops!"

"So? Willie's my husband. He's not gonna arrest me! If he does, he won't get his dinner!"

"Yeah, and Chris is my mom's boyfriend. . . ."

Hadleigh, overjoyed at the sight of the uniformed policemen, didn't hear the door open behind her, or see the rough hands that grabbed her and yanked her backward.

She shrieked, hanging on to Caroline for dear life.

It was some three hours later before they were able to get their pet supplies and head for home. Brutal drove, taking turns letting the girls steer the van along the nearly deserted blacktop.

Treet sat with Hadleigh in the backseat, tired but curiously content to listen to his girls—*his girls*—fuss over who was next, and who was the best driver. He felt Hadleigh's gaze on him and turned to find her watching him intently.

He lifted a brow in question. "What? Do I have mustard on my nose or something?"

She shook her head. "No. I was just thinking about what a nice guy you are, for doing that. Does your hand hurt?"

"A little." He stretched his fingers to work out the stiffness, casting her a wry grin. "I have to admit, this is the first time I've autographed clothing."

"Panties," Hadleigh corrected, straight-faced. "And bras."

"I think I saw a slip or two."

Brutal dared to take his eyes off the road as Caroline guided the slow-moving vehicle. "Don't forget Grandma's girdle."

"Was *that* what that thing was?" Treet chuckled at the memory of the feisty, blue-haired lady. "She was ninety if she was a day."

Hadleigh laughed with him. "Well, you have to admit you certainly made the manager's day. I'll bet he doesn't have a pair of panties left in the store."

"Or a bra," Sam added, peeping over the headrest. Her eyes danced with mischief. "Are you going to make him sign *your* underwear, Mommy? One of the peoples there said she was going to keep it, and after Treet died, she was gonna sell it and make lots and lots of money!"

At the sight of Hadleigh's shocked face, Treet threw back his head and roared with laughter.

Chapter Seventeen

Treet Miller and candlelight were a dangerous combination, Hadleigh discovered as she shook out her cloth napkin and spread it on her lap. She glanced across the elegantly set table at Treet and watched him do the same.

In the kitchen a short distance away from where she and Treet sat in the formal dining room, Hadleigh could hear Sam and Caroline giggling, interspersed with Trudy's carefully worded instructions.

She caught Treet's amused glance and smiled. "They'll probably giggle the whole time they're serving us," she said.

"Probably," he agreed, chuckling. "But they're having fun, and that's what counts."

Hadleigh took a sip of her water. "Including the girls in this rehearsal was a great suggestion." Treet shrugged, as if embarrassed by her compliment, which in turn intrigued Hadleigh. The man was constantly surprising her.

Trudy banged twice on a pot, signaling that the girls were ready. Hadleigh exchanged another amused glance with Treet as Caroline entered the dining room.

Halting before the table, Caroline brought out a pad and pencil and looked from one to the other, her expression so solemn, Hadleigh had to bite her lip to keep from smiling.

"Good evening. What would you like to drink?"

"I'd like a glass of white wine, please," Hadleigh said politely.

Treet drummed his fingers on the table, his gaze unwavering on Hadleigh's face. She suspected he was struggling with laughter.

"And I'd like a scotch. Neat. No ice," he said.

Caroline frowned, hovering over the pad as she pretended to scribble their order. After a moment, she looked up at them. There wasn't a trace of recognition on her face. "Okay. Got it. Your waitress will be out to take your order in a minute."

"Thanks."

"Yeah, thanks."

When Caroline disappeared through the door, Hadleigh leaned forward to whisper, "Was that uncanny, or what?"

"Yes, it was. She's pretty good."

Sam appeared, nearly invisible in one of Trudy's oversize aprons. She snapped to attention like a soldier, obviously not to be outdone by Caroline. "May I recommend the roast duck tonight?" she asked importantly, pen poised over her notepad.

Straight-faced, Treet said, "No, I'd like a hamburger."

Hadleigh kicked Treet beneath the table. Sam glared at him.

"All right," Treet relented. "Roast duck is fine with me. How about you, Zoey?"

"Sounds good."

"We'll start with an appetizer of oysters on the half shell," Treet added, casting Hadleigh a meaningful look, followed by a leering wink.

Thank goodness Sam didn't have a clue, Hadleigh thought, fighting a blush. When her daughter disappeared through the doorway, Treet kicked into high gear: he became Russell Linuchi with a vengeance.

She'd thought she was prepared, but soon discovered she wasn't.

He scooted his chair around close to hers and placed a warm, arousing hand on her thigh beneath the table. Bold as brass and really, really high up on her leg. Too close for comfort.

She jumped, wishing she hadn't worn a dress.

"You know what they say about oysters, don't you?" Russell rumbled intimately in her ear.

Zoey pretended ignorance. "No, I don't, but I've got a strong hunch you're going to tell me." As the script in front of her instructed, she shifted her leg to the right—away from his hand.

His hand stayed clamped to her thigh. In fact, if she wasn't dreaming, it inched even higher. Another fractional move and he'd be toying with the elastic of her panties. What she wouldn't give for a hot platter of linguini noodles right now.

Russell's other hand began a slow, erotic dance along her spine. Zoey arched her back, then forced herself to relax against the disturbing motion. Up. Down. Lower each time. Higher again until his fingers burrowed into her hair, then back down again. Despite Russell's outrageous attitude, he had magic fingers.

"You know, Zoey, I think we're going to work well together," he breathed into her ear.

She felt him grasp her earlobe with his teeth and tug. She shivered, and a tiny moan escaped. The sound jarred her back to reality. Or to the reality she was in at the moment. "I think so . . . too," she said breathlessly, turning her face to his. There was a kiss coming up, she knew, although she'd argued with Treet that it was rather crude of Russell to kiss Zoey in a crowded restaurant. "It's what Russell would do," he'd stated with a shrug, as if to remind her that *he* hadn't written the script.

"I've got a fantastic deal coming up, so we'll be spending a *lot* of time together."

"Really?" Zoey allowed his lips to feather hers, then teased him by turning her face away so that his next kiss landed on the corner of her mouth.

Not that it wasn't great anyway.

"Yes, really." Russell let out a low chuckle that turned her bones to liquid. He caught her chin and turned her to face him again. His tongue darted out, sliding across her lower lip, a look of intense pleasure on his handsome face.

Really, Hadleigh thought, bracing herself against a rush of pure lust, Russell was making a spectacle of himself. He was being crude and nasty in public.

And she loved it.

She ran her tongue where his had been only seconds before, forcing herself to look at him at close range. He ceased being Russell the moment she gazed into his languid, sexy-as-hell eyes. In fact, she forgot her next line altogether. And what *was* her name again?

"So what's this . . ." Treet prompted in a husky whisper, nuzzling her nose with his.

Hadleigh swallowed, forcing herself to concentrate on how Zoey would act. "So what's this fantastic deal we'll be working on?"

On cue, Caroline and Sam entered, each carrying an empty plate. They set them down and left the room again.

Sam giggled just as she reached the door. Caroline shushed her and yanked her on through and out of sight.

Russell sighed and moved his chair back in place. He picked up a fork and pretended to eat. "I'll tell you all about it when we get to my place," he flung at her casually.

Zoey pretended to choke on her food. She gasped out, *"Your* place?"

"Well, actually, it belongs to a friend of mine." His expression turned grave. "You see, my invalid mother lives with me."

Hadleigh had been looking forward to her next line from the moment she'd reviewed the scene earlier. She widened her eyes until they burned, looking convincingly stunned. "Amazing!" she breathed. "My invalid mother lives with me, too!"

She was having a ball, Treet mused, recalling the sparkle in her eyes, and the flush on her cheeks—a flush he was fairly certain he'd caused with his wandering hands and wicked tongue. He fell onto his bed and propped his arms under his head, staring at the ceiling. The fact that Hadleigh was enjoying herself helped ease some of the guilt he felt at having tricked her.

But not all of it.

Man, would she be furious if she knew! Treet smiled grimly, thinking of the remarks she'd made about the script. Little did she know the very things she claimed felt wrong were the things he'd changed to help further his own devious motives.

He wanted to get close to Hadleigh, to kiss her and stroke her, to hold her so tightly not a flicker of light could squeeze between them.

He wanted, quite frankly, to be inside her, loving her, making her moan and scream his name. He wanted to make her forget who he was, who she was, and for a brief time, the reason they'd met.

But he'd settle for a little stroking and a lot of kissing. For now. Sooner or later he would wear her down.

Sooner or later she'd realize this thing between them was bigger than both of them.

They had chemistry. A lot of chemistry.

They had common interests.

They had Caroline and Sam, but she was wrong about everything else. Yes, he wanted Sam with him permanently, but he would never make the mistake of thinking he was falling in love with a woman just to get his wish.

No, he knew that he was falling in love with Hadleigh.

He believed that she cared for him too; he wanted to find out how much.

So he'd tricked her. Shamelessly doctored the script so that Russell had more opportunity to put his hands and lips on Zoey. Plenty of opportunities to weaken her defenses, to show her that the explosive chemistry between them shouldn't be denied.

And unless she had more talent than he realized, Treet believed his plan was working. He'd recognized the want, the sweet flame of desire in her gorgeous green eyes. Oh, she fought it. Damn, did she fight it! But sooner or later she'd weaken. . . .

She *had* to.

Thank God they'd finally fallen asleep, Hadleigh thought, sighing as she closed the book and laid it on the nightstand. She tucked the covers around the sleeping girls and tiptoed to the door. Outside their window, occasional flashes of lightning brightened the night, heralding an approaching storm.

Once or twice Hadleigh thought she'd heard the low, distant rumble of thunder.

She'd placed her hand on the light switch when Caroline spoke in a loud whisper from her position on the bottom bunk with Sam.

"Is it going to storm, Haddy?"

"I don't know. Maybe." Hadleigh hoped not; Sam was terrified of storms.

"Haddy?"

"Yes, Caroline?"

"I wish you were *my* mommy, too."

Her voice was drowsy with sleep and filled with a heartbreaking wistfulness that seared Hadleigh to her very soul.

Hadleigh wanted to shout, "I am, I am!" Instead, she whispered, "Me too, sweetie. Me too." On impulse, she walked back to the bed and sat on the edge, gathering Caroline in her arms. She squeezed her tight, fighting a sudden rush of tears. "I love you," she said.

Caroline squeezed her back with all her might. "I love you too, Haddy. Sam said it was okay."

Smiling through her tears, Hadleigh released her and turned away before Caroline could see her crying. Treet was waiting, but she needed a moment or two to recover before she joined him in the bedroom for the next scene.

She slipped out the front door and walked to the porch railing, watching the brilliant flashes of lightning to the east. In the distance, she heard a horse nicker softly, nervously. The wind kicked up, bringing with it the smell of dust and rain. She lifted her face and closed her eyes, asking herself again what the hell she thought she was doing.

Playing with fire.

Dancing with the devil.

Fooling herself into believing she was doing the right thing, being here with Sam and helping Treet, when in fact she was basking in the contact, glorying in the closeness they shared with the girls, and the more intimate closeness they shared as Zoey and Russell.

There wasn't a moment that went by when she didn't feel his presence, sense him, or think about him.

Treet Miller. Hunky movie star and Daddy of the Year. A man full of passion and humor. A man who was gentle, yet fierce.

Hadleigh dropped her chin and finally admitted what she had been trying desperately to deny. She loved Treet Miller. She loved him, and she feared she was going to pay dearly for her weakness when it was all said and done. Her fingers tightened on the railing. She just hoped Sam and Caroline didn't have to pay along with her.

Just conjuring the girls' names made her chest hurt. Since meeting Treet and Caroline, Sam seemed happier, more settled, and less prone to tantrums. And she actually seemed to like Treet, something Hadleigh still found surprising.

Then there was Caroline. Sweet, tolerant Caroline, yearning for a mother and revealing a mischievous side Hadleigh was fairly certain hadn't been apparent in the Years Before Sam.

It was obvious they complemented each other, Hadleigh decided, smiling slightly. Her smile faded quickly as she thought about the scene she was about to rehearse with Treet.

Could she do it?

Could she romp around on the bed with Treet without embarrassing herself? Without winding her arms around his neck and begging him to make love to her? She dreamed about it at night, and thought about it often during the day. It was a dangerous hobby, she knew. Making love with Treet would change her life.

She didn't doubt it for a moment.

Not because of his sexual prowess—although she wouldn't be surprised to find him above average—but because he possessed the ability to arouse, enhance, and stimulate each and every emotion known to her, and a few she *didn't* know about.

From tenderness to laughter.

From love to aching desire.

And the thousand and one emotions in between.

She jumped as arms circled her waist from behind and squeezed. A hard, warm body pressed against her from shoulder to calf. Treet nuzzled her ear, his voice low and sexy, his lips hot and erotic, instinctively seeking out the most sensitive spots.

"Hiding out?" he taunted.

"No," she lied.

"The girls asleep?"

"Yes." He sounded as if he'd been asleep, too.

"So what's on your mind?" His hands inched upward, resting boldly beneath the curve of her breasts.

"Caroline told me that she loved me."

He grew still. "I think I hate you."

He meant to be funny, but Hadleigh sensed his hurt. "Sam likes you," she assured him.

"Maybe. But she doesn't *love* me," he grumbled. "On the other hand, I think Caroline's ready to trade me in for you."

Hadleigh hesitated, knowing that she was about to tread on shaky ground. "Caroline misses her mother."

"She couldn't miss her mother," Treet retorted harshly. "She's never met her."

"She misses *having* a mother," Hadleigh amended. She tilted her face around to peer at him in the darkness. In the dim light, his features had taken on a tense, wary look—a far cry from his customary naughty-boy smile. Feeling reckless, Hadleigh deliberately pushed his button. "Are you ever going to tell me what happened with Cheyenne?"

"I'd rather neck." He raked his teeth lightly against her neck to emphasize his preference.

Hadleigh recognized a distraction when she felt one. "Treet? Please? Humor me? I've heard her side of the story. I'd like to hear yours."

"And who will you believe?"

Without hesitation, Hadleigh said, "You. You've given me no reason to believe you would lie. On the other hand, Cheyenne has given me proof that she would go to any lengths to satisfy her need for revenge." It was all true.

Sighing, he began to walk backward, holding her to him. He sank into a deck chair and pulled her onto his lap.

Treet was definitely a hands-on man, Hadleigh thought, allowing him to cuddle her against his chest. Besides, it felt nice being this close to him. She could feel his heartbeating against her side. His breath fanned her neck, making her shiver.

With longing.

With need.

With a strange and desperate yearning to be loved by this man.

"Cold?"

"No, I'm fine."

"Guess you're waiting."

She smiled at his grumbling tone. "Yes, I am."

"It's not a pretty story," he warned, his tone deepening, growing somber.

"I'm a big girl. Tell me, Treet. I want to know about Sam's mother." The confession nearly stuck in her throat. Most of the time she could forget that someone else had given birth to Sam.

This was one of those times when she couldn't.

She couldn't tell Treet the other reason she wanted to know about Cheyenne. She couldn't tell him that it was personal, this curiosity about the other women in his life.

"We met at a dinner hosted by a director friend of mine, Sands Echo. Cheyenne was . . . looped when I bumped into her. She started crying, so I took her into another room, thinking she needed a shoulder. She introduced herself, then sobbed out her story, of how her boyfriend had dumped her for her best friend." Treet shifted in the chair, his arms tightening around Hadleigh as if he were bracing himself—or her—against something unpleasant. "She wouldn't stop drinking, even after I got her calmed down and we returned to the party. I didn't want her to drive in that condition, and she'd come to the party alone, so I offered to take her home. She passed out before she could give me directions, so I took her home with me. I woke up in the middle of the night and she was in bed with me."

Hadleigh squeezed her eyes tightly shut against the image his words evoked in her mind. "You slept with her," she whispered, hoping she didn't sound as hurt as she felt.

"Yes. I slept with her." His sigh seemed to come from the very depths of his chest. "She was emotionally unstable. I knew better, but I can't undo what's done. Brutal warned me—"

"So *that's* why he's so mistrustful of me!" Hadleigh exclaimed, sitting up to look at him. She could just make out his frown in the darkness.

"Yeah," he said dryly. "Brutal hasn't let me live it down. But hey, he's not as tough as he looks. And if telling yourself that doesn't work, imagine him sitting beneath a Christmas tree trying to put a diaper on a baby doll."

"So that's the big secret you threatened to tell me that first day?"

"Yep. Caught him red-handed—on video. Remind me to show it to you sometime."

"When Brutal isn't around."

He chuckled. "Yeah, when Brutal isn't around. Anyway"—he pulled her back against him—"back to my

246

sordid past. Instead of being firm and making Cheyenne leave, I let her hang around. When she told me that she was pregnant, I told her that I would do my part in raising the baby, but that I couldn't marry her. I didn't love her," Treet added flatly. "It went from bad to worse after that. She screamed and threatened. There wasn't a lamp or a vase left in one piece. She finally stormed out. I didn't see her again until she went into labor."

"She told the nurses that you promised to marry her."

"She lied. Cheyenne knew from the start how I stood with her, she just wouldn't accept it. When she found out that I couldn't be bullied into marrying her, she gave me the baby. That's when I found out I wasn't Caroline's father."

Shock jolted Hadleigh out of his lap and onto the porch. She was speechless for a few seconds. Finally, she got out, "You *knew* Caroline wasn't yours? And you weren't suspicious?" She'd heard the rumor from her friends, but she hadn't wanted to believe it.

Treet crossed his ankle over his knee, and ran a distracted hand through his hair. He sighed again. "Like I said, Cheyenne was emotionally unstable. It was easy to believe that she'd lied to me from the start. That she'd switched babies in the hospital never crossed my mind." He stared at her long and hard, as if he was trying to judge her reaction in the dark. "Would it have crossed *your* mind?"

He had a point, Hadleigh realized, still reeling from the news. Treet had known Caroline wasn't his, yet he'd raised her as if she were. Loved her unconditionally. Guarded her with his life.

He couldn't be that noble . . . could he?

Hadleigh felt suddenly chilled. She shivered and hugged herself. She had to ask. "When you found out . . . she wasn't yours, why did you keep her?"

"Because I already loved her. By that time it didn't matter that she wasn't mine biologically." His voice dropped so low, she had to lean close to hear him. "She needed me . . . and I needed her. Since then, we've been a hell of a team."

"Does Caroline know?"

"No. Nobody knows but myself, Brutal, and my agent. Todd's the one that pushed for the blood test." Treet rubbed his jaw and rose from the chair. "When the hospital called to tell me that Caroline wasn't my daughter, I thought Todd had been running his mouth. I was ready to pound him into the ground."

Hadleigh believed him. She knew how fierce he was about protecting Caroline. "Why didn't you tell me sooner?"

He took a step and began rubbing his hands along her chilled arms, staring into her face. His body heat reached her and began to seep into her bones. She swayed toward him, then steadied herself.

"Because I don't think about it. Because I don't want anyone to know. As far as I'm concerned and as far as Caroline's concerned, *I'm* her father."

With a moan, Hadleigh dropped her head to his chest. "Oh, hell," she said. Treet's soothing hands grew still. His fingers tightened around her arms.

Those Baby Blues

"What's wrong?" When she didn't immediately respond, he gave her a little shake. "Tell me," he demanded, sounding worried.

A weak chuckle escaped her. "Cheyenne is Sam's mother, Treet. Sam's *mother!*" It took her a moment to realize that the shaking came from his chest this time.

Treet was laughing.

"It's not funny," she growled, burying her face against him. She tried not to laugh, but his mirth was contagious. "I guess I don't have to wonder any longer where Sam got her temper."

"Or the red hair."

"Or the red hair," Hadleigh repeated. She didn't resist when Treet shuffled closer, warming her all over. Knowing she shouldn't, she slid her arms around his waist. He was wonderful to snuggle with, she mused. "Or her flair for getting her way," she continued. "And her mile-long stubborn streak."

"Hmm. She could have gotten that one from watching you," Treet drawled teasingly. "From what I've heard so far about your ex, I feel extremely grateful that Caroline takes after you."

It was the best compliment Hadleigh had ever heard. She inhaled his rich, masculine scent and let her breath out in a silent shudder. She felt as if she could stand there in his arms all night long, with the lightning her background, thunder her music, and Treet for support. Even the wind, though a little cool, was refreshing against her hot face.

Treet had other, better ideas. "Let's rehearse, shall we? Shouldn't take more than fifteen minutes or so."

"Slave driver," Hadleigh mumbled, reluctantly releasing him and stepping back. When he picked up her hand and laced his fingers through hers, she let him as if it were the most natural thing in the world.

It *felt* natural. *Right.*

They paused to look in on the girls, smiling simultaneously at the sight of their sleeping forms. Sam was snoring softly, her arm flung across Caroline's unsuspecting face.

"I don't know how Caroline sleeps with her," Hadleigh whispered, her throat tight with emotion. "She takes up the entire bed."

"So do I," Treet whispered back.

Hadleigh shot him an accusing look. "So *that's* where she gets it."

He chuckled and nudged her along the hall until they reached his bedroom door.

Suddenly rooted to the spot, Hadleigh swallowed hard and glanced his way. Their eyes met; heat flared between them, instant and intense. "Maybe we should wait until tomorrow," Hadleigh said, her voice husky and uncertain. "When we're not so—so—"

"Emotionally charged?" he supplied, then shrugged. "I'm fine. Primed and ready."

The word *primed* made her heart skip a beat, and caused a startling, sudden jolt in her midsection. She resisted the urge to glance down and see for herself if he was indeed *primed*.

"Don't worry, I promise you'll have fun." His knuckles raked her spine, then dropped away, while his expression remained innocent . . . questioning.

The jolt settled lower in her belly.

Very low. She licked her lips and nodded. "Okay. Let's do it."

"*Now* you're talking my language."

He grinned at her shocked expression and opened the bedroom door, waving his hand for her to go first.

Taking a deep breath, Hadleigh went inside.

Chapter Eighteen

The moment the door closed behind them, Treet became Russell Linuchi again.

Startled anew by the split-second transformation, Hadleigh wondered if she would ever get used to this man's amazing talent.

He looked purposeful as he turned and locked the door.

He could have pretended, she thought, swallowing hard. Just like they had pretended to eat roast duck earlier. Now the door was truly locked and she was in Treet's bedroom.

Not a pantry.

Not a closet.

But a bedroom. *His* bedroom.

Lordy. Her throat went bone-dry. She silently reminded herself that this was a rehearsal, and Treet was acting. Which was what she should be doing. She knew her lines—she had memorized them earlier. Besides, there weren't many. *Say them, get them over with, and get the hell out before you do what you know you shouldn't do.*

"Relax, babe, I won't eat ya," Russell drawled, giving her that comical leer again as he advanced on her.

She began to stumble backward. The backs of her knees hit the bed. She buckled, falling onto the king-size mattress.

He pounced, landing lightly on top of her, his face close to hers. It was like gazing into a stranger's eyes, she mused, trying to catch her breath and remember her lines.

Oh, yeah. "Shouldn't—shouldn't we talk first?"

"We can talk afterward." Efficient fingers began to unfasten her dress, which had a tiny row of pearl buttons all the way to the hem. He'd reached the fourth button before Hadleigh grabbed his hand. Belatedly, she remembered that she wasn't supposed to let him get that far.

"Um, could you slow down a bit?" She didn't have to fake a blush; she was already blushing. "I'm a little nervous."

"Sure, babe," Russell said with just the right amount of disappointment in his voice. He rolled away from her and sat up.

And began removing his shirt.

"Wh—what are you doing?" she asked in a squeaky voice. Frantically, she scooted along the bed until she reached the headboard.

"You know what I'm doing, babe."

If he said *babe* one more time she was going to scream. But she knew that he would . . . because he was Russell Linuchi, and *babe* was Russell's favorite word.

Sleeping with a different woman each night was also Russell's favorite pastime. "But I thought we were going to talk about this deal you've got coming up with Unique."

"You said something about talking," Russell corrected. He pulled off his shirt and threw it aside, then started on his jeans.

"Wait!" This time Zoey didn't bother trying to hide her obvious panic. "Mr. Linuchi . . . Russell, I never sleep with a man on the first date." She flashed him a weak smile, slowly creeping to the edge of the bed.

She made a dash for the bathroom.

He caught her just before she reached it, laughing and pulling her back to the bed, completely oblivious of Zoey's panic. "My, you *are* going to make this interesting, aren't you?"

Zoey struggled in his arms, finally stomping the heel of her shoe onto his foot. He let out a muffled yelp and let her go. She turned, mortified as she watched him hop around the room.

His expression was one of intense pain. It looked too real to be fake.

"Treet?" she ventured, trying to figure out if she'd really hurt him. "I didn't . . . you're not really hurt, are you?" She'd tried to warn him she wasn't a professional!

He hopped close enough to grab her—which he did. Tackling her onto the bed, he grinned wickedly into her startled face. "Gotcha."

"You're a creep," Hadleigh said with feeling. He'd let her believe she'd really hurt him. "Now get off me, *creep!*"

His wicked grin widened, spreading to his eyes. "I don't think you're in a position to give orders, *babe.*"

"Don't call me that when you're not Russell. It's bad enough I have to hear it from him."

Treet's brow rose. "You still don't like Russell?"

"Who's asking, Russell or *you?*"

"Does it matter?"

She frowned in thought. "Well, yeah, it does. If you're still Russell, that means I'm still Zoey, and since Zoey wouldn't want to blow her chances of becoming Russell's secretary, she wouldn't tell him that she didn't like him."

He whistled between his teeth as if he was impressed. "You're really getting into this, aren't you?"

"Doesn't it help?" She was genuinely curious about his work. Besides, she needed *something* to take her mind off the fact that Treet was lying on top of her. "Wasn't that the whole point of my playing Zoey's part, to make it seem real for you?"

"Oh, you make it real, Hadleigh. You make it *very* real."

The sudden silence that fell between them made Hadleigh want to squirm. Desperately, she said, "I still think that Russell is moving too fast with Zoey. How can she fall for this guy? He obviously has only one thing on his mind."

Treet appeared to consider her criticism. "Maybe Zoey's thinking the same thing," he suggested.

"Russell hasn't given Zoey time to think of her own name! If he isn't pawing her, he's making suggestive remarks—"

"The scene's over, Hadleigh. Come back to earth."

She immediately snapped her mouth closed. Very evenly—or so she thought—she said, "If the scene is over, then why are you lying on top of me?"

"Because it feels good?"

Hadleigh wished she had the nerve to disagree, but she knew she'd be lying, and worse, he'd know she was lying just by looking down and seeing her hard nipples jutting against her dress. Tentatively, she reached out and placed her hand against his bare chest, right in the middle of the dark patch of soft, curly hair over his heart.

It pounded beneath her fingers. Her eyes went wide, staring into his watchful, sexy gaze. He brought his hand up and did the same, pushing her unbuttoned dress aside and placing his hand against her breast over her own galloping heart.

"We've—we've been running around the bedroom," she began in a rush.

"Like hell," he growled, shifting her sideways on the bed but keeping her held tightly to him. His mouth captured hers in a long, hot, exploratory kiss. When they came up for air, he whispered against her mouth, "You are the absolute *best* kisser."

"Mmm," she mumbled, breathing hard. *"You* are." She didn't see him do it, but somehow he managed to reach out and touch the bedside lamp twice, bringing it to a low glow.

They did a lot of kissing. Just holding each other and kissing as if they couldn't get enough. Nibbling kisses. Little kisses. Big, urgent kisses. Soft, tender, teasing kisses. They left no stone unturned in the art of kissing. They became experts at it.

"Hmm, you taste sweet," Treet murmured, his hand finally searching for and finding her aching breast. Each movement was slow and tentative, as if he was giving her plenty of time to protest. As if he expected her to protest.

Protest? Ha! She sighed into his mouth and arched against his hand, wishing he'd just rip the bra from her and get it out of the way. Now that she was here, in his bedroom, in his arms, she wanted to get with the program.

Get naked with him.

Lordy, Lordy, she had lost her mind!

She never knew losing her mind could be so . . . so *mind*-blowing.

Impatient with his torturous pace, Hadleigh struggled to finish the job he'd started on her buttons. There had to be a million, she thought, working blindly. When his hands closed over hers, she let out a sigh of relief, thinking he would help.

257

But instead he stilled her hands and reluctantly drew away from her mouth. She opened her eyes, staring into his smoky baby blues, confused and aching.

"Hadleigh, I don't want you to do anything you're going to regret," he whispered.

She didn't know whether to kiss him for being so sensitive, or slap him for holding them up. She opted to kiss him. Maybe she could do something about his hesitation.

It worked. As if her assurance had snapped something inside him, Treet began to work frantically at the aggravating buttons.

"I'll never wear this dress again," she vowed breathlessly against his throat. "So tear it. Rip the damned buttons loose."

With a groan and a chuckle, Treet obeyed. Within seconds, she was free. Her wisp of a bra quickly followed the dress to the floor. Now they were bare breasts to bare chest and it was glorious.

"God, you feel fantastic," he croaked, his hands seemingly everywhere at once. Stroking her nipples. Cupping her buttocks. Trailing fire down her spine with skillful fingers. Pulling her tight against his erection, making her inhale a sharp gasp. Sucking hard on her nipples, giving each the same bone-melting attention until they quivered.

Shaking, on fire with an urgent need, Hadleigh fumbled with his button-fly jeans.

To hell with fighting it.

* * *

Now that the moment had arrived, Treet was suffering. Really suffering.

From guilt. Immense guilt. He was a creep. A manipulator. A selfish bastard. He'd tricked her into his bed, and now he regretted it.

Which was the biggest lie he'd ever told himself.

No, he didn't actually regret the fact that she was here, in his arms, he just regretted the way he'd done it. But God, was she warm! And sweet. And receptive.

And she truly was the best kisser.

The first button of his jeans popped open beneath Hadleigh's impatient, determined fingers. His throbbing erection strained against his jeans. He'd never felt so hard in his life.

Or so guilty.

Like the scandalous rakes from a bygone era, he'd seduced Hadleigh Charmaine, and not very honestly, either. He'd used his profession, his talent, and an outrageously doctored script to bring her to this point of no return.

"Oh, my." Her appreciative exclamation sank into his fogged brain at the exact moment her silken, hot fingers closed around him.

He gasped, his fingers toying with the elastic of her panties. Her belly was flat and smooth . . . soft and silken. And so were the curls he tangled his fingers in.

"Lordy," she breathed, squeezing him gently, then slowly working her fingers up and down his length.

Treet nearly bit his tongue in two. He eased her panties down her hips, smiling when she quickly wiggled her way out of them and tossed them from her foot. She reminded him of a fledgling stripper.

He grinned, thinking he'd best keep that comparison under his hat.

"Now it's your turn," she said in a commanding voice that was new to Treet. She pushed him onto his back, then straddled him.

Intrigued, Treet watched her, enjoying her expression as much as she seemed to be enjoying undressing him. She scooted along his legs, giving him an enticing view of her dangling breasts as she dragged his jeans with her. She stood briefly at the edge of the bed while she pulled them free. With a sexy, yet shy smile, she held them up by her finger, then let them drop to the floor.

That left his briefs.

But not for long. Sliding back along his legs like a kitten at play, she hooked his briefs with her thumbs and rolled them down, her eyes growing so big and wondering, Treet couldn't resist a chuckle. "Talk about ego trips," he murmured. Then, as he unrolled a condom over his erection, he grew even bigger.

"My, my." She clucked her tongue, tossing his briefs onto the floor with the same flourish that she'd used with the rest of their clothes. "Looky what we've got."

Licking his lips, Treet ventured, "Zoey?"

"Not on your life, buster. Zoey will have to get her own man." She paused a moment, eying him through narrowed cat eyes. "By the way, don't you think it's time I knew your real name?"

"Treet Miller *is* my legal name," he said evasively.

"You know what I mean."

"Promise not to laugh?"

"I promise."

"It's Tyrone."

"Oh, God," she breathed, clutching her bare chest in mock horror.

Treet laughed, grabbing her arms and hauling her back onto the bed, flipping her onto her back and pinning her down with his thigh. Flesh met bare flesh, and heat shimmered and sizzled between their bodies. The sexual tension had been building for so long, Treet was afraid he wouldn't live through the explosion.

Gazing down into her sparkling eyes, he traced her lips with his finger as he told her, "I don't believe in one-night stands, Hadleigh." Her lips twitched. She tried to capture his finger, but he quickly drew it away. He was having trouble concentrating as it was.

"Isn't that supposed to be *my* line?"

She thought he was teasing, Treet realized. He shook his head. "I'm serious, sweetheart. I'm just not that kind of guy."

This time she giggled outright. "I swear you're stealing my lines." When she saw that he wasn't amused, she sighed. "Okay, okay. I believe you. But you really don't have to—"

"I'm not forcing myself to say anything," Treet insisted. He wouldn't be satisfied until she believed him. "I just want you to know that being with you—like this—means a lot to me."

"All right." Her lips puckered in a provocative pout. "If I promise to call you afterward, will you *please* shut up?" She thrust her fingers through his hair, cupping the back of his neck and drawing him to her warm, hungry mouth and effectively silencing him.

Treet gave up. She was determined to avoid a serious discussion, and for now he'd let her get away with it. But afterward—just the thought of what came before *afterward* made Treet suck in a sharp breath—he would force her to listen.

As their tongues did an erotic, teasing dance, Treet traced the contours of her waist and hip with his hand, then very slowly inched his way to the triangle of curls between her legs.

Her breath came hard and fast in his ear. He closed his eyes and sighed blissfully as his fingers found the hot bud of her desire. The moment he touched her, Hadleigh stiffened. Her arms tightened around his neck and her breathing ceased altogether.

Thinking he'd hurt her, he lifted his head and looked at her. It was the most amazing sight he'd ever seen. The most amazing—and the most arousing.

Hadleigh was in the throes of a climax, her bottom lip clasped between her teeth as if to hold back a moan.

Treet groaned, cupping her with his hand as she shuddered against him. He buried his face in her neck and tried to forget what he'd seen—what was still happening.

He was about to explode against her hip.

Her breath came out in a rush, along with a confession and a dozen more tiny shudders. He could feel the tremors against his hand. "I'm—I'm sorry. You . . . seem to have the most amazing effect on me."

Treet almost laughed from the sheer joy her words brought.

"Sweetheart," he muttered in a strangled whisper, "the feeling is mutual. I'm about two seconds from joining you."

She grew still, as if uncertain about his meaning. "You . . . too?" She hugged him tight, then continued to test his amazing control by adding, "This isn't the first time for me . . . with you."

Her second mind-shattering confession stunned him, and gave him the distraction he needed to avoid an embarrassing catastrophe. For the moment, anyway. "You—you're saying that you've—"

"Yes." A fiery tongue circled his ear, making him groan. "In the closet," she panted. "At your house."

The sudden, electrifying memory of him rocking against her made sweat pop out on his forehead. He'd brought her to a climax, and she hadn't told him. He hadn't known!

Hell *fire*. She'd cheated him out of the glorious event.

With a low, primitive growl, he rose above her, settling himself between her legs. He rose on his arms and gazed at her, so very, very conscious of her heat closing over the tip of his raging erection.

He let out a ragged moan and pulled back, concentrating on her face, hoping it would distract him.

Her cheeks were flushed, and her eyes were smoky with mystery and anticipation. He felt as if he were seeing Hadleigh for the first time. He'd always found her sexy, beautiful, and intelligent, had sensed that with

263

a little coaxing and tender wooing she would be a sensual, selfless lover beyond compare.

But he hadn't known about this amazing, feisty, lusty woman. It was as if she truly had become someone else. Someone without inhibitions. Someone without worries or regrets or what-ifs.

Not the woman he remembered, but he wasn't complaining.

Oh, hell no.

He attempted to douse the flames by joking. "Then I guess that means the heat is off."

Her eyes on his face, she lifted her hips, whimpering when he quickly dodged her sneaky maneuver. "Heat?" she asked distractedly. She licked her lips, taking her time running her tongue along her bottom lip until she elicited another groan from him. She was breathing fast again . . . making him wonder if—

No, don't go there. Don't think about it.

"Meaning I don't have to worry about disappointing you," he explained through gritted teeth, easing into her inch by torturous inch. She was incredibly tight . . . amazingly hot. Nope. Joking would *not* help. He was going to have to cut this one short and make up for it later.

He liked the idea of there being a *later,* but he hated the idea of crossing the finish line alone.

He needn't have worried.

The moment he sank to the limit inside her, she began to spasm around him. He watched her, stunned speechless as her eyes widened in surprise again. There—her bottom lip disappeared between her teeth, but this time he caught the tail end of her stifled moan.

The screams of a thousand fans could not compare to that little, erotic sound that slipped through her lips.

"Hadleigh," he ground out, swooping down to close his mouth over hers in a soul-stealing kiss.

He exploded. There was no other description for the way he came apart inside her, spilling his seed deep. The aftershocks just kept coming, spurred by the clamping of her inner walls around him as she climaxed hard and fast a third time.

"Ahhh . . ." she breathed against his mouth, arching her lithe body and rotating her hips.

Distantly, he heard her gasping for air. Or was that him? He was still stunned by the length and intensity of his climax. He didn't think he was exaggerating when he thought it was the best, the absolute best.

He didn't even think it had a thing to do with the fact that he'd been celibate for months.

No, he knew with certainty that it had everything to do with the incredible woman beneath him.

And he loved her. No man could feel this extraordinary unless he loved a woman. Hell, even *he* knew that.

Now, if only he could convince Hadleigh.

Chapter Nineteen

If scientists could figure out a way to manufacture sex in capsule form, it would make the best sleeping pill in the world.

At least this was what Hadleigh would think later, long after the unimaginable happened. Long after her embarrassment became bearable.

Long after she stopped thinking of ways to make herself invisible.

She was deeply asleep when she heard the rattling of the doorknob, and it seemed to take forever to fight her way up through the thick fog of slumber to consciousness. When she finally did, she was disoriented. Her bones felt like peanut butter. She couldn't remember the last time she'd awoken from such a deep sleep. Gingerly, she stretched, then froze as her elbow encountered something solid beside her. *Large* and solid.

Not Sam.

Not her bed.

Not her room.

And then it all came back to her. The wild, intense but brief lovemaking. The wild and intense *longer* bout of lovemaking. The third time . . . an image of herself, on her knees clutching the headboard, a scream building in her throat—

"I'm coming," Treet mumbled beside her, sounding as groggy and disoriented as she felt. And no wonder, she thought, flushing all over at the memory. He'd been fantastic and quite energetic all four times. He probably felt just as deliciously lethargic as she, perhaps more so.

The bed dipped as he rose. She heard him stumbling around, looking for his briefs, muttering curses.

The knock sounded again, a small knock from a small fist.

Small knock. Small fist.

The sound of Treet padding across the floor and the subsequent realization of where he was heading scattered the last fog of sleep from Hadleigh's mind. "Treet, don't!" she called out in a frantic whisper.

She was too late.

"Daddy, it's storming," Caroline complained as Treet swung open the bedroom door.

Her thudding footsteps took her to the bed. She dived into the middle, scrambling beneath the covers and pulling them to her chin. "I'm gonna sleep with you. Sam's hogging the bed and I don't like the thunder."

Hadleigh knew the exact moment Caroline realized there was someone else in the bed. Caroline let out a frightened little yelp, which forced Hadleigh to say in a very reluctant voice, "It's just me." If there had been a way to sink into the mattress and disappear, Hadleigh would gladly have done it.

She was mortified to be found in bed with Treet by his daughter. How could she let this happen? How could *he* let it happen?

It got worse.

Beneath the hall light shining into the room, Hadleigh could see Treet's bemused expression as he looked from the door to the bed. In the doorway, a small shadow appeared, paused for a second, then followed Caroline's path to the bed.

Sam, of course.

But Sam had yet to notice Hadleigh, intent on scolding Caroline. "You left me by myself," she complained, settling herself into bed beside her friend. "I don't like storms. Just ask Mom if you don't believe me."

Caroline giggled. "Okay, I'll ask her. She's right beside you, silly!"

Frozen with horror, naked, and mortified beyond speech, Hadleigh clutched the covers beneath her chin and prayed for a quick death. Heart attack was a pretty quick way to go, she thought. And she wasn't far from having one!

Sam peered at Hadleigh, her brow puckering. "Mommy? Did you get scared of the storm too?"

When Hadleigh didn't answer—she couldn't because her throat had closed up—Caroline whispered loudly, "I think she did, Sam. That's why she's in Daddy's bed, but she's a grown-up, so she don't want to say she's scared."

Oh, thank you, God, for their innocence, Hadleigh thought fervently. She tried to make her mouth move, to say something, but she couldn't talk. How could she have let this happen? She should have gotten up afterward—after the fourth time, she amended—and gone to her own room.

Treet, bless his heart, saved the day—er—night. He shut the bedroom door, cutting off the light, apparently wide awake now and aware of the situation and Hadleigh's shock.

"It's dark, Daddy."

"That's because it's in the middle of the night, pumpkin."

He sounded so normal. A flash of lightning lit the bedroom briefly, revealing Treet sorting through a drawer. Probably in search of something to put on over his boxers, Hadleigh thought, struggling with the incredible urge to giggle.

Hysterically, of course.

"*I'm* not afraid of the dark," Sam announced even as she shuffled closer to Hadleigh.

As subtly as she could, Hadleigh edged closer to the side of the bed—away from Sam.

Treet must have found something, for he came back to the bed—muttering a curse as he bumped his shin on something—and collapsed onto it with a loud, put-upon sigh.

Tense as a bowstring, Hadleigh waited to see what he would do. She prayed he remembered her state of undress—he should, since he'd helped get her that way!

Very casually, Treet grumbled as he yanked the covers over his legs, "I guess I've got *three* scaredy-cats on my hands."

Hadleigh had never appreciated his talent for acting more than she did at that moment, because he nearly convinced *her*.

But had he forgotten one, majorly important fact? She was afraid that he had, and any moment Sam would realize that her mother was naked! Then Caroline would know. Hadleigh didn't think Treet would be able to act his way out of *that* one. She knew *she* couldn't. What could she possibly say by way of explanation?

Please, God, I'm sorry. If you'll just help me out—

"Daddy. I got to go to the bathroom."

"Sounds like a personal problem to me," Treet said with a sleep-husky chuckle. "You've been going by yourself for a few years now, sweetheart."

One down, one to go, Hadleigh thought, holding her breath.

"I'm scared to go by myself," Caroline whispered loudly.

"Sam can go with you, can't you, Sam?"

Yes, yes, yes!

Hadleigh crossed her fingers beneath the covers and squeezed her eyes so tightly she made them ache. *Go, go, go!*

"I'll go with her."

The moment the two girls closed the bathroom door, Hadleigh leaped from the bed, dragging the sheet with her. Judging by the speed with which Treet followed, she realized she'd been wrong about him forgetting.

They quickly dropped to their knees and searched the carpet for her clothes, particularly her dress. "I found it!" Treet whispered, bumping into her, then reaching out to hold her steady.

His hand landed on her bare rump, where the sheet had slipped down. His breath whistled sharply between his teeth. Hadleigh caught her breath as well, erotic memories flooding her mind.

She quickly pushed them away. "Hurry, help me into it!" They stood, hands tangling, elbows knocking into each other. Finally, Hadleigh pulled the dress together, then began to fasten the buttons.

Only she couldn't find any to fasten! With a hiss of dismay, she whispered, "The buttons! You ripped them off!"

"You told me to," Treet whispered back.

And damned if he didn't sound on the verge of laughter. "Treet, this is *not* funny! What are the girls thinking?"

"That you were afraid of the storm?" he suggested, finding a top button intact. "I think you have a few at the top . . . before I went crazy."

271

The slight huskiness in his voice speared a hot shaft into her belly. "Not now! What are we going to do?"

The sound of a toilet flushing moved them to action.

"Get under the covers," Treet instructed. "Hold your dress together." He turned her toward the bed and gave her a slight push.

She dived back under the covers and Treet dived with her. They immediately moved to their appointed corners of the bed as if they hadn't covered every inch of it earlier in every position imaginable.

A few heart-pounding seconds later, the bathroom door opened and out came Caroline and Sam, holding hands and huddling together.

Lightning flashed, illuminating their pensive expressions. When a booming crash of thunder followed, it was Sam's turn to desert Caroline. She broke free and raced for the bed, leaping the last few feet with a shriek of fright.

Hadleigh heard Treet muffle a laugh, which quickly turned into a yelp of pain when Sam landed her knee in a delicate part of his anatomy.

The moment the girls grew quiet, Hadleigh said, "Sam, we should move to my bed."

"Why?"

"Well, because—"

"I don't want to leave Caroline," Sam said in a petulant voice Hadleigh recognized only too well.

Caroline joined her, sounding incredibly like Sam. "Let her stay, Haddy! And you stay too. We'll all sleep in Daddy's bed. He don't care, do you, Daddy?"

Treet didn't get an opportunity to answer. The bedroom door burst open, revealing a large, hulking shadow silhouetted in the doorway.

Sam and Caroline screamed simultaneously.

Hadleigh gasped.

"Boss," Brutal said, sounding frantic. "I checked on the girls and they ain't in their room! Hide your eyes, I'm gonna turn on the light."

Before the last word left his mouth, before Hadleigh or Treet could protest, the overhead lights came on, blinding everyone huddled in the bed.

For a shocked moment, Brutal didn't speak. His terror-stricken eyes narrowed on the crowded bed, lingering on her—or so Hadleigh imagined—just a tad longer than the rest. "Oh."

That *oh* carried a wealth of meaning for Hadleigh. Censure, disbelief, disgust . . . more disbelief. She could well imagine how things looked from Brutal's point of view. She looked at Treet, urging him to explain, to say *anything* to take that awful look from his bodyguard's eyes.

To her immense relief, he did.

"The girls were scared," Treet said, casually bracing his hands behind his head on the pillow. "Of the storm," he added unnecessarily.

"Yeah, Caroline was scared," Sam added.

Caroline snorted. "So were you!"

Hadleigh realized she was staring at Treet's tanned, perfect chest, visible above the sheet. She swallowed and pulled her gaze away.

The *girls* were scared. No other explanation. Just that the *girls* were scared. And she was a girl. It wasn't the best excuse, but it was better than nothing.

Unfortunately, it didn't ease the heat that scorched her face.

"The storm," Brutal echoed. "Of course. The storm." He reached out and flicked off the light, that one little snapping action speaking volumes. "Sorry, boss."

The door clicked shut.

"He sounds upset," Hadleigh ventured, wondering when the nightmare would end. "Maybe you should go talk to him."

"He'll get over it," Treet growled.

She heard the covers rustling, the girls whispering; then all was quiet again. Hadleigh lay still, hugging the edge of the bed and feeling like the woman in *The Scarlet Letter*. Caroline and Sam snuggled together between them, face-to-face.

This was ridiculous, she decided, sliding from the bed. As close as she was to the edge, it didn't take much sliding to hit the floor.

Sam jackknifed in the bed, followed by Caroline, followed by Treet.

Incredulously, they all three demanded in unison, "Where are you going?"

Except Treet said "Hadleigh," Caroline said "Haddy," and Sam said "Mom."

With a nervous laugh, Hadleigh clutched her dress together and fumbled her way around the bed in the dark. "I'm—I'm going to the bathroom. I'll be right back."

"There's a bathroom right there," Sam pointed out.

Hadleigh could have slapped Treet when he drawled, "Yeah. You could use my bathroom."

"There's—there's something I need to get from my room," she stammered. Like clothes that didn't have all the buttons ripped off, and a pair of panties—as if he didn't know! Where in the hell was that door?

Luckily a flash of lightning revealed her path. She grabbed the doorknob and yanked the door open. "I'll be right back," she told Sam, closing the door firmly again.

In the dimly lighted hall, she put a hand to her thundering heart. Without hesitation, she flayed herself alive for her totally inexcusable, reckless behavior. What if the girls had been older, wiser? What if they'd left the door unlocked, and the girls had burst in earlier? What if Sam had come to her room instead, and found her gone? Sam would have been hysterical.

She covered her face with her free hand—the other clutched the dress tightly closed—and moaned softly. What kind of morals was she teaching her daughter, and Caroline? She wasn't fit to be a mother!

"You need something, Miss Charmaine?"

Hadleigh slowly lowered her hand. Brutal stood a few feet away in the hall, his arms, as usual, crossed over his chest. His face was impassive, expressionless.

But he didn't fool Hadleigh. The sharp bodyguard would have noticed her dress—what was left of it. No doubt he'd already drawn his own conclusions.

And she'd bet her next royalty check he was right on target with each and every one of them. Except for thinking she was holding out for marriage. Hadleigh drew a shaky breath and nearly smiled. Well, she guessed she'd blown *that* theory to hell and back.

Four times.

Unflinching, she looked the bodyguard in the eye and lifted her chin. "We fell asleep," she said evenly, without shame. Oh, she felt shame all right, but her pride helped her hide it from Brutal. And it wasn't shame for making love with Treet. It was shame for not using more caution concerning the girls. "Does . . ."

She cleared her throat and tried again. "Does Caroline normally wake up in the middle of the night?"

Brutal's shoulders relaxed a fraction. Hadleigh thought some of the censure faded from his eyes. Or maybe it was just wishful thinking.

He shook his head. "Not usually. Not unless it storms, or she has a nightmare."

"Same with Sam," she said, glad to know that Treet hadn't acted any less responsible than she had. Caroline and Sam waking had been a fluke, an unfortunate coincidence. "They . . . they think I was scared of the storm, too."

"You don't have to explain to me," Brutal said with a shrug of his massive shoulders. "I just work for the boss. I ain't his mama." With that asinine remark hanging in the air, he turned and disappeared down the hall.

Hadleigh felt like an idiot. She felt like calling Brutal an idiot, as well, if only to vent a little of her frustration. Why did she feel compelled to explain herself to Treet's hired help? But she knew why. She had sensed from the first moment that Brutal was more than Treet's bodyguard. He was Treet's trusted friend. Perhaps his *only* friend. He cared about Treet. He watched over Treet, had sworn to protect him from harm.

Apparently Brutal took his duties very seriously.

It took every ounce of willpower Treet possessed to remain in the bed. He wanted to leap up and go after Hadleigh, assure her that everything was not as bad as it seemed.

Hell, he had a pretty good idea of how she felt. When he'd realized Caroline had jumped into the bed—with Hadleigh in it—he'd nearly bitten a chunk out of his own tongue. Then Sam had joined them.

Talking about Heart Attack City!

At least *he'd* had his boxers on. Poor Hadleigh, she must have been close to fainting in her naked state.

And she was probably at that moment tearing herself to shreds, condemning her stupidity, vowing to stay clear of him in the future to avoid another near disaster.

Treet sat up suddenly at the thought. No, he couldn't let that happen. He'd made too much headway with Hadleigh to allow this mishap to come between them. The girls were okay. Too young, thank goodness, to even remotely consider the real reason Hadleigh had been in his bed.

But what if they'd been older? Treet was forced to ask himself. Then there would have been questions. Uncomfortable questions he would have had to answer. He muttered and punched his pillow, telling himself that it was a waste of time worrying about what-ifs. The girls, in their innocence, had assumed Hadleigh

277

was frightened by the storm, just as they had been.

A reluctant smile tugged at his lips. He could well imagine Mrs. Shoreshire's reaction to their show of closeness. Treet doubted the counselor expected them to go *that* far!

But they had . . . and it had been awesome. So awesome he ached in every muscle, and felt more sated both physically and emotionally than he'd ever felt before in his life.

He lifted his head as the bedroom door opened a crack and Hadleigh slipped through. He caught a glimpse of her—just enough to make him stuff the covers in his mouth to muffle a chuckle.

She was wearing a pair of oversize flannel pajamas.

Chapter Twenty

The fishing trip on the Morning After was a howling success. Sam discovered something daddies could do that moms *wouldn't* do: thread squiggly worms onto hooks, and remove wiggly fish *from* hooks.

Afterward, they'd all ridden in the back of Mr. Spencer's truck with Brutal at the wheel, a string of fat perch flopping on the bed of the truck, and the cool mountain air rushing through their hair.

Treet couldn't keep his eyes from Hadleigh, who blushed each time she caught him watching her. He wanted to stand in the back of the truck and shout to the world that he was the luckiest man on earth.

He wanted *her* to see how perfect they all were together.

And he wanted to get her alone again, so that he could jar her memory—although from the way she blushed, he suspected her memory was perfectly fine. What was she thinking? How did she feel? Did she regret it? He was dying to hear the answers to his questions.

When they arrived at the ranch, Treet took his time unloading the truck, signaling Brutal to remain behind with a jerk of his head. Hadleigh and the girls went inside to tell Trudy and Mrs. Spencer about their fishing trip.

Brutal propped himself against the side of the truck and shoved his hands in his pockets. "Got something on your mind, boss?"

Treet heard what his bodyguard *didn't* say. He decided it was time to lay down the law. "Why don't you just admit that she's nothing like Cheyenne? That she's not some sneaky, manipulative vampiress waiting for the right time to suck my bank account?"

With a shrug, Brutal conceded. "She's not like Cheyenne."

"Smart of you to notice."

"But I still don't trust her."

Cursing, Treet slammed the tackle box back onto the truck bed. "Why?"

"Because she's got you over a barrel, boss. Can't you see that for yourself?"

He honestly couldn't. "Explain."

"She's got Sam."

"And *I've* got Caroline," Treet reminded him. "Maybe you should talk to someone about your problem with women."

Brutal snorted. "I don't have a problem with women, but you seem to have a problem with your vision. You're blind."

"I'm not blind."

"And bullheaded."

"Have you looked in the mirror, lately?"

The bodyguard ignored his remark. He stared off into the distance, toward the corral and the milling horses. "I just don't want to see you make a mistake, boss. I can't help asking myself if you'd be this crazy over her if it wasn't for that little girl."

"That *little girl* is my daughter."

"Ain't much doubt about that . . . *this* time."

Brutal's quick agreement took the wind from Treet's sails for a second. He rallied fast. "And despite what you *and* Hadleigh think, I'm not prone to fantasies. I care for Hadleigh." Treet leaned close and growled out distinctly, "Not even *I* can fake a hard-on, buddy."

Without moving so much as an eyelash, Brutal stared him down. "So she's hot. I'm not going to argue with you there."

Which would explain his hard-on. For the first time since he'd met Brutal ten years ago, Treet wanted to punch him, to shake him up just a bit. "She's a lot more than hot, Brutal, and nothing you say will change my mind about how I feel."

"So where's it going? And what happens to the girls when it's over?"

"Who says it's going to be over?" Treet asked succinctly, goaded beyond caution or discretion. "As a matter of fact, I'm thinking about popping the question."

Ah-ha! he thought with immense satisfaction as the pupils of Brutal's eyes dilated. He'd finally gotten to him. Rattled the big, narrow-minded ass!

Then Treet realized what he'd said.

Oh hell.

"Trudy and Brutal are taking the girls to dinner and a movie in town."

The lead in her pencil snapped at the sound of Treet's voice. Hadleigh glanced up from her work, feasting her eyes on Treet, who was lounging in her bedroom doorway, looking outrageously sexy in his faded button-fly jeans and a comfortable sweatshirt. He'd pushed the sleeves up, revealing the dark hair on his arms. Her mouth literally watered at the sight. "That sounds like fun." Infinitely safer than staying here, she thought, swallowing hard.

But Treet was shaking his head, a peculiar gleam in his eye. "You're not going. Neither am I. We're going to have dinner here . . . alone."

A naughty little shock wave stole over her. Despite the betraying tremor, she lifted a brow at his bossy tone. "I am? We are?"

"Yes. We need to talk."

Talk. About last night? Suddenly and irrationally, Hadleigh discovered that she didn't want to talk about last night. She didn't want him to ruin everything by telling her that he regretted it, or that it shouldn't happen again, or that he liked her a lot, but . . .

Trying to appear casual, she laid her now useless pencil on top of her sketchbook. "What's wrong with now?" If she had to hear it, she didn't want it to be in an intimate, romantic setting.

Treet pushed himself away from the door and walked into the room. Just before he reached her, he stopped, hooking his thumbs in his pockets and pulling his jeans scandalously low on his hips.

Hadleigh wet her lips, unable to tear her gaze away from that arousing line of hair that disappeared into the waistband of his jeans. It was no longer a mystery. She knew what lay beyond. Had stroked it. Felt it deep inside her. Could almost feel it now.

"Not now. Tonight. Over dinner. And stop looking at me like that."

Startled by his sudden, thick tone, Hadleigh jerked her gaze up. Her body was hot . . . expectant. Tense. Uptight. Aroused.

Very aroused.

Just by looking at him. What had he done to her? Turned her into some wild, sex-crazed woman who drooled at the sight of a little bit of hair?

His eyes burned into hers, singed her with liquid blue heat. "Last night was incredible," he said in that same, thick, low tone that made her knees go weak. "But it wasn't enough. I want you again and again and again."

"The girls," she murmured weakly.

"The girls are looking forward to going out with Brutal and Trudy. We've spent nearly every waking moment with our daughters since we arrived, so I think we can spend a few hours alone without feeling guilty."

Hadleigh closed her eyes and bit her lip. She had to, just to think a rational thought that didn't involve his incredible mouth and hard, thrusting body. She was proud that her voice was a bit stronger when she said, "We should concentrate on the girls."

"And forget last night?" He sounded on the verge of laughing, as if he realized how preposterous the idea would be.

"Not forget." As if she could! "We should regroup. Give ourselves time to figure out what this means."

"We'll talk tonight," he repeated more softly.

When Hadleigh opened her eyes again, he was gone.

The first time they'd met, Hadleigh had been understandably nervous. Later, when she and Sam had gone to his house, her nerves had been taut as a bowstring again—with good reason; she'd been meeting Caroline for the first time.

But this time . . . *this* time she was beyond nervous. This time she was meeting Treet for a date . . . the day after she'd engaged in wild, unforgettable sex with him.

She dropped her mascara brush for the third time, fumbling as she untangled it from the bathrobe she wore. What did Treet want to talk about? Why did he sound so serious, so . . . purposeful? She took a deep breath and sat down in front of her mirror. Okay. Calm down. Calm down. Maybe he wanted to talk about Sam and Caroline.

Maybe he thought the girls were ready to hear the truth. Instead of calming her, the new possibility made her dizzy. How would they react? How would Caroline feel about having her for a mother? How would Sam feel about having Treet for a father? While she felt confident Caroline wouldn't be upset to discover that Hadleigh was her mother, Hadleigh feared she would definitely be upset to find out Treet wasn't her father.

Treet would have to reassure Caroline that their relationship wouldn't change, just as she would have to reassure Sam that she would always be her mother.

Finally, she was ready. She knew the girls, Trudy, and Brutal had left a half hour ago. She could think of no other reason to linger in her room.

Like a scaredy-cat, as Treet would say.

Long before she reached the kitchen, Hadleigh knew that Treet was preparing his favorite dish: spaghetti. The aroma of basil and oregano spiced the air, evoking memories of another time and place. Was it possible that only two weeks had passed?

"Hi," she said from the doorway. She eyed the distance between the doorway and the breakfast bar, wondering if she would make it before her knees buckled. She was a basket case!

Treet glanced up from chopping fresh mushrooms for the salad. Unsmiling, he nodded toward the stool. "Have a seat and I'll get you a glass of wine or something."

Wine sounded good. In fact, a shot of tequila sounded better. Probably not a good idea, though, so she said nothing, moving on shaky legs to the stool.

So far so good, she thought, glad to have something solid beneath her butt. She took the wine he offered, nearly spilling it when his hands closed over her shoulders.

Leaning close, he whispered, "You look great in that dress."

This old thing? she wanted to say. It was just a simple dress, one of many she'd considered wearing. Her bedroom resembled a changing room at J. C. Penney.

But she didn't say anything, because her throat had closed shut. Warm, teasing breath fanned her neck. Hadleigh closed her eyes, breathing fast. How could she be so turned on after last night? Could she ever get enough of this man?

The answer, it seemed, was obvious.

"You're incredible," Treet murmured, his own breathing none too steady as his hands slipped from her shoulders to her breasts. "In fact, you're so incredible I'm tempted to forget dinner and go straight to dessert."

Hadleigh held onto the bar counter to keep from sliding from the stool onto the floor like a pool of melted butter. Damn him for being so good at seduction.

"The girls," she murmured like a mantra. A shamefully weak mantra.

His hands . . . those wondrous, talented hands closed over her breasts possessively, his thumbs gently strumming her nipples. Her head fell back. She closed her eyes and sighed in sheer ecstasy. Against her back, she could feel him hard and throbbing. Without instruction or prompting, her legs parted.

The silent, bold invitation did not go unanswered.

Treet shifted his arm around her waist and found the hem of her dress. He lifted it up and over her thigh, running his finger in a teasing, tantalizing line along the elastic of her panties.

He dipped inside, targeting her moist center with unerring accuracy.

Hadleigh sucked in a sharp breath and let it out on a low moan. The bulge against her back quivered in reaction. She wanted to reach around and touch him, but she was afraid to let go of the counter.

Afraid of slipping to the floor in a helpless heap.

But Treet seemed to read her mind, to anticipate her needs. He slowly spun the stool around, shifting until he stood between her spread legs. He kissed her parted lips, and her arms closed around his neck.

His mouth was so incredibly exciting, providing erotic foreplay in a class of its own. She ran her tongue over his teeth, onto his bottom lip, tasting him, feeling the smooth, moist texture of his lip, gasping when he caught her wandering tongue and began to suck, mimicking the act of love.

Two seconds later Hadleigh pulled free, breathing hard. She gazed into his desire-fogged eyes, her arms clasped tightly around his neck, and said hoarsely, "We'll eat later."

His husky chuckle was smothered by another soul-eating, passionate kiss. Meanwhile, Hadleigh got busy with the buttons on his jeans, quickly freeing his magnificent erection so that she could close her hands around him.

He was hot and throbbing.

She was hot and throbbing. For him. Only for him.

Hadleigh stroked him, her fingers skimming over now-familiar territory. She laughed softly into his mouth when he finally captured her teasing hands and, with a low warning growl, transferred them to his chest.

Where she proceeded to remove his shirt, breaking free of his mouth long enough to slip it over his head.

"No fair," he grumbled, bending his head to tease her nipples through her dress. With a growl of frustration, he lifted the dress over her head and tossed it over his shoulder.

A faint gleam of sanity penetrated Hadleigh's desire-fogged mind. "Shouldn't we—"

"The doors are locked," he breathed, lifting his head from her breast long enough to scorch her with a glance. "Nobody will bother us for another two or three hours. I promise. Besides," he added, his hands slipping around to cup her bottom, "I think this stool is just the right height."

Before Hadleigh could absorb his meaning, he lifted her from the stool and slipped her panties down over her hips, stripping them from her legs. Dazed, she looked down, staring at the proud thrust of his erection, remembering every intimate detail of the pleasure it had brought her the night before.

Pleasure she wanted to feel again.

She continued to watch, mesmerized, as he nudged her legs wider and cupped her buttocks, joining their bodies in one powerful thrust.

He moaned and dropped his head to her shoulder, holding himself still, buried deep inside her. Trembling against her.

Hadleigh whimpered, embarrassed by her hair-trigger reaction to Treet. She could feel herself pulsing around his thick length, feel the incredible waves beating against the walls of her resistance. No elaborate foreplay for her—she'd never make it.

Or maybe she would . . . several times over.

"Let it go, baby. Just let it go." He began to move, standing before her, plunging into her, his voice ragged and thick and perfectly aware of her sensual battle. "I've got you. Just let it go."

"But I don't want to—" Hadleigh bit the inside of her cheek, her arms tightening around his neck as the sensational waves ignored her resistance and picked her up, rushing her out to sea.

Treet didn't lie. He held her, continued to fan the flames with each sure, delicious stroke.

And incredibly, as the waves receded, they began to build again.

"Treet . . . ?" Hadleigh moaned, hearing the sound and thinking, *That's me.* She shouldn't have been surprised, but she was. Frantically, she clutched him, kissed his mouth, his neck, his jaw, his mouth again.

Finally, her hands dropped to his butt. She grabbed each steel bun and urged him harder, faster, beyond embarrassment, beyond rational thought.

There was just her and Treet, fiercely loving each other.

"Only you," Treet ground out, holding her face steady and staring into her wide, shell-shocked eyes as the force of his seed sent her over the edge with him—again. "Only you."

"Only you," she choked out, and knew that she spoke the truth.

Taking a shower with Hadleigh was another awesome experience, Treet discovered as he stepped from the steamy bathroom into the cooler air of his bedroom. Before closing the door, he glanced back, watching the outline of Hadleigh's curvy figure through the frosty glass shower doors as she finished rinsing the shampoo from her hair.

They'd made love against the shower wall as the warm shower spray pelted their slick bodies, her moans mingling with his own, her cries of pleasure raw and uninhibited. She was truly amazing. Incredible. The most giving, generous lover he'd ever had.

And she touched him in a way no other woman had ever done—touched his *heart,* more deeply, more profoundly than he'd ever thought possible.

When they finally got around to eating, Treet decided, reluctantly pulling the door shut, he was going to remind her of the numerous things they had in common, list everything they had going for them, paint a vivid, detailed picture of what their life could be like together.

Then he was going to ask her to marry him.

She would say yes . . . wouldn't she? How could she deny the significance of what they had?

"Boss . . ."

Treet inhaled sharply and spun around.

Brutal stood in the bedroom doorway. As usual, his face was impassive, but his very presence alarmed Treet. Treet knew that Brutal would never interrupt him during a private moment unless it was important. Belatedly, Treet remembered the intrusive, incessant ringing of the phone earlier.

He'd steadfastly ignored it, and had convinced Hadleigh to do the same.

"I had to use my key to let myself in," Brutal said, his words both an explanation and an apology. The bodyguard took a deep breath, and the action sent a cold chill down Treet's spine.

"What is it?" Treet demanded, glancing back at the closed bathroom door.

"It's Sam, boss. We lost her."

"Excuse me?"

Brutal's gaze slid to the floor, then back to Treet's face. "One minute she was there, and the next she was gone. I don't know what happened, boss." At his side, his massive hands were clenched, the only outward sign that he was upset. "I tried to call—"

"How long?" Treet croaked, grabbing his clothes from the bed, his mind racing in a hundred different directions as he hastily dressed.

"About an hour. We were watching the movie—"

Behind Treet, the bathroom door opened.

"Treet," Hadleigh said, appearing in the doorway wrapped in a towel, her voice soft and sexy. "I thought I heard you talking to someone." When she saw Brutal, her gaze widened. She clutched the towel tighter. "Treet, what's going on? What's Brutal doing here . . . in your bedroom?"

There was no gentle way to say it, Treet thought. "Sam's disappeared."

"Sam's dis—what do you mean, *disappeared?*" Her voice rose shrilly. "A child just doesn't disappear!"

"Get dressed," Treet instructed her grimly. To Brutal, he said, "Wait in the van. We'll be out in a minute." As Brutal started to leave, Treet added, "I'll drive."

Hadleigh grabbed his arm, her face pale, her lips trembling. "Treet, the town's not that big. Sam's probably hiding, thinking it's a game." Her voice wobbled, and her big green eyes filled with tears.

Treet swallowed hard, unable to look away from the stark terror he saw building there.

"Little girls just don't disappear . . . unless—"

He put a finger to her soft, trembling lips and whispered, "Don't say it. Don't even think it. It's probably just like you said. Sam is hiding somewhere. We'll find her."

In the end, he had to help her get dressed. She was shaking so much that he nearly had to carry her to the van. God, he wasn't far from coming apart himself!

As he drove like a madman toward town, his mind continued to torture him with horrifying images of Sam lost and crying, or worse, kidnaped by a sadistic baby killer, or some greedy son of a bitch after ransom money.

It happened, he knew, especially to celebrities.

Dear God, she was only four years old!

He hit the steering wheel with his fist, causing the van to swerve.

"Boss," Brutal said from the seat behind him, "we won't do Sam any good if you land us in a ditch."

Treet glowered at him in the rearview mirror. "Where's Trudy and Caroline?"

"Waiting at the police station."

"Tell me again exactly what happened."

Brutal was silent for a moment. Finally, he said, "We were watching the movie, all sittin' together. Sam said she had to go to the bathroom, so Trudy went with her. While Sam was in the bathroom, Trudy decided to get popcorn—the concession stand was only a few feet away from the bathrooms. She said she waited and waited, and when Sam didn't come out, she went in to look for her. Then she came back to where I was, thinking Sam had gone back to her seat without her."

"And Sam wasn't there." Treet watched the speedometer climb to eighty, then ninety. He glanced at Hadleigh's set, pale face, glad to see that she had automatically buckled her seat belt.

"It wasn't Trudy's fault," Brutal said.

Through gritted teeth, Treet snarled, "I didn't say that it was, but somebody's responsible." To Treet's surprise, he felt Hadleigh's hand on his arm.

"He's right, Treet. It isn't anyone's fault. Sam is, well, you know how Sam is. She probably gave Trudy the slip. She's done the same to me more times than I could count."

Treet heard the sound of her swallowing before she continued.

"But she wouldn't have carried the game this far. She would have gotten bored and revealed herself."

The fingers on his arm tightened painfully. Treet forced himself to concentrate on his driving. What he really wanted to do was pull the van to the side of the road and comfort Hadleigh, promise her that everything would be all right.

But he was afraid he couldn't keep that promise.

"Someone must have taken her."

Hadleigh's blunt announcement echoed Treet's own wild thoughts. He wanted to scoff at her fears, but he couldn't. She was right; someone must have taken Sam, lured her from the rest room right beneath Trudy's nose.

And since Treet had been seen in public with Sam by a lot of people—thanks to Super Dollar Mart's lingerie sale—it could be practically anyone.

Chapter Twenty-one

Hadleigh had believed she knew the meaning of fear.

When she'd found out that Samantha wasn't her biological daughter and that she might have to give her up, she'd felt plenty of that gut-churning emotion.

But it was nothing compared to what she felt now, knowing Samantha was out there somewhere all alone. What she felt now could only be described as raw terror.

Samantha was lost. Gone. Disappeared.

Or taken.

The last thought was harder to consider, because for Hadleigh it was the most terrifying of them all.

So she tried not to think about it.

Up ahead, she saw the twinkling lights of Burlington. She flung out her hand to brace herself against the dash as Treet rounded a curve in the road. The disbelief that had numbed her brain from the moment Treet told her that Sam was missing finally began to clear, allowing her once again to think rationally.

The sick, rolling sensation in her belly remained.

"Brutal, did you ask the cinema manager to turn on the lights in the auditorium?" Hadleigh asked as they passed the sign welcoming them to Burlington.

"Yes. We had everyone looking under their seats."

"And the men's room?"

"I checked it myself."

Hadleigh bit her lip until she tasted blood. "What about other rooms? The manager's office? Supply room? Projection room?"

"We searched every nook and cranny."

Her eyes burned, but she determinedly blinked until they cleared. Crying wouldn't help Sam. Cold, logical thinking would. "Treet, have you had any threats against you lately? Any crazed fans sending you letters, hanging around—"

"Boss—"

"No." Treet's voice was flat. "I haven't had any threats in a long time, and besides, we're the only ones who know the truth about my connection with Samantha."

When Hadleigh realized Treet had nothing else to add, she twisted around to look at Brutal. "What were you going to say?"

Brutal stared back at her for a long moment. From the corner of her eye, Hadleigh saw Treet shake his head.

The movement was slight, barely noticeable, but it was a definite warning meant for Brutal. She was suddenly very certain that Treet was hiding something, and that Brutal had been on the verge of blurting it out.

Before she could confront Treet with her suspicion, they arrived at the Burlington police station. Treet and Brutal jumped out of the van, leaving her no choice but to follow suit.

Once they were inside the building, a uniformed policeman immediately led them to the sheriff's office. Caroline caught sight of Treet and came racing toward him, her little face tear-stained and solemn.

"Daddy, we can't find Sam," she said, winding her arms around Treet's neck as he lifted her.

"I know, sweetheart, but we will."

Sheriff Striker, whom Hadleigh remembered from the Super Dollar Mart incident, greeted her warmly. Of medium height, with gentle brown eyes and a quiet, soothing voice, he reminded her more of a minister than a lawman.

"Miss Charmaine." Sheriff Striker nodded. "Nice to see you again, although I don't like the circumstances. Don't like them one bit."

Hadleigh braced herself; the sheriff's low, sympathetic voice made her want to weep. "Sheriff," she said, her voice thick and unsteady, "I don't like it either." She swallowed. "Have . . . have you heard anything?"

"Sorry to say I haven't, ma'am. We've got every man on the force out swarming the streets with floodlights and asking questions, but so far nothing."

The sheriff led them into the office and shut the door, motioning Hadleigh to take a seat next to Trudy. It was obvious that Trudy had been crying; her face was red and blotchy, her eyes swollen. Hadleigh reached out and took the woman's hand, giving it a reassuring squeeze just as Treet's hands closed over her own shoulders from behind and did the same. Caroline had moved to stand next to Brutal.

Treet's touch, meant to comfort and support, was a nasty reminder of what *she* had been doing when her child had disappeared. If she hadn't fallen for Treet . . . if she hadn't lusted after him, then Sam would be at the ranch right now, playing with the kittens or looking for that elusive, monstrous turtle.

The sheriff drew everyone's attention. "Now, let's get down to business." Sheriff Striker settled into a chair behind his desk, picked up a pencil, and began to scribble on a notepad. "According to the bodyguard and the nanny, Samantha was last seen going into the rest rooms at the movie house. She never came out, or if she did, nobody saw her."

Trudy muffled a sob into her handkerchief, and Brutal nodded. Hadleigh closed her eyes and took a deep, shuddering breath. She prayed that she wouldn't be sick.

"I don't think she . . . Sam would have left the movie house," Hadleigh told him. "Not on her own."

Sheriff Striker's eyebrows met in the middle. "So you believe that someone took her?"

Hadleigh's heart knocked against her ribs. She had to force the words past her constricted throat. Saying them would make them real. "Yes, I think someone took her."

"Have any idea who?" Striker asked.

Before Hadleigh could respond, Caroline let go of Brutal's hand and approached the desk. "Maybe it was that woman with the candy. She said we could have all we wanted."

"Oh, God!" Hadleigh gasped. She covered her mouth as the sheriff motioned for her to be quiet. She could feel the tension in Treet's fingers where they gripped her shoulders.

"Good thinking, Caroline," Striker said, flashing her an encouraging smile. "Where did you see this woman?"

"At the movies."

"Can you remember anything else about her?"

Caroline shook her head, looking pensive. "She was sitting behind us, so I couldn't see her very good."

"Thank you, Caroline. You're a big, brave girl."

There was speculative silence for a moment; then Treet let go of Hadleigh's shoulders and stepped forward. "Sheriff, I think there's something you need—"

The jarring ring of the sheriff's desk phone interrupted Treet. Sheriff Striker snatched it up. "Sheriff Striker here." He listened for a second, then frowned. "Yes, Bunny, put the call through." He covered the mouthpiece and explained, "Bunny says some kid dialed 911 from a cell phone. Probably a prank call, but I don't want to miss anything."

Hadleigh's heartbeat picked up speed. Samantha knew how to dial 911. She also knew her home address and phone number. It would be incredible luck, but—

"Hi, young lady. This is Sheriff Striker. Can I get your name?"

Everyone in the room seemed to stop breathing as they strained to hear the other end of the conversation. It was impossible, of course. There was nothing left to do but try to read Sheriff Striker's expression.

Sheriff Striker's eyebrows rose. He looked straight at Hadleigh. "You say you're Samantha Kessler?"

"Sam!" Hadleigh leaped from the chair and reached for the phone in the sheriff's hand. Her voice shook. "Let me talk to her, please!"

The sheriff held up a hand, motioning her to sit down. When she was seated again, he punched the speaker button on the phone, then gently replaced the receiver. He leaned over and spoke into the mike. "Honey, can you tell me where you are so your mother can come and get you?"

Sam's voice came erratically through the static. "I don't know."

"It's Sam!" Hadleigh cried, not daring to believe it until she heard her daughter's voice.

"Mommy?"

"Sam? Can you hear me?" Hadleigh leaned forward. "Sam, what happened to you? Where are you? Did— did someone force you to go with them?" The sheriff shot her an approving look and motioned for her to continue. "Sam, listen very carefully to Mommy. Are you alone right now?"

"Yes, Mommy. That woman went to clean her dress off." There was a brief pause, a lot of static; then Sam

300

said, "I spilled my Coke on her by accident. She got mad."

"Sam, honey, did this woman say her name?"

"She said . . . she said she was my real mommy."

"Oh, God." Hadleigh stuffed a fist in her mouth. Behind her, Treet mumbled a few choice words.

Brutal pushed forward and took control. "Sam, it's Brutal. Are the keys in the ignition?"

"What's a 'nition?" Sam asked, sounding small and scared.

"The car keys," Brutal repeated. "Do you see them near the steering wheel?"

"Yeah. Yeah, I see them."

Brutal stuffed his hands in his pockets. "Do you know how to lock the doors?"

"Uh-huh. I locked them already, and I'm not lettin' her back in. She's mad at me, and it was an accident."

There were more rustling noises, and Hadleigh had no trouble imagining Sam stirring restlessly in the seat.

"I wanna talk to Mommy again."

"I'm here, sweetie."

"I wanna come home. She said she'd take me to get a puppy, but I changed my mind." Sam sniffed.

"Sam," Brutal said, leaning over the phone. "When she comes back, do not let her in the car, no matter what she says."

"I won't. I don't like her."

"I want you to look around you. Do you see any signs?"

Hadleigh grabbed Brutal's shirtsleeve in her excitement. "She can read, Brutal. She can read! Sam, listen to what Brutal says. Do you see any signs? Is there a sign on the building where the woman went to clean up?"

"Just a minute."

The seconds crawled by. Hadleigh held her breath, as she suspected everyone else was doing. Finally, Sam came back on the line.

"I can't say it, Mommy." Sam sounded peeved.

"That's okay, sweetie. Just spell it out."

"E-X-X-O-N."

Hadleigh let out her breath, then drew air into her burning lungs again. There had to be a million Exxon stations. She caught the sheriff's eye. He rose and went to a map on the wall.

"She's been gone an hour and a half. If we can determine which direction, then we can map out the Exxon stations and narrow her location."

"She doesn't know her directions!" Hadleigh said, her heart sinking.

"I've got an idea." Sheriff Striker resumed his seat. "Sam, this is Sheriff Striker again. Can you hear me okay?"

"Yeah."

"When you left town, did you see a red flashing sign?"

Once again the silence seemed to stretch forever. Finally, Sam said, "No. I didn't see no red flashing sign. I saw a big cow, though."

"A cow?" Sheriff Striker frowned and shook his head. "Was it a picture of a cow, or a real cow?"

Sam giggled, and the sound was so sweet Hadleigh thought she would pass out. "A picture, silly! A *big* picture, and the cow was wearing a silly hat—"

The sheriff's eyes widened. He snapped his fingers. "The Angus Feedlot! It's a steak house on the outskirts of town. That means they went north."

"Mommy?"

Hadleigh struggled to keep her voice even, to hide her fear from Sam. "Yes, baby?"

"That woman's coming back. She looks mad."

"Don't let her in, Sam!" Brutal and the sheriff ordered simultaneously.

The sheriff hurried to the door, motioning another officer into the room. He led him to the map on the wall and they began to converse in low tones.

In the background, Hadleigh heard a thudding noise, then indistinct screeching. Sam shouted, "No! I'm not supposed to let you in! Go away!" The thudding noise came again, louder this time.

Hadliegh realized someone was banging on the car window and screaming at Sam. The woman. The woman who had told Sam she was her *real* mommy. Slowly, with her heart galloping at an incredible rate, Hadleigh turned and looked at Treet. She didn't know why she had missed the implication the first time.

He gazed back at her, his eyes bleak, his expression grim.

He looked guilty as hell, and she thought she knew why.

"It's Cheyenne, isn't it?" she asked. "Cheyenne took Sam."

Brutal spoke before Treet had a chance. "It could be a crazed fan who really thinks Sam's her daughter."

But Hadleigh shot his idea to hell and back. "But a crazed fan wouldn't know the circumstances, would she? And Cheyenne does, obviously." Her gaze remained locked on Treet's. "Cheyenne knows, doesn't she, Treet? She knows and she's not happy that her scheme was thwarted."

Sheriff Striker, apparently overhearing her statement, stopped talking to the officer, frowning at Treet. "Who's Cheyenne?"

"Mommy? I wanna go home."

It was Sam, her voice getting grumpier by the minute. When Treet gestured for the sheriff to step outside the office and away from Caroline, Hadleigh wanted to go with them. She wanted to hear his explanation.

But she couldn't leave Sam.

"I said *no!*" Sam shouted suddenly to the woman Hadleigh now suspected was Cheyenne. "Stop banging on the window, you're giving me a headache!"

Any other time, Hadleigh would have reprimanded Sam for her rudeness. But not this time. Cheyenne didn't deserve Sam's respect. "Sam, just ignore her, okay, honey? We're trying to figure out where you are so that we can come and get you."

"She's making ugly faces at me," Sam said in an aggrieved voice. "She's shaking her fist, too. She looks really mad."

"Don't look at her." Hadleigh clenched her hands, wishing she could put them around Cheyenne's neck for scaring her daughter. "She can't hurt you, sweetie. The doors are locked, remember?"

"Yeah, 'cause I locked them. You aren't mad?"

"No, I'm not mad. You did the right thing." Hadleigh searched for a happy topic. She had to keep Sam talking, because if she lost contact with her, she was afraid she'd lose her mind. "Sam, did you like the movie?" The thudding in the background continued. Hadleigh could only pray that Cheyenne didn't break through the car window.

"I didn't get to watch all of it."

"Oh. But did you like the part you *did* see?"

"Uh-huh. Mommy, it's raining. That lady's gettin' wet."

"Don't pay any attention to her, darling. She did a bad thing when she took you away."

"Will she go to jail?"

Hadleigh hesitated. "I don't know, Sam. Maybe." If Hadleigh had any say in the matter, she most definitely would.

"Ha-ha! My mommy says you're going to jail!" Sam's singsong voice rose as she taunted Cheyenne from the safety of the locked car. "And you're gettin' wet!"

Suddenly, Sam screamed.

Hadleigh's heart lodged somewhere near her tonsils. "Sam? Sam! Talk to me! What's happening?"

"She—she cracked the window, Mommy, with her shoe!"

Oh, God. Mouth dry, Hadleigh tried to think. What should she tell Sam?

Brutal came to the rescue. "Take the keys out of the ignition, Sam," he ordered. "If she breaks through the glass, take the keys and run. Go inside the gas station and lock yourself into the bathroom."

Hadleigh heard the sound of keys jingling.

"I got 'em," Sam said, her voice quavering. "She's still hitting the window with her shoe."

"Which side is she on?" Brutal demanded. When Sam didn't immediately answer, Hadleigh clarified the question.

"Is she on the side where the steering wheel is, Sam?"

"Uh-huh. Mommy, can you come get me? I'm scared, and I wanna go home. I wanna play with Caroline!"

"Yes, baby. We're coming to get you. Just do what Brutal said, okay? If she gets inside the car, run into the service station and hide in the bathroom. And stay put." Hadleigh grabbed the desk, wishing she could jump through the phone and hold her daughter tight. "And, Sam . . ."

"Huh?"

"If she catches you, be bad. Be very bad. You won't get into trouble."

Getting permission to be bad immediately cheered Sam. "Really?"

"Yes, really."

"Okay, Mommy."

The door behind Hadleigh opened. The sheriff stuck his head inside. "I think we've got her location."

"Thank God." Hadleigh leaped from her chair. She urged Caroline forward in her place. "Caroline, talk to Sam, okay?"

"Okay. Haddy?"

Hadleigh looked down into Caroline's puzzled gaze. "Why did my mommy take Sam instead of me?"

Her heart did a crazy flip-flop. Hadleigh shook her head. "I can't explain it to you now, sweetheart. Later, okay?" And later it would be Treet explaining to his daughter why Caroline's supposed mother had kidnaped Sam instead.

Followed by Brutal, Hadleigh joined Treet and the sheriff in the hall. "I'm going with you," Hadleigh stated.

"It would be better if you stayed here and kept her on the phone," Treet said.

Hadleigh shot him a look that should have given him frostbite. "I don't think I need you to tell me what to do, Treet. If you had been honest with me in the beginning, I doubt Sam would be in this position." She angled her chin and transferred her gaze to the sheriff. "She's my daughter, and I'm going with you."

Trudy emerged from the office, her expression so stricken, Hadleigh flinched. "Sam not on phone now. Phone . . . gone dead."

"Let's move it," the sheriff said.

Brutal started to follow, but Treet stopped him. "You need to stay here in case she calls back and needs instructions on what to do."

Without argument, Brutal nodded.

In the backseat of the sheriff's car, Treet eyed Hadleigh's stony profile and sighed. He didn't blame her for being angry with him. Hell, he was angry with himself for ignoring the possibility that Cheyenne could be involved with Sam's disappearance. The crazy model hadn't shown an interest in her daughter in four years; he'd never dreamed she would start now.

As they sped through the rainy night, sirens wailing, lights flashing, Treet attempted to apologize. "I guess I should have considered Cheyenne."

"Yes, I *guess* you should have," Hadleigh retorted, staring straight ahead. "And while you're guessing, maybe you should have guessed that I had a right to know Cheyenne had been informed about the switch."

She was right again, Treet thought, mentally kicking himself. "I didn't want to worry you. . . ." He stifled a curse. "No, the truth is, I didn't think we *had* a reason to be worried. Cheyenne has never come around, or called. In fact, I don't think this would have happened if Todd hadn't taunted Cheyenne about us—" He stopped abruptly as she swung around to stare at him in disbelief.

"Something else you failed to mention?"

"I didn't think it mattered."

"Well, think again. Obviously it *did* matter."

"Hadleigh—" Treet reached out, then let his hand drop back to the seat. The chasm between them kept growing wider, and what he was about to say wouldn't help matters. But he knew he had to tell her now, rather than later. "Hadleigh, there's something else."

She lifted a sarcastic brow, her eyes bright with tears he knew she was determined to hold back. The hands folded in her lap shook visibly. "And in your infinite wisdom, you think this is something *I* should know?

I'm flattered, Treet." Her burning gaze bore into his. "So what is it? Something else you didn't think would matter? Are you going to tell me that you and Cheyenne are secretly married, and this little kidnapping scheme was all planned so that you could take Sam from me?"

Her ridiculous suggestion roused Treet's anger. "You know that isn't true."

"Do I?"

"Yes, you do," he growled. "Because if there were a grain of truth in your statement, I wouldn't be in the car with you—I'd be in the car with Cheyenne."

"So what is it? What's the big confession?"

Aware that the sheriff and his deputy were shamelessly eavesdropping, Treet lowered his voice, "When Cheyenne and I signed the papers giving me custody of Caroline, there was a tiny clause . . . giving Cheyenne the right to visitation."

"And since Sam is your rightful daughter—and hers—she now has the right to visit Sam." Her voice shook. The tears she'd been holding back spilled over and streamed down her face. She seemed unaware of them, making no move to wipe them away. "Well, that's just great, Treet. Just great. I guess that means I can't file kidnapping charges against her, doesn't it?" Then, beneath her breath, yet loud enough for him hear, she whispered, "I wish I'd never met you."

Her words stabbed Treet, driving pain deep into his heart.

The sheriff slowed the patrol car, pulling onto the shoulder and braking. He twisted around to look at them through the protective grill. His deputy followed suit. "You mean to tell me that I'm not after a kidnapper?" Sheriff Striker asked.

"She hasn't attempted to see Caroline since she was six weeks old," Treet stated coldly. "I had all but forgotten about the custody clause."

"Doesn't mean diddly-squat, Miller. If the woman has visitation rights to see her daughter, then she hasn't kidnapped her."

"She took my baby from the hospital when she was born," Hadleigh said. "I'd say that was kidnapping!"

"Maybe, but that's out of my jurisdiction. You'll have to talk to a lawyer about filing charges." The sheriff continued to look at them, and something in their tense, desperate expressions must have touched him, for he sighed and said, "I guess I can pretend I never heard that outrageous story about switched babies. I can't deny that this woman sounds dangerous." He slanted them a stern look. "But once we get Samantha back, you'd better figure out a way to keep her, because I'm only gonna do this once."

"Thank you, Sheriff."

Treet unclenched his teeth. "Yeah, thanks, Sheriff. And don't worry, when we get her back, we don't intend to let her out of our sight again."

"Looks like we found her," Sheriff Striker said, cruising slowly past a silver Cadillac. He pointed to the shattered window. "See?"

Hadleigh followed his finger, resisting the urge to leap out and scream for her daughter. Cheyenne had parked in a shadowed area, away from the bright lights of the service station.

The car looked empty.

"She—she might be hiding behind the seat," Hadleigh managed to croak. Terror held her in its grip, threatening to paralyze her limbs. What had happened when Cheyenne broke through the window? Where were they? Had Sam gotten away? Hadleigh tried the door handle on the cruiser, vaguely aware that Treet was doing the same on the other side.

The handles wouldn't budge.

"Sheriff—open the door! I've got to see if my daughter's in the car."

She nearly tumbled from the patrol car as the sheriff popped the release. It didn't take her long to realize the car *was* empty. Her terrified gaze met Treet's over the hood of the car.

Dry-mouthed, she said, "She's—she's probably inside."

"Yeah, let's go."

Together, they loped across the parking lot to the brightly lit coffee shop inside the service station. Sheriff Striker and his deputy parked the car and hastily followed them inside.

Hadleigh spotted Cheyenne immediately, sitting in a booth nursing a cup of coffee. The supermodel was hard to miss, even as bedraggled as she was. Her flaming hair lay plastered to her head, darkened by the rain and knotted by the wind. There was a streak of mud across one high cheekbone, and her peasant-style blouse was torn at the shoulder seam. A shoe—minus the heel—perched on the seat beside her.

Cheyenne looked up and spotted them, revealing a developing bruise beneath her eye. Her gaze widened, then narrowed on Treet. "I figured she was talking to you," she snarled, tossing her soggy hair over her shoulder. It hit the vinyl booth with an audible splat. "You should count yourself lucky, Treet, that you didn't have that demon child for the last four years."

Treet's fingers curled around Hadleigh's arm to stop her headlong rush toward the booth. "Don't," he whispered in her ear. "She'd like nothing better than to slap an assault charge on you."

Sheriff Striker and his deputy crowded in behind them. Hadleigh was trembling from head to toe, itching to fly at this woman and scratch her eyes out. Cheyenne had taken her child, and then had the audacity to call her baby names. The woman's list of transgressions was growing by the minute.

Apparently Hadleigh's fury was more than obvious, for the sheriff took her other arm.

"Where's Sam?" Hadleigh demanded, wishing looks could at least inflict injury. "Where *is* she?"

Cheyenne stared at Hadleigh, looking her over before making a face. "Good grief, Treet. I'd heard you weren't getting out much, but I hadn't realized how bad it was. Who is this, the maid?"

"This is Samantha's mother," Treet ground out. "The woman I intend to marry."

The model flung back her head, exposing her slim throat as she laughed. "You'd do anything to get what you want, wouldn't you, Treet? Even to the point of marrying a little nobody."

Hadleigh was speechless, both over Treet's announcement, and Cheyenne's too-close-to-the-mark observation. With a powerful surge, she broke free and stalked to where Cheyenne sat in the booth. She leaned over, placing one hand on the table and the other on the booth behind Cheyenne, trapping the woman's hair between her palm and the vinyl seat.

"I'm going to count to three," Hadleigh snarled, bringing her face close so that Cheyenne could see that she wasn't making an idle threat. She was satisfied to see Cheyenne's pupils dilate with alarm. "And if you don't tell me where my daughter is, I'm going to—"

"She's in the bathroom," Cheyenne said hastily. "That's where she ran *after* she tripped me, and *after* she hit me in the eye with my cell phone. That kid is a—"

"Good. She did what I told her to do." Hadleigh whirled and headed for the rest rooms; she'd noted the sign on entering the store. Cheyenne shouted after her.

"She's *my* daughter! You can't stop me from seeing her!"

"Wanna bet?" Hadleigh mumbled beneath her breath. If it took every cent she had, she would see that Sam would never have to face this woman again.

Reaching the bathroom, she stopped and knocked on the door, her heart pounding in anticipation of holding her daughter again. "Sam, baby? It's Mom. Open the door."

After a short silence, a muffled voice asked, "How do I know it's really you?"

Smart girl, Hadleigh thought, smiling through her tears. "Because *I* know that you're scared of storms."

"Lots of little girls are scared of storms," Sam reasoned.

Hadleigh leaned weakly against the door, chuckling. "Sam, it's really me. I promise." When Sam didn't respond, Hadleigh prompted, "Sam? Can you hear me?"

"Yeah."

"Will you open the door?"

"No."

"Why not?"

"Is *she* still out there?"

"Yes, but Treet and the sheriff are out there too. We won't let her take you, sweetheart."

"I made her pretty mad, Mommy."

Now they were getting somewhere; Sam had called her Mommy. "You did good, baby. You did exactly what Mommy wanted you to do."

"You wanted me to make her fall in the mud?"

"If that's what it took to get away from her."

Sam was silent for a long moment, and Hadleigh suspected she was trying to make sense of everything.

"Mommy?"

"Yes, baby?"

"If I come out, can I have a dog?"

This time Hadleigh laughed outright, the tears running unchecked down her face. "Right now I would promise you the moon if you would just come out so I can hug you."

Those Baby Blues

Wonder of wonders, Hadleigh heard the lock click. The door opened just enough to reveal Sam's big blue eyes peering through. Then she flung the door wide and ran into Hadleigh's open arms.

Hadleigh gathered her close, nearly squeezing the life out of her. She began to rain kisses over her face, making Sam giggle and squirm. "I love you, sweetheart."

"I love you too, Mommy."

Chapter Twenty-two

"So, that's it in a nutshell," Hadleigh concluded, placing her hands on her hips and surveying Sam's and Caroline's confused faces. She sighed. "You didn't understand, did you?"

"Nope."

"Uh-uhn." Sam shook her head for emphasis.

Treet pushed away from where he'd been leaning against the fireplace mantel and approached the sofa. He folded his arms over his chest. Hadleigh moved aside, still furious with Treet but determined to hide the fact from the girls; they had enough confusion in their lives.

"What part do you not understand?" Treet asked.

Sam frowned. "How can Caroline's mommy be *my*

mommy when she's *her* mommy? And I've got a mommy already."

"Yeah, she's got Haddy for a mommy," Caroline added.

"Besides, I don't like *her*, and I don't want her for a mommy." Sam's bottom lip trembled. Her big blue eyes filled with tears as she looked at Hadleigh. "Mommy, I don't *like* Caroline's mommy!" She began to sob openly, which tore at Hadleigh's heart. "I like *you!*"

Hadleigh dropped to her knees in front of her, her heart aching. She gathered Sam close. "Sweetheart, I'm still your mommy. I'll *always* be your mommy. We were just trying to explain to you why Cheyenne tried to take you away with her."

Caroline reached out and patted Sam on the back, whispering, "That's okay, Sam. I don't like my mommy neither, 'cause she doesn't like me."

Helplessly, Hadleigh looked at Treet. He shrugged, apparently at a loss as well.

"Hey, dry those tears." Hadleigh wiped Sam's face and kissed her wet cheeks. "Just forget about it, okay, sweetheart?"

"Okay." Sam smiled tremulously. "Can we go play now?"

Hadleigh smiled back. "Yes, you can go play." She released Sam and reached for Caroline, hugging her. Together, the girls raced from the room.

She watched them go, her insides churning. What was she going to do? She didn't want to leave Caroline, but she wanted to get away from Treet, and take Sam away so that Cheyenne would leave them alone. Hadleigh wasn't naive; she suspected the only thing that drove Cheyenne was spite.

"I talked to my lawyer today," Treet said, his voice low and deep.

The sound of it speared a hot arrow of desire into her belly. Hadleigh stubbornly ignored it. Desire had nearly cost her Sam. To her, the facts were simple: get away from Treet, and Cheyenne would once again be out of their lives.

Caroline . . . Caroline was all that was stopping her.

Okay, so she wasn't all, but the rest Hadleigh was determined to ignore.

Slowly, she turned to face Treet, hooking her thumbs in the back pockets of her jeans. She regarded the handsome devil of her dreams impassively, taking a leaf from Brutal's book. "What did he say?"

"He said that if Cheyenne files a new custody suit, then we might have a fight on our hands. A judge rarely decides to keep a mother from her birth child."

Hadleigh's mouth flooded with the bitter taste of fear. "I can't let that happen, Treet. You saw Sam—how frightened she was. I can't let that woman get her hands on my daughter again." Her voice shook as she added, "Even if I have to leave the country with Sam."

"You won't have to do that." Treet slowly approached her.

She tensed, bracing herself for his touch, telling herself she wasn't disappointed when he kept his hands to himself.

"If we get married and present a united front, we'll have a better chance of fighting Cheyenne."

She had wondered if he'd remembered saying those shocking words. She hadn't believed he'd meant the proposal then, and she didn't now. She licked her lips. "If we get married, Cheyenne will *never* leave us alone."

"I disagree."

"That's your privilege." Prudently, Hadleigh widened the distance between them, strolling around the sofa. She was disconcerted to find that Treet had followed her. He turned her around—touching her, reminding her that she wasn't the cold, unemotional woman she was pretending to be.

"You'd rather run, and give up Caroline, than marry me?" He shook her slightly, his gaze drawn to her mouth. His eyes darkened, sending a shock wave rocketing through her body. "That's not the impression I got last night."

Hadleigh drew in a sharp breath. "You fight dirty, don't you?"

"I fight any way I can, when I'm fighting for something I want."

"And you want Sam."

"I want *you* and Sam. In my life. In *our* lives."

His thumbs began to draw circles on her arms, raising goose bumps and reminding her how she'd squirmed and moaned beneath him.

"If you'd just be honest with yourself, you'd see that you want the same thing. We've got a lot going for us, Hadleigh. For God's sake, just admit it!" And then he threw the final punch, one that hit below the belt. "If you love Sam, you'll marry me."

"That's not fair!" she cried, closing her eyes against the intensity of his gaze.

"And it's fair for me to keep quiet while you take my daughter and run? Is *that* fair, Hadleigh? Don't *you* love Caroline?"

"You know I do!" Hadleigh struggled to get free, but he was relentless and ruthless in his quest to change her mind.

"I don't think Caroline will believe you. Cheyenne didn't want her, and if you leave she'll believe that you don't want her."

Before Hadleigh could think, she jerked one arm free and slapped him. She immediately felt horrified. "I'm sorry—I didn't mean to—Oh, God, I'm so sorry." She covered her face with her hands. When she tried to turn away, he grabbed her arms once again and forced her to look at him.

"Just give me one good reason why you don't want to marry me, and I'll let you go."

Hadleigh stared into his blazing eyes. "Because you don't love me," she blurted out.

Treet's lips twisted ruefully. "After everything that's happened, would you believe me if I told you that I *did* love you? That I fell in love with you the moment I saw you sitting in Mrs. Shoreshire's office?" When she didn't respond, his smile faded. "Just as I thought. You don't believe me. You also wouldn't believe that I had planned on asking you to marry me last night, before Brutal interrupted us."

"Why?" Not that she would believe him, of course, but she was curious to hear what incredible story he'd tell.

"Because I love you, Hadleigh."

His hands dropped away. She told herself that his defeated look was an act, a calculated act to trick her into believing him, to gain her sympathy. Well, it wouldn't work.

Taking a deep breath, she said, "I'm sorry, Treet. Things are just too complicated for me. I don't want to make a mistake we'll both regret for the rest of our lives."

"Promise me that you'll at least think about it."

She was determined, but she wasn't unfeeling. "Okay, I promise that I'll think about it." For Sam's and Caroline's sake, she'd think about it. But not for Treet's, or her own.

It was a relief to escape the thick tension that always sprang up between them. Emotionally drained, confused, and scared, all Hadleigh wanted to do was crawl into bed and cry herself to sleep.

Lost in her tormented thoughts, she didn't see the big shadow that stepped in front of her until it was too late. She barreled into what felt like a solid wall. Strong hands reached out to steady her, then quickly let go.

"Sorry. I thought you saw me," Brutal said, keeping his voice low.

"No, I didn't."

"I wanted to talk to you."

She managed a faint smile. "I think I'm all talked out for tonight, Brutal. Can I take a rain check?"

321

"No."

Startled by his abrupt answer, she glanced at him. "What's this about?"

"Let's go into the office where we can have some privacy."

Curious now, Hadleigh let herself be led into the office, watching as Brutal shut the door and turned to her.

"I was eavesdropping," he informed her bluntly. "And I heard what the boss said. I just wanted you to know that I can vouch for him. He told me yesterday that he was going to pop the question."

"That still doesn't change anything, Brutal. Treet should have told me about Cheyenne, what she knew, and that she could be a threat to my child. The fact that he didn't indicates to me that he was hiding something. And while we're confessing here, I overheard you talking to Trudy, so I know what you really think of me."

Brutal had the grace to look uncomfortable. "Yeah, well, that was then. I've had the chance to get to know you, and I think I might have judged you a little too harshly. The boss loves you, and does Caroline."

"What makes you think that Treet loves me?"

"Because he's been acting like a fool." In an uncharacteristic action that surprised her, Brutal rolled his eyes. "I've seen him act a lot of ways, but this takes the cake. He's either in love, or he's lost his mind."

Hadleigh allowed herself the luxury of considering Brutal's words for the space of two seconds. Finally, she whispered, her voice husky, "What if you're wrong? What if *Treet's* wrong? What if he's convinced himself that he loves me . . . so that he doesn't lose Sam?" She jumped as Brutal whistled between his teeth.

"The boss was right; you *are* a scaredy-cat. That's a lot of what-ifs. You gonna pass up a chance to be happy for a bunch of what-ifs?" He gave his shiny head a mournful shake. "That's sad. Real sad." He reached for the doorknob, pausing just before he opened the door. "Well, I gave it my best shot. I might as well say good-bye, since I guess you'll be leaving us."

As Brutal disappeared into the hall, Hadleigh realized her mouth was hanging open. She snapped it shut. Who was next? she wondered, half expecting Trudy to appear with her two cents' worth.

Thoughtfully, she left the office and went to her room, her mind whirling and her heart in turmoil. She undressed and turned out the light, crawling beneath the covers wearing an oversize T-shirt that featured a big yellow smiley face on the front.

She discovered she wasn't alone.

"Is it all right if I sleep with you, Haddy?" Caroline whispered.

Hadleigh felt tears prick her eyes. "Of course, it's all right." Silently, the tears coursed down her cheeks and onto her pillow. She cried as quietly as she could, not wanting to upset Caroline. Her daughter. How could she think of leaving her? Treet was right, Caroline would be devastated if she left.

"Haddy?"

"Yes, sweetheart?"

"If you married us, would that make you my real mommy?" A small, searching hand reached out and circled Hadleigh's neck. Caroline scooted closer.

Apparently Brutal hadn't been alone in his eavesdropping activities tonight. Hadleigh thought about trying once again to explain to Caroline that she was already her real mommy, but ditched the idea as a lost cause. Until the girls were older, she didn't think they would understand something as complicated as babies switched at birth.

She had to swallow several times to get past the emotional lump in her throat. "Yes, that would make me your mommy."

"Then . . . would you please, please marry us?"

She could deny Treet. She could deny Brutal.

But she couldn't deny Caroline.

With a heavy, defeated sigh, she said, "Yes."

Treet had a split second to protect himself before Caroline landed on him. He opened his gritty eyes to find the bedroom shadowed in early dawn light and Caroline's bright, smiling face hovering over his. It couldn't have been more than half past six. What the hell?

"She said yes, Daddy! Haddy said she would marry us!"

He blinked and shielded his face, struggling to clear the fog of sleep from his mind and concentrate on his daughter's babbling. Another small figure attacked his legs, effectively pinning him to the mattress.

"That means me and Caroline will be sisters!" Sam shouted, bouncing on his shins.

Treet thought he heard something crack. Like his bones. Sam was no lightweight, and he wasn't as young as he once was. He made a mental note to start drinking more milk.

And to start locking his bedroom door.

"Did you hear me, Daddy? Haddy said she would marry us." Caroline giggled. "Well, *you,* she said she would marry you. But that means she's marrying me, too, don't it, Daddy?"

"We're *all* gettin' married," Sam inserted, leaping from his legs to the bed and nearly clipping his ear with her hand.

Treet rubbed his eyes and peered at his daughter, wondering if he'd gone over the edge. "Caroline, sweetheart, what are you talking about?" And how had *she* known he'd asked Hadleigh to marry him?

"I said," Caroline repeated slowly, as if he were dull-witted, "that Haddy said she would marry you!"

"When did she say that?"

"Last night, when I slept in her bed. She said I could. I asked her and she said *yes!*" Caroline shouted the last word, bouncing up and down on his stomach and knocking the breath out of him.

He grabbed her shoulders and held her still, hearing, but not believing. *"You* asked her to marry me?"

Beside him, Sam heaved an aggravated sigh, flopped onto her back, and folded her arms. "She's *told* you twenty times, silly!" Suddenly, she let out an earsplitting screech and sat up. "Hey, who's the oldest?"

"I was born on April fifteenth!" Caroline shouted happily.

"That's *my* birthday," Sam yelled back, unhappily. "You can't have my birthday!"

"Yes, I can!"

"No, you can't!"

"Well, I do!" And as usual, Caroline immediately saw the bright side. "That means *two* birthday cakes and *twice* as many presents!"

She'd said the magic words: *cake* and *presents*. Sam let out another war cry that Treet suspected the Spencers must have heard. "I'm gonna open my presents first because *I'm* gonna be the oldest!" she announced, daring Caroline to argue.

Which, of course, Caroline didn't. A peacemaker at heart, she merely grinned and said, "Okay, you can be the oldest. Let's go tell Trudy!"

"Wait—" Treet grunted as Caroline used his stomach for a trampoline and vaulted to the floor. Before he could catch his breath, Sam hit him square in the ribs with her elbow and shimmied over him, sliding to the floor like a snake. They were up and running for the door before he could gather his breath to remind them that Trudy, bless her heart, was probably still asleep at this ungodly hour.

Treet propped his hands behind his head, a slow grin spreading across his mouth. So, Hadleigh hadn't been able to say no to Caroline's proposal. And if he knew Hadleigh—which he felt he did—she'd agreed with reservations still intact.

It was up to Treet to convince her she wasn't making a mistake. His grin became a wicked, Russell Linuchi leer. Definitely something to look forward to.

And the early bird catches the worm.

Hadleigh came awake at the sound of her bedroom door clicking shut. Her eyes popped wide when the distinct click of the lock followed.

Her body knew before her mind that Treet was in the room.

By now, Hadleigh thought, he would know that she had agreed to marry him, and that she had been too big a coward to tell him herself.

The bed dipped; her body went on red alert.

"Hell of a way to find out I'm going to be married," Treet drawled in a sexy, teasing way that made her toes curl beneath the concealing quilt.

Hadleigh knew she couldn't play possum forever, so she rolled onto her back, rubbing the sleep from her eyes. She blinked, then looked away from the disturbing heat of his gaze, focusing on the quilt.

"What changed your mind?"

"Does it matter?"

"Yes."

She took a deep breath. "Caroline, mostly. I can't leave her."

His chuckled. "What a little hypocrite you are, Hadleigh."

"What—what do you mean?" She braced herself and looked at him, thrusting out her chin. His dark hair was tousled, as if he'd just rolled out of bed. His eyes, so bright and intense, seemed to burn with an inner flame.

327

The man was, without a doubt, simply dynamite. Dressed or undressed. Morning, noon, or night.

"You just confessed that you're basically agreeing to marry me because of Caroline."

"That's not—"

A gorgeous dark brow lifted, daring her to continue. Hadleigh moistened her lips, inadvertently drawing his gaze to her mouth. "That's not the only reason," she finished in a whisper.

His eyes went from blazing blue to the color of a simmering storm. He cupped her face in his palm, the gesture unmistakably tender and surprisingly erotic. "What are the other reasons?" he whispered.

"I—I like being with you." The confession wasn't easy for Hadleigh. "I just can't stop wondering if you're lying to yourself—"

"Let it go, baby," he murmured, leaning over her until his mouth was mere inches from hers. "There's no way in hell I can prove it, so just let it go and give me the benefit of the doubt."

Let it go. Hadleigh melted at his words, words that conjured memories of a hot night in the kitchen with her on the bar stool and him between her legs.

"Are you thinking what I'm thinking?" Treet asked in a sexy whisper, nuzzling her jaw with hot, hot lips. His hands drifted downward, onto her breasts.

"How—how did you know?" She was already breathless and aroused. Amazing. Simply amazing. Would this . . . this intense lust for him last? she found herself wondering.

"Because we're in tune with each other, babe."

Those Baby Blues

But it wasn't Treet that answered with such outrageous confidence; it was Russell Linuchi.

Hadleigh went weak with laughter. One thing she knew for certain: life would *never* be boring with Treet.

She quickly sobered as his hot, exciting mouth closed over hers.

Chapter Twenty-three

They decided to get married at the ranch, agreeing with Treet's lawyer that the sooner they presented a stable, united front, the better; they all suspected Cheyenne would waste no time gathering her defenses.

Within moments of formally announcing the news of their impending marriage to Brutal and Trudy, Trudy and Mrs. Spencer were on the phone making plans for a "small" wedding a week from Saturday. Mrs. Spencer not only had dozens of relatives living in town, she had many, many useful friends. Her niece managed a florist shop, and her brother-in-law was a preacher. Mrs. Spencer bullied her husband into begging his sister— who ran a small boutique—to drive out to the ranch and bring every suitable dress in her shop.

330

Those Baby Blues

Hadleigh, her head spinning at the sudden whirlwind of preparations in the previously semiquiet house, quickly settled on a simple, but elegant champagne-colored silk suit, thanking the flustered woman over and over again for her troubles.

Finally, on the Friday before the wedding, Hadleigh retreated to her room to finish a few sketches she should have mailed days ago to her publisher in New York. It was nearly impossible to concentrate, knowing she was about to marry the most eligible bachelor in the country.

Treet Miller, the movie star. Sexiest man of the year.

How long had it been since she'd last thought of him as *that* Treet Miller? She chewed on the end of her pencil, thinking hard. A long time, she finally conceded, relieved. Since they'd arrived at the ranch, or maybe even longer. The name *Treet Miller* no longer intimidated her.

But *he* still weakened her knees.

She knew now it had nothing to do with his fame *or* fortune, and everything to do with his lips, his voice, his hands, his—er—other body parts. The only shadow blighting her anticipation was her inability to believe that Treet truly loved her. Yes, he desired her. Yes, he admired her.

But . . . love? He claimed that he did, had loved her from almost the first moment. And Brutal seemed convinced as well. So why wasn't *she* convinced? Was she just too stubborn? Too scared?

Three fidgety hours later, Hadleigh finished her sketches. Perhaps there was a fax machine in the office, she mused, gathering them up. She was certain her publisher would appreciate getting them today.

Cautiously, she opened the door to her bedroom and looked both ways. The last thing she wanted was to be cornered by Trudy or Mrs. Spencer about the wedding cake or flower decorations. The two women consistently ignored her pleas for a small, simple ceremony.

Treet was no help at all, flashing his wicked grin when she mentioned to him that perhaps Trudy and Mrs. Spencer were getting a little carried away with this wedding thing.

Finding the hall empty, Hadleigh rushed to the office and closed the door behind her. She spotted the fax machine sitting on a filing cabinet beside the computer desk. Settling in a chair, she slid the sheets into the appropriate slot and punched in her publisher's number.

While the faxes were being transferred, she pulled a blank sheet of paper from a stack by the computer and picked up a pen, intending to make a to-do list while she waited.

The paper wasn't blank at all, she realized, turning it over. It was part of the script *In the Scheme of Things*. With a nostalgic sigh, she leaned back and began to read the beginning of the first scene.

By the second line, Hadleigh was gripping the page in disbelief.

The scene was the one she and Treet had rehearsed . . . yet it *wasn't*. The wording was different.

In *this* scene, Russell Linuchi did not kiss Zoey during her job interview. He didn't put his hands on her butt, either, or unfasten the top three buttons of her dress.

Her suspicions growing, Hadleigh reached for another page and quickly scanned it. More changes. More discrepancies in the script Treet had handed her to read. *This* Zoey did a lot more dodging, and Russell did a lot less groping. In fact, the more she read, the more she found that Russell Linuchi wasn't all that bad.

Treet had changed the script. It was clear *why* he had—it didn't take a genius to figure it out. A hot flush seeped into Hadleigh's face as she realized how naive she'd been to trust him.

He'd obviously changed the script in an underhanded attempt to seduce her into his bed.

And it had worked.

Foolish man, she thought, surprised to find she wasn't truly angry, *you could have talked me out of my pants without pretending to be someone else.*

So he'd done it . . . because? Hadleigh chewed on her bottom lip, considering the possible reasons. Because Treet was basically a shy person, and could only show confidence when he was pretending to be someone else?

She shook her head, dismissing that possibility. Once he'd gotten her into bed, he'd definitely been Treet, not Russell, and there had been nothing shy about him, just as there had been nothing shy about him since.

So why?

The answer continued to elude her. Snatching her sketches out of the fax tray, she left the office just as someone leaned on the front doorbell.

After a long pause in the hall, Hadleigh realized no one was going to put a stop to the persistent ringing.

Thinking it had to be Sam or Caroline—or both—she went to the door and yanked it open.

"Surprise!" Doreen, Barbi, and Karen all cried in unison.

They nearly toppled Hadleigh, crowding in at once and surrounding her with breath-stealing hugs. Through a gap in the circle, Hadleigh saw Treet leaning against the doorjamb, watching the reunion with a lazy smile and looking as if he'd just stepped out of a *Playgirl* magazine.

Hadleigh was overwhelmed by his gesture. He'd flown her best friends in for the ceremony. Half listening to the incoherent babbling of her friends, she saw something—an envelope, she deduced—clutched in Treet's hand. An official-looking envelope.

He shoved the envelope between Barbi and Doreen, silently urging her to take it. With trembling fingers, she opened it and withdrew a document. It was a deed, she saw.

To the ranch.

"You—you *bought* this ranch?" she squeaked. She hardly noticed the sudden, stunned silence around her.

Before Treet could answer, Sam and Caroline pushed past his legs, barreling into the room and nearly knocking Hadleigh to her knees in their mad rush to reach her. They didn't seem to notice the three women watching silently from the side.

"Mom!" Sam panted, holding up a small ball of fur. She was grinning from ear to ear, and her eyes were sparkling blue diamonds. "See *my* wedding present?"

The "wedding present" whined and wagged its tail.

It was a puppy.

Caroline shoved Sam aside and held her puppy up for Hadleigh's inspection. "I got one too, Haddy! Me and Sam both got puppies, 'cause Daddy says we're gettin' married, too!"

"We're *all* gettin' married," Sam echoed.

Hadleigh should have been overjoyed; she was marrying the man she loved, who just happened to be her daughter's father; she had her best friends with her to share her joyful moment, a ranch, and two very happy daughters. There was also the ever-growing possibility that Treet *did* love her.

But instead of embracing her good fortune, she found herself petrified. It all seemed too good to be true. Something *had* to go wrong.

So when Brutal added his bulk to the crowd gathered in front of the door, she wasn't surprised to hear say him in a growling voice that clearly stated his displeasure, "Boss, we've got company."

Filled with an awful premonition, Hadleigh moved to the open doorway. A white limo had pulled into the drive, all two hundred miles of it. As Hadleigh watched, a uniformed driver got out and walked around to the passenger door.

When he opened it, one dainty, high-heeled foot emerged, followed by a tall, model-thin red-haired beauty dressed in form-fitting, low-slung bell-bottom pants and a short top of the same emerald green silk.

Cheyenne Windsor.

Hadleigh felt her vision turn gray as she recognized the model, although she looked very different from the bedraggled woman in the coffee shop. No doubt about it, *this* was the bad thing. In fact, at the moment she couldn't think of anything worse.

Until Sheriff Striker's patrol car pulled in behind the limo. Sam tugged on her sleeve, snagging her dazed attention. Feeling as if everything were moving in slow motion, Hadleigh looked down at her terrified daughter.

"Mommy, it's *her!* Don't let her take me!"

With his jaw clenched so tightly he thought he heard his teeth cracking, Treet watched Cheyenne and the sheriff approach. Sheriff Striker held an official-looking document in his hand, his expression grim. Treet shot a quick glance at Hadleigh's chalky face and swallowed a nasty, four-letter curse.

"Treet?"

Treet flinched at the stark fear in her voice. "Take the girls and get out of here. I'll handle this."

"No. I'm not leaving." Hadleigh lifted her chin, her eyes glittering with anger. "Brutal, will you please show my friends where they'll be sleeping? And, um, take Sam and Caroline with you."

Sensing the seriousness of the moment, Karen, Doreen, and Barbi kept their mouths shut and followed Brutal down the hall, herding Sam and Caroline with them. A few feet away, Doreen paused to throw over her shoulder, "If you need some help kicking her ass, just holler."

Cheyenne wasted no time when she reached the doorway. Looking ill at ease, Sheriff Striker stood beside her. He shot Treet and Hadleigh an apologetic look.

"I want to see Sam," Cheyenne demanded, staring at Treet and ignoring Hadleigh. "I've got papers that say I have visitation rights one weekend out of the month. I'm exercising those rights now."

Treet took the papers—papers he hadn't seen in four years. Scanning them, he handed them to Hadleigh. Maybe she would see a loophole where he hadn't. Otherwise, he knew they would have no choice but to give Cheyenne Samantha for the weekend.

"Why now, Cheyenne?" he asked coldly. "Did you just wake up one morning and think, 'Hey, just to spite Treet, I want to see the child I abandoned four years ago'?"

Cheyenne's lip curled. "I have a right to see my daughter," she repeated, giving Treet the impression she'd been coached by someone. Her lawyer, probably.

Sheriff Striker cleared his throat. "I'm afraid she's right, folks—"

"Wait." Hadleigh held up the paper, her eyes gleaming with something Treet thought might have been triumph. "The papers state you have visitation rights to Caroline Nicole Miller."

"So, you can read," Cheyenne drawled nastily. "How charming."

Treet felt a surge of adrenaline as he realized that Hadleigh had discovered the loophole he'd missed.

Practically purring now, Hadleigh said, "Well, then, you can't possibly mean Samantha, because obviously she's not Caroline Nicole Windsor. Her name is Samantha Leigh Kessler."

"Caroline's not my—" Cheyenne's eyes narrowed to slits. "You know damned well that Sam is Caroline."

"Confusing, isn't it?" Hadleigh asked sweetly. "It's a shame you made the switch. If you hadn't, everything wouldn't be such a tangled mess right now."

"My lawyer will rip you to pieces in court," Cheyenne snarled, her beautiful face twisted into an ugly mask of hate.

Hadleigh smiled, and Treet silently applauded her gutsy attitude. "And *my* lawyer will put you behind bars for kidnapping. You made a big mistake taking my baby home with you from the hospital, Cheyenne. You made an even bigger mistake terrifying *my* daughter."

"You can't prove anything!"

"Can't I?" Hadleigh lifted a brow. "With a witness, I can. It seems someone at the hospital remembers seeing you bending over the wrong bassinet."

Cheyenne turned a vivid red. "You're lying!"

With a shrug, Hadleigh said, "We'll find out in court, won't we? What do they give a person for kidnapping these days, Sheriff Striker?"

Startled to find himself suddenly the focus of attention, Sheriff Striker shifted, then pulled at his collar. "Well, let me see. Depends on who's the judge. Five to ten years would be my guess." He shot Cheyenne a quick, calculating glance, then added gravely, "Maybe more."

"Then there's the child-endangerment charge," Hadleigh said.

"Oh, yeah." From the gleam apparent in his eyes, the sheriff was beginning to enjoy himself. "That would add another year or two."

"Child endangerment?" Cheyenne shrieked.

"Yes, child endangerment." Hadleigh waited a beat, long enough for her threat to sink in. "Sam says you left her alone in a locked vehicle."

Cheyenne gasped. "*She* locked *me* out! That—that demon child—"

"Then you smashed the window, shattering glass all over her," Treet added. "I think she had a cut or two."

"Four," Hadleigh corrected, folding her arms and fixing Cheyenne with a cold stare. "You saw the smashed window, didn't you, Sheriff?"

"Yes, ma'am."

This time, Cheyenne could only manage to sputter. With a scorching glance at Hadleigh, then Treet, she spun on her heel and stalked to the waiting limo. She climbed inside, jerking the door from the driver's hand and slamming it shut.

They all watched as the limo made a circle in the drive, then disappeared down the road.

Sheriff Striker shook his head, then squinted at Hadleigh. "You'd make a fine prosecuting attorney, Miss Charmaine. A damned fine one."

"Thanks, Sheriff."

Treet heard the revealing wobble in her voice. He circled her waist and pulled her against him. She sagged into him, letting out a sigh of relief. "You were fantastic," he said. His voice dipped low as he added, "Brave. Remarkable. How can you wonder why I love you?"

Instead of answering, Hadleigh burst into tears.

Converging in Hadleigh's room that night for an informal bachelorette party, Barbi, Karen, and Doreen listened in shocked silence as Hadleigh told them about Cheyenne's attempt to kidnap Sam.

"When we got to the service station," Hadleigh concluded, "Cheyenne sported a black eye, a torn blouse, a missing heel, and she was soaked to the skin. Sam had locked herself in the bathroom with Cheyenne's car keys."

By this time, Doreen had tears rolling down her face, but they were tears of laughter.

Hadleigh failed to find humor in the story. "Sam could have been hurt, Dorey. I don't think it's funny."

Barbi, in the midst of applying a final topcoat to Hadleigh's nails, paused to look at her. Her lips were twitching. "But she wasn't hurt, and you have to admit, it *is* funny. I seriously doubt Cheyenne will have the guts to take on Sam again."

Put that way, Hadleigh could see how someone might find humor in the situation. Maybe someday she would, as well. "I hope you're right. Ouch!" She tried to duck as Karen aimed her tweezers at her eyebrow again. "Take it easy, will you?"

Karen gave Hadleigh a pitying look. "Honey, there *is* no easy way to pluck eyebrows."

"So, Hadleigh," Doreen said, having recovered from her fit of laughter. She sat on the edge of the bed and propped her chin in her hands, her eyes taking on a dreamy expression. "Share with us. How does it feel to have a famous movie star madly in love with you?"

A lump suddenly lodged in Hadleigh's throat. "I'm—I'm not sure he is."

Doreen snorted. "Bull!"

"Yeah, right!" Barbi muttered, carefully painting Hadleigh's toenails a pearly shade of mauve.

"Gimme a break!" Karen rolled her eyes and mimicked Doreen's snort.

It was amazing, Hadleigh thought dryly, how quickly her friends had reversed their opinions of Treet after a little game of cards. Now they were ready to pull him into the pack as if he'd belonged all along. Deciding to test their loyalty, she told them about finding the doctored script.

Once again Doreen howled with laughter, but this time the others joined her. Hadleigh patiently waited for their mirth to subside, drumming her wet nails on her thighs.

"Oh," Doreen gasped, clutching her knees, "that's priceless!"

341

"Typical man, if you asked me," Barbi said, her laughter drifting into chuckles.

Karen wiped her streaming eyes. "Honey, only a man in love would go to that much trouble to get close to a woman. I'd feel flattered. In fact"—she wiggled her eyebrows suggestively—"I wished Conway *would* pretend to be someone else once in a while."

"*Not* Russell Linuchi, I hope," Hadleigh said with heartfelt sincerity. "The man's a sex maniac."

Hadleigh finally managed to convince her trio of friends that she would fall asleep at her own wedding if she didn't get to bed.

She *was* exhausted, but she had far too much to think about to consider sleeping. Once in the blessed quiet of her own room, she began to wear a path in the carpet.

To the door from the windows, from the windows to the door.

Back and forth.

Thinking. Remembering. Considering.

Did Treet love her? Was he *in* love with her, as her friends seemed to believe? As *he* claimed? Could she possibly be lucky enough to have found her soul mate?

A soft knock at her bedroom door interrupted Hadleigh's musings. Barbi? Doreen? Karen? Undoubtably all three, back for another around of laughter at her expense.

"Treet," she exclaimed as she opened the door.

His sudden, lazy grin weakened her knees in two seconds flat. He propped his shoulder against the doorjamb and crossed his ankles. "I figured you were in here wearing a path in the carpet, trying to warm those cold feet."

He was so dead right that she blushed.

"Ah. So I *was* right."

She took a deep breath and waved him inside, shutting the door. There was only one thing between them that needed to be aired, and it might as well be now. "I found the original script in the office."

"Oh."

"Yes, 'oh.'" Hadleigh crossed her arms and waited. She wasn't angry, but she decided it wouldn't hurt to shake his confidence a bit. Make him sweat. *She* sure had done enough sweating as a result of his handiwork.

With a shrug and a wicked grin, he said, "I couldn't resist. You were being so stubborn about not getting involved with me." He came to stand close to her. Very close. So close his brilliant baby blues nearly blinded her. Tenderly, he brushed a strand of hair from her cheek. "I'm not going to apologize. That would be paramount to saying I regret what happened as a result of my devious, underhanded, cowardly plot to get you into my arms."

Hadleigh's lips twitched. She put a hand up to stop the betraying movement. Treet brushed her fingers away and replaced them with his own.

He drew an erotic, tingly line across her bottom lip, watching it as if mesmerized. "I've never met anyone who makes me feel the way you do." His voice dropped to that warm-honey level of intoxication. "I've never met anyone that I care about, the way I care about you."

343

Hadleigh unglued her tongue from the roof of her mouth, struggling to stay focused on the issue. And what *was* the issue, anyway? Had there ever been an issue, aside from her stubbornness?

Running his hand down her spine, Treet pulled her close, shamelessly flaunting his magnificent erection. "I can't imagine life without you, Hadleigh."

Her lips parted, and a sigh slipped through. "That—that *sounds* like love," she whispered, reaching for his tempting mouth. He stopped just short of letting their lips meet.

"Your turn," he murmured thickly, his hungry gaze on her moist lips.

"I feel the same way." Her hands crept between them; her fingers curled into his shirt over his heart. She could feel the heavy *boom boom* of his heartbeat. Slowly, she pressed her forehead against his chest—right over the beat. "I just don't want to make a mistake, Treet."

He kissed the top of her head. "I don't think love comes with a guarantee, baby. I can only swear to you that I intended to ask you to marry me before Cheyenne came into the picture."

The tension drained from Hadleigh like air from a balloon. She finally allowed herself to believe him, and it made her giddy. "What if . . . what if Cheyenne doesn't give up?" She heard a low growl rumble in his throat.

"Then we'll keep fighting her—together." He chuckled. "I don't think she'll be back, especially after you threatened her with that witness from the hospital."

Hadleigh felt her face heat. He saw it and laughed. "So, that was a bluff?"

She nodded, sliding her arms around his waist and hugging him tightly to her. "Yes." She hesitated. "Treet, do you think it's fair to keep her from Sam?" The words nearly stuck in her throat as she added, "After all, she *is* Sam's mother."

Treet shook her slightly. "No. *You're* Sam's mother. Cheyenne is just—just—"

"Every man's dream?" Hadleigh teased, tilting her head to look at him.

Just before his mouth crushed hers, she heard him growl, "Not *this* man's dream."

Epilogue

The marriage ceremony—which Hadleigh firmly kept repeating whenever someone referred to it as a "wedding," was scheduled for two o'clock.

At one fifty-five, Sam slipped into Hadleigh's room. "Mommy," she whispered, looking like an angel in a white chiffon dress edged with pink lace. Matching ribbons adorned her auburn hair.

There was a smudge of icing at the corner of her mouth, and a black scuff mark on her shiny white shoes.

"I see you've been sampling the cake," Hadleigh said, dropping to her knees and scrubbing Sam's mouth with a tissue. She didn't know why, but every time she blinked, her eyes teared up again.

Sam inched closer, wrapping her arms around Hadleigh's neck and nearly pulling her off balance. "I'm nervous, Mommy."

"Me too, sweetheart."

"Then can I walk out with you?"

Hadleigh managed a tremulous smile. "You took the words right out of my mouth." Standing, she took Sam's little hand in hers and headed for the door.

"There's a lot of people out there, Mommy," Sam said, frowning. "Are they all gettin' married?"

"No. They're just here to watch *us* get married."

"Oh."

Sam wasn't kidding about the crowd, Hadleigh realized as they walked slowly down the hall. She could see them spilling into the foyer, some she recognized, a lot she didn't.

In the family room where the ceremony would be performed by the local preacher—Mrs. Spencer's brother-in-law—Karen, Barbi, and Doreen huddled together, dressed in their best. Hadleigh took heart from their encouraging smiles. Their support went a long way toward relieving the flutters in her stomach.

Finally, her gaze landed on Treet, who stood before the cold fireplace with his back to her. The preacher faced her, a benign smile on his face. Brutal stood to the right of Treet, looking huge and handsome in a suit and tie. Caroline, dressed identically to Sam, stood before Brutal, holding a bouquet of tiny pink rosebuds.

Treet turned to look at Hadleigh, his expression both tender and hungry.

At that moment, she knew how Sleeping Beauty must have felt when she opened her eyes and saw her beloved prince again. *She* had found her prince as well.

The actual ceremony was short and sweet, just as they'd planned in deference to the short attention span of their daughters. When it came time for Hadleigh to say, "I do," Sam and Caroline's exuberant "We do, we do!" coincided with the ringing of the doorbell.

Instead of looking surprised, Treet glanced at his watch and shot Hadleigh a loving, satisfied smile. "Clint's right on time."

Clint the producer, Hadleigh thought, a trifle bewildered at the producer's timing. The preacher pronounced them husband and wife and Treet leaned in to kiss her long and hard. When they broke apart, he looked deeply into her eyes and said, "I love you."

Hadleigh's heart lurched in response, and Karen's sudden, muffled scream hardly registered as Hadleigh whispered hoarsely, "I love you, too."

Beside her, a deep, familiar voice drawled, "Now it's *my* turn to kiss the bride."

Startled, Hadleigh turned just in time to feel cool, firm lips on hers. Definitely not Treet's mouth, because she felt no answering surge of desire. When she opened her eyes, she nearly swooned.

Clint Eastwood grinned at her. "Not bad for an old man, huh?"

Hadleigh's lips moved, but no sound emerged. She'd just been kissed by Clint Eastwood—

"Ouch!"

To her amazement, the movie icon howled and began to hop on one foot. In a daze, Hadleigh watched her scowling daughter move in for another well-aimed kick to Clint's shin.

"Don't you kiss my mommy! We're married to Treet!" she shouted, red-faced. She doubled her fist and aimed for his groin.

In the nick of time, Hadleigh caught her arm before it could do irreparable damage to the movie star legend. When she glanced helplessly at Treet, she found him nearly doubled over with laughter.

Brutal had actual tears streaming down his face, and his big body was shaking with suppressed laughter.

Hadleigh was mortified. "Mr. Eastwood," she began to babble, "I'm so sorry! I don't know what gets into her—"

Clint had finally recovered, but remained wisely out of reach of Sam's flaying legs and arms as she fought to free herself from Hadleigh's grip. "I think I'll live." His benevolent gaze slid to Treet's laughing face. "Yours?" he asked.

Treet wiped his eyes, still chuckling. "Mine. They're *all* mine," he added, indicating Caroline and Hadleigh.

With a rueful lift of his famous brow, Clint shook his head. "I should have known."

"Is it working?" Samantha asked Caroline, leaning forward to see how much of the black brew her new sister had consumed. She took a sip of her own drink, shuddering at the awful taste. "It always works for Mommy."

349

Caroline braved another sip, her expression nearly identical to Sam's. "I think so. I don't feel sleepy, do you?"

Sam shook her head. She and Caroline were seated on the floor in front of the television in the den, watching *Sleeping Beauty*. Behind them on the sofa, the newlywed couple sat wrapped in each other's arms, sound asleep. "I guess getting married makes people tired," Sam said. She reached for the jar of instant coffee sitting between them and poured a fair amount into her cup, stirring it with her finger.

"Yeah. I guess so. Look!" Caroline pointed to the TV screen. "Everyone's crying over Sleeping Beauty. They think she's dead."

The atmosphere became hushed. They watched, fascinated, as Prince Phillip slashed his way through huge thorn trees to get to the castle.

"He won't make it," Sam said glumly.

"Yes, he will!" Caroline leaned forward in expectation. When Prince Phillip kissed Sleeping Beauty, both girls squealed as Princess Aurora opened her eyes.

"Told ya!"

"So." Sam stuck out her tongue. The movie came to an end. She put down her cup of coffee and grabbed Caroline's hand, hauling her to her feet. "Wanna make pancakes?" she asked, glancing at the sleeping couple. "We could surprise them."

"You know how?"

"Course I do!"

Caroline shrugged. "Okay." She took another big gulp of her cold coffee, making a face. "I'm not a bit sleepy, anyway. Maybe after we make pancakes, we can make some cookies. I watched Trudy do it and it looks easy."

Hand in hand, the two girls left the unsuspecting newlyweds.

The Misconception

Darlene Gardner

Evolutionary scientist Marietta Dalrymple views romantic love—like the myth of the monogamous male—as a fairy tale. Men are only good for procreation. And she has found the ideal candidate to satisfy her strongest biological urge—motherhood. On paper Jax Jackson has all the necessary advantages, including a high IQ and a successful career. In person his body drives her to reconsider the term animal magnetism. But in the aftermath of their passion, Jax claims there has been a mix-up; he is not the sperm supplier with whom she contracted, but an aspiring family man. The erudite professor is stupefied. Until she recognizes that she has found the wrong donor, but the right man for her heart.

Baby, Oh Baby!

ROBIN WELLS

The hunk who appears on Annie's doorstep is a looker. The tall attorney's aura is clouded, and she can see that he's been suffering for some time. But all that is going to change, because a new—no, two new people are going to come into his life.

Jake Chastaine knows how things are supposed to be, and that doesn't include fertility clinic mixups or having fathered a child with a woman he'd never met. And looking at the vivid redhead who's the mother, Jake realizes he's missed out on something spectacular. Everyone knows how things are supposed to be—first comes love, then comes marriage, then the baby in the baby carriage. Maybe this time, things are going to happen a little differently.

EUGENIA RILEY
The Great Baby Caper

Courtney Kelly knows her boss is crazy. But never does she dream that the dotty chairman will send her on a wacky scavenger hunt and expect her to marry Mark Billingham, or lose her coveted promotion. But one night of reckless passion in Mark's arms leaves Courtney with the daunting discovery that the real prize will be delivered in about nine months!

A charming and sexy British entrepreneur, Mark is determined to convince his independent-minded new wife that he didn't marry her just to placate his outrageous grandfather. Amid the chaos of clashing careers and pending parenthood, Mark and Courtney will have to conduct their courtship after the fact and hunt down the most elusive quarry of all—love.

UNDER THE COVERS
RITA HERRON

Marriage counselor Abigail Jensen faked it, and she is going to have to keep on faking it. She wrote *the* book on how to keep a relationship alive, and now the public is clamoring for more than her advice—they want her to demonstrate her techniques! But Abby has just discovered that her own wedding was a sham. Adding insult to injury, her publicist produces a gorgeous actor to play her husband, and with him Abby experiences the orgasmic kisses and titillating touches she previously knew only as chapter titles. Longing to be caught up in a tangle of sheets with her hunk of a "hubby," Abby wonders if she has finally found true love. She knows she will have to discover the truth . . . under the covers.

ROBIN WELLS
OOH, LA LA!

Kate Matthews is the pre-eminent expert on New Orleans's red-light district. It makes sense that she'd be the historical consultant for the new picture being shot on location there. So why is its director being so difficult? His last flick flopped, and he is counting on this one to resurrect his career. Maybe it is because he is so handsome. He's probably used to getting women to do as he wishes. And now he wants her to loosen up. But Kate knows that accuracy is crucial to the story Zack Jackson is filming—and finding love in the Big Easy is anything but. No, there will be no lights, no cameras and certainly no action until he proves her wrong. Then it'll be a blockbuster of a show.

SHOCKING BEHAVIOR
JENNIFER ARCHER

J.T. Drake has always felt he pales in comparison to his father's outrageous inventions. But with the push of a button, one of the professor's madcap gadgets actually renders him *invisible*.

Roselyn Peabody's electrifying caress arouses him from his stupor. The beautiful scientist claims his tingling nerve endings are a result of his unique state, but J. T. knows sparks of attraction when he feels them. And while Rosy promises to help him regain his image, J.T. plots to dazzle her with his sex appeal. Only one question remains: When J.T. finally materializes, will their sizzling chemistry disappear or reveal itself as true love?

Dorchester Publishing Co., Inc.
P.O. Box 6640
Wayne, PA 19087-8640

52507-0
$5.99 US/$7.99 CAN